Totally Bound Publishing books by Caitlyn Willows

Single Books
To Die For

Rules of Engagement
Always Faithful
Ice Princess
Beneath the Layers

Rules of Engagement

BENEATH THE LAYERS

CAITLYN WILLOWS

Beneath the Layers
ISBN # 978-1-83943-843-1
©Copyright Caitlyn Willows 2019
Cover Art by Erin Dameron-Hill ©Copyright February 2019
Interior text design by Claire Siemaszkiewicz
Totally Bound Publishing

Published in 2020 by Totally Bound Publishing, United Kingdom.

BENEATH THE LAYERS

Chapter One

Midge Ellis stared in shocked disbelief at her reflection in the bedroom mirror. 'Hooker' was the only way to describe her. It wasn't even remotely what she'd had in mind when she'd grudgingly agreed to celebrate her birthday at the Lost Oasis, and she was beyond pissed to learn Susan Bolotnik had discovered it *was* her birthday by snooping in her medical records. Susan's *'but you're my friend and I wanted to help you celebrate'* dowsed some of Midge's ire, yet irritation still hovered at the fringes of her mind.

How am I even friends with these two?

Susan and her boyfriend slash BFF Jeremy had descended on Midge one day while she'd been enjoying a good book and a sandwich during her lunch break. They'd overwhelmed her with friendship. She'd yet to shake them in those six weeks. She hated confrontation and had had enough to last a lifetime. Midge didn't want any more. It was easier to go with the flow and put up with crap than to deal with it. But for Susan to use her job at the base hospital to extract personal information had crossed a big line, despite her 'good' intentions. Midge was beyond tempted to file a formal complaint through Susan's chain of command. Being a Navy corpsman didn't give her the right to access Midge's medical records.

Then there was Jeremy. A Marine didn't go absent without leave and not expect some ramifications. From what Midge had heard, it hadn't been his first time being charged with unauthorized absence. He'd deserved being busted from staff sergeant down to private first class. By all rights, she shouldn't be associating with him. Even after all these years, she worried someone would try to pin something on her. Hanging out with a dirtbag like Jeremy would be a career killer. Plus, he was now a private first class and she was a staff sergeant. Fraternization was a big no-no, punishable by court-martial. It was the perfect excuse to send the two packing. But that involved the dreaded *confrontation.*

I am such a fucking wimp.

The thought made her want to cry. She used to be a hard-charger — the person who stood up for someone and did the right thing. Then she'd found herself caught in an impossible situation and her world had turned upside down. Few had remained her friends during and after the debacle. The ordeal followed Midge wherever she was stationed. In a world where everything was a mouse click away, her past was there, waiting to be rediscovered. She'd learned to lock herself away, keep her head down, do her job and not draw attention to herself. Once her current enlistment was up the next year, she was leaving the Marine Corps behind. *Far behind.*

Midge reached for the wig. She'd had enough.

Susan swatted her hand away. "Relax and get a grip."

She tugged the red wig into place. Midge blew the flaming red bangs off her eyebrows then flicked them aside when that didn't work. The get-up was outrageous and much too revealing.

"Please tell me there's more to this somewhere."

Susan's glower screamed exasperation. "You look fabulous." She tilted her bleached-blonde head to one side and smiled. "I should become a makeup artist."

"What *would* the Navy ever do without you?" Midge let the sarcasm speak for itself while she evaluated the results of Susan's over-the-top cosmetic work.

Where am I underneath all this makeup?

Heavy liner highlighted with a luminescent silver powder made her gray eyes enormous behind her black-rimmed glasses. Dark red lipstick gave her lips a lush, sultry pout.

She twisted away from the mirror and paced the confines of her bedroom. Walking to-and-fro always made her feel better. The problem with her circuit in the small room was the tell-all mirror giving her glimpses of the transformation from mild-mannered court-reporter to... *Hooker from hell? Vamp? Wicked city woman?*

The crimson wig was straight and heavy. The flipped-up ends brushed past her shoulders. Midge's dark curls were stuffed under a wig cap that threatened to suck out her brain.

Susan had delved into her vast wardrobe for Midge's transformation. The stylish, black silk tank top with a scoop neck felt like heaven against her skin. But the soft leather mini-skirt that looked cute when Susan wore it was much too short on Midge. All the tugging in the world wasn't going to lengthen it. Though she and her nemesis were about the same height, Midge's curves filled out the form-fitting clothes to the point of indecency. What was sophisticated on Susan oozed provocative on Midge. It was amazing the clothes fit at all. Susan's body was H-shaped while Midge's was hourglass.

The crowning touch to the evening's ensemble was a pair of thigh-high leather boots with three-inch heels. They hugged Midge's calves. With every step, their *shush-shush* told the world she was coming. A bell around her neck would have been less intrusive. The ensemble demanded male attention and forced a sway into Midge's walk that made her want to crawl into a hole and die.

"I'm not wearing this. I'll get arrested for indecent exposure." Midge stumbled to the bed, sat and tugged at her left boot.

"You're wearing more right now than you do when you're at the pool."

"I don't go to the pool." The boot refused to budge. "Can you see me swimming around in front of two billion twenty-year-old Marines? No way."

"Yes, God forbid any man should see what a great figure you have underneath that frumpy uniform."

Midge couldn't disagree. It was part of who she'd become. She didn't want anyone to notice her — at least no one in the Marine Corps community. It had been easy to be anonymous when stationed near a big city. Now she was in the fishbowl of a small town, living in Twentynine Palms. A person couldn't go anywhere without running into an acquaintance. It made hooking up impossible.

But you're anonymous now, her conscience whispered.

Standing, Midge studied her reflection through narrowed eyes. No one would recognize her. Hell, she didn't recognize herself. A hookup would be nice, though. She hadn't had sex since the incident. All the masturbation in the world hadn't cut the edge on her horniness, and she'd masturbated a lot since she'd arrived at this duty station, lusting after a man she couldn't have. Her rules forbade it.

Questions assaulted her… *Can I get away with it? Will the wig stay in place? How will I face the guy if we run into each other later? Isn't this lying?* With the disguise, her hookup would never know it was her.

"These boots have to go."

"No, no, no." Susan's bobbed hair bounced with every shake of her head. "Let's get Jeremy's opinion."

Midge frowned at her. "I don't care about his opinion. Why did you have to invite him anyway? You said girls' night out. At least it was before you turned it into sluts' night out. I'm not in the mood for Jeremy's running commentary."

The man never shut up, even when he was eating. Left to his own devices downstairs, he'd probably devoured half the contents of her refrigerator.

Susan laughed and leaned toward the mirror to blot her glossy lipstick with a tissue. "Cut him some slack. Being busted rattled him. I thought we could give him some company. Anyway, going out is a good stress reliever, right?"

She fiddled with the neck clasp on her halter-cut cranberry jumpsuit. Her adjustment deepened her cleavage.

Midge lowered her foot with an exasperated thump. "Jeremy needs to be rattled. If he keeps up his crap, he'll be dishonorably discharged. I'm not in the mood to play babysitter to him tonight." *Or ever.*

"He's harmless, and don't try to change the subject by starting an argument." Susan shook her finger. "You're trying to wiggle out of our big adventure."

Midge glared at her. "I'm not comfortable with this. When you mentioned having some fun for my birthday, I thought you meant going to a movie in Palm Springs, not all *this*. It's not me." It never had been.

Susan whirled around and parked her fists on slender hips. "You're impossible. You don't date, you don't socialize and you're either squirreled up in this wannabe home or that damn bookstore."

Anger flared to the forefront. Midge willed her temper to cool. "How dare—"

"Forget work, forget those stupid books, forget about being a mousy little court reporter…just for this one night."

She grabbed Midge's wrists, hauled her to her feet then let go. Midge flailed her arms for balance. Susan righted her before she fell.

"I want you to have some fun. Come out tonight and have the time of your life. Be someone else. Make this evening a birthday gift to yourself."

On firm feet once more, Midge stood there, stomach clenching, heart pounding with a raw combination of rage, indecision and anxiety. She studied her reflection again—at the wig, the over-the-top makeup, the skin-tight mini—and knew true fear. She'd wanted to go incognito, not shout her presence to the world. This getup would garner too much attention. She couldn't pull it off.

"I'd really rather stay home and read."

"Seriously?" Susan screeched. "It's your birthday. You need to go out and get laid."

Midge wouldn't argue that. But no matter how horny she was, relationships took too much energy. What she *needed* was a one-night stand. What she *wanted* was a forever kind of guy. She wanted a man who had her back, one for whom the past didn't matter, a man who understood and supported what she'd done, one who didn't condemn her for having done the right thing. Oh hell, she wanted that delicious-looking Kurt Davidson, but work relationships were off her list. It might be all right, since they worked for different agencies, but she still had to see him on an almost day-to-day basis. She wouldn't risk it. But he *was* a sweet fantasy with his light blue eyes, sandy blond hair and a smile that turned her insides to mush. When they'd first crossed paths, he'd been somewhat attentive, sharing gum and mints with her. She'd been too tongue-tied to speak and too fearful of having attention on her in the office to respond. He'd said little to her since but had occupied the prime spot in her nightly fantasies. That was too much information to share with her pushy, so-called friend.

"Fine," she snapped.

"Lovely." Susan sniffed. "With an attitude like that, you can forget about getting laid."

Midge looked her in the eye. She was crossing one line after the other. "You're starting to piss me off." They were well past that point.

"Because I want you to get out and have fun?"

"All I want is a normal life."

"Then start living that way," she replied.

Susan had a point. Normal was what made people happy. Midge couldn't honestly say she was happy anymore. She watched her coworkers with their families and longed for that kind of life—especially children. She knew what she wanted, and maybe now it was time to go out and get it. She wasn't going to find the man of her dreams by sitting at home every night with her cat and a good book...or by bringing herself off to images of a man she could never play with.

Midge tugged at the annoying boots once more. "Enough. I promise I'll try to be charming and exciting, not nerdy and boring."

Susan clasped her hands to her chest. "Thank you. One more thing… Let's lose these."

Before Midge could stop her, Susan snatched off her glasses and tossed them to the queen-size bed. Midge grabbed them and put them back on.

"Are you two done in there yet? It's getting late." Jeremy cracked open the door.

"Not yet." Susan dashed to the door and smacked it shut.

A muffled 'ouch' came from the other side. "You're the meanest corpsman I've ever met. What happened to being kind and gentle?"

"I'm off-duty," Susan replied. "Are you ready to see the new Midge?"

"If I say yes, can we get going? I want to hit the bar. Plus, this fucking cat keeps giving me the evil eye. He's already scratched my hand, and I think he's going to bite me or something."

"Hades doesn't bite," Midge replied. But he was a pro at letting his displeasure be known. Susan and Jeremy had been on his hate list from the second he'd met them.

Midge wiggled her foot, trying in vain to get some breathing room between it and the leather boot.

Susan performed a drum roll on the dresser. "And now, for the first time in public…" She threw open the door and Jeremy fell in. He rolled to his back, laughing.

God, is he already drunk?

"Are you all right?" Midge wobbled toward him and was forced to grab the dresser to keep from crumpling on top of him. She still managed to slide down the wall and land on her backside with a thump.

Susan had always referred to Jeremy as her pretty surfer boy. His wavy white-blond hair was cut in the longest style Marine Corps regulations allowed. His eyes were blue-violet fringed with thick, dark gold lashes. Jeremy matched Midge's five-foot-five inches, but what he lacked in height he more than made up for in muscle. If he spent half as much time working on his education as he did lifting weights, he might attain reasonable intelligence. While funny and good-natured, he wasn't the brightest bulb in the pack. Instead, he excelled at being a testosterone-laden jerk.

Take a stand. Dump these two.

As she clambered to her feet, Jeremy's laughter faded and his eyes widened in lecherous appreciation.

"Wow. If I didn't know it was you —"

"Stand up, you idiot, and quit trying to look under her skirt." Susan yanked on his arm, hauling him to his feet. "What do you think of her outfit?"

He ran a slow gaze down her body, making her feel dirty and shamed and damned uncomfortable. *Just say no. These aren't real friends.*

"If I were drunk in a bar, I'd hit on you," he declared. "Love the wig. Hot, hot, hot."

"High compliments, indeed," Midge muttered.

"Are we going or not?" Susan demanded. "If we hurry, we can get to the club before the DJ sets up." She snatched her purse from the bed. "Once he starts spinning tunes, it'll be impossible to find a table."

Jeremy draped an arm around each of them. "If any guys from my unit are there tonight, I may have to tell them I'm dating you both."

"Cut the crap. It's irritating." Midge shrugged off his arm and sank to the edge of her bed to remove the torturous boots.

"What're you doing?" Susan screeched. "You *have* to wear those. They're part of the outfit."

Midge glared up at her. "I'll wear your wig and this hideous outfit, but I am *not* wearing these boots. Give me your heels or I'm staying home."

Faced with that ultimatum, Susan grudgingly complied. Wearing four-inch heels didn't help Midge's equilibrium, but at least her legs could breathe. She took a fortifying lungful of air and picked up her small black leather purse — a birthday gift from her father and stepmom.

"Let's go before I lose my nerve and run for the shower to get this gunk off my face."

"I'll join you in the shower anytime, hot stuff." Jeremy waggled his eyebrows at her.

The thought curdled her stomach. She curled her fingers into a fist, ready to plow it into his solar plexus if he dared come near her. A sibilant hiss from the doorway drew everyone's attention and saved Midge from a response. Hades stood there, back arched, black fur puffed out and yellow eyes huge. He hissed again before leaping to his accustomed perch on the windowsill. Tail curled around his legs, he continued to watch her, emitting little angry chuffing noises.

"There's a critic in every bunch," Susan said. "And get these rid of these damn glasses."

She had them off before Midge could stop her.

"Are you crazy? I can't see without those." She also couldn't see what Susan had done with them. Everything was a fuzzy blob — like a picture in desperate need of focus.

"Put in your contacts."

Jeremy edged toward the door, rubbing his right hand. He must have done something to deserve that scratch. Hades didn't lash out unless someone he didn't like invaded his space.

"I don't have contacts," she answered.

It was a lie, but she was careful about when and where she wore them — and certainly wouldn't in this town. She kept her guard up for a reason. It was one of the things she'd sacrificed to keep attention off her — and one of her biggest regrets. In reality, it was a small price to pay for her peace of mind.

"You look like a nerd. No way." Susan caught her arm and dragged her from the room.

"I can't see." Midge squinted. Her surroundings were a blur at best.

Susan gave her a little shove. "Go."

"Don't worry, cutie-pie." Jeremy followed. "We're your friends. We'll take good care of you during your birthday bash."

Midge winced. "That's what I'm afraid of."

The Lost Oasis was within walking distance of her place, but maybe they could get a cab. Navigating the two miles without glasses and in four-inch heels wasn't the smartest thing to consider, but if this night went further downhill, she was out of there. As a Marine, she'd handled worse on forced marches.

With 'friends' like them...

Chapter Two

Pounding drumbeats shook the dance floor. Couples swayed to the beat, eyes closed, lost in the music and each other. Despite the ban against smoking, thick clouds of cigarette smoke tinged the air blue – a haze charged by spinning strobe lights. Too many hot bodies in a crowded club made the atmosphere stifling. The Lost Oasis was open for business – and business was booming.

Kurt Davidson slumped over a table and surveyed the crowd, looking for his target. Couples jostled for space, trying to stake out prime locations for the evening. He examined each new face carefully. It was past nine. His target should be arriving soon. This was her usual time, and from her victims' statements, she never deviated from that pattern. She'd also never used the same name twice. But the look was still the same – red hair, dressed for sex and wearing thigh-high boots.

He scanned the packed dance floor and bar, shifting his focus from face to face. *Not her. Not yet. Where is she, damn it?*

The club's clientele varied. Locals sought a change from the pool table and darts bars, excited to check out a new venue. Marines crowded in, eager to get away from the neighboring Marine Corps base, enjoying the music and the opportunity to dance with someone who wasn't in uniform. Most would party until the wee hours of the morning. Their energy made him feel old at thirty-two.

He caught his reflection in the table's mirrored surface. The older he got, the more he hated disguises and undercover assignments. The hairpiece was a nondescript shade of brown, meant to stay in place in a hurricane. Dark brown contacts and matching beard applied with spirit gum that too often gave him a headache completed his club-hopping persona. The jeans and long-sleeved green shirt were all him, though. Anything else would have made him stand out too much. His target had to be attracted to him and comfortable enough to consider him easy to fool.

The worst thing about the evening's attire was the lifts in his shoes. They added two inches to his five-foot-eleven but killed his arches and aggravated the year-old injury to his thigh. He never knew how women could stand to wear high heels for hours at a time, though he loved the look of a tight calf they created. Having had to don heels a time or two in his career, Kurt would have to say women deserved a medal for wearing them.

People described him as an imposing man, often intimidating, focused. He thanked his acting skills for creating that impression. Those tools had served him well. Most times that meant going undercover.

Kurt generally enjoyed his work and believed what he did was important for the integrity of the military, as well as the civilian community. Investigating crimes and felons was difficult and often dangerous, but he craved the thrill of the hunt and the challenge of finding the perpetrator before his own identity was discovered. What he didn't like was the isolation.

Few knew the real man beneath the layers. He hid his frustrations well from most, though his struggle to get back in shape after the previous year's injury was starting to tell on him. He'd put on weight while he'd been convalescing from bullet wounds. Working out wasn't helping him lose it. His dad had warned him that once he hit thirty, he could kiss lean and mean goodbye. His father hadn't lied.

Where have the years gone?

It seemed like yesterday he'd been a sophomore at University of Southern California, depressed over having lost another acting gig. He'd been ready to chuck it all when new options had opened to him, appealing not only to the patriot in Kurt, but also offering the thrill of challenging work as a special agent for the Naval Criminal Investigative Service. He loved uncovering the pieces in a criminal investigation and reassembling them to find the truth beneath the lies. The job was the best of all his worlds and had led to some great adventures. That was also how he'd met his closest friends, Zach and Claudia Taylor.

Odd how the world maneuvered people together. He'd quietly freaked out when he'd heard they had orders to Okinawa, then fell to his knees and thanked all the world's deities when Zach's promotion to major got those orders canceled and they remained in Twentynine Palms. He knew one day the Marine Corps would send them elsewhere. Kurt didn't want to think about that, much less deal with it — especially when the couple was expecting their first child. He grew lonely just thinking about them being gone.

The waitress inched toward him among the dimly-lit tables. She narrowly avoided getting bumped by two giggling women with enormous margarita glasses.

"Sorry it took me so long to reach you. What can I get you to drink?"

"Whatever's on tap." Kurt pulled a handful of bills from his jeans pocket and handed them to the harried woman. "Thanks. Keep the change."

Smiling, she sidled off as fast as the limited space allowed. One of the margarita drinkers edged up to his table, tracing dagger-like silver fingernails along its edge.

"Don'cha know it ain't good to drink alone?" She slurred each word and ogled him through glassy eyes. "We think a good-lookin' guy like you should have some company."

She offered up an inebriated grin and angled her chest so her generous cleavage was exposed to its best advantage. If he'd been the least bit interested, her display would have turned him off. He didn't care for women who showed off their assets. He rather liked the mystery of clothing and discovering what was underneath.

Her companion leaned heavily on Kurt's left arm, sloshing her red concoction out of its glass and forming a puddle on his table. The air was redolent with the sickly-sweet smell of strawberries and cheap tequila.

At least I can't smell the cigarette smoke.

"Yeah, baby, you look like you could take care of us both, no problemo."

She yanked up Kurt's shirt, exposing his stomach. Both women gasped and giggled, then pursed their lips as they *oohed* and *aahed*.

"Yum, yum," Fingernails said. "A six-pack."

She reached over to stroke Kurt's stomach. He intercepted her wrist, holding it immobile.

"Sorry, ladies. I'm already taken." He added a phony smile, turned on the charm and stroked the molester's hand with his thumb. "And she's *very* possessive."

He slipped on his role of the regretful but appreciative boyfriend. It settled over him like a comfortable shoe, well-worn and familiar. *If only it were true.* He was tired of being alone but had little energy to correct that situation. A recent attempt at flirting had proven he'd lost his touch. Her ignoring him had probably been for the best, despite the sting of rejection that refused to go away. What woman would put up with the things he had to do for the job? Still, her snubbing his efforts had cut a little deeper than he wanted to admit, and he hadn't taken the rejection with grace, either. In fact, he'd been pretty nasty about it, dashing any hope of winning her over.

"Too bad, hot stuff. You look like more man than one woman could handle." They cackled like witches over a cauldron, feigned pouts and made obligatory noises of disappointment before staggering back to their table, drinks in hand.

Kurt sighed. Undercover work wasn't sitting in a car with a sack of donuts, waiting for the perp to show. Sometimes things got tricky.

Jess Alderman was going to love hearing about *this* little undercover incident. *Instead of finding the femme fatale of the desert, the intrepid hero ends up getting harassed and groped by a pair of drunken bimbos.*

Six young Marines at the bar began a boisterous beer chug. One sunburned contestant gulped beer from a yard glass. His buddies pounded the bar in time with each gulp and broke into a roar when the last of the foamy brew slid down his throat. Kurt winced at the thought of the hangover to follow. It hadn't been long since he'd been at bars like this one, playing the same stupid games with his buddies and paying the price the next morning. Thank God he'd gotten beyond that point in his life.

The waitress reappeared, bringing a frosted pint of beer and a small dish of pretzels. She smiled as she set the glass on top of a bar napkin inscribed with the palm tree logo of the Lost Oasis.

"The pretzels are fresh. Took them out of the bag myself. Give me a holler if you need another beer." She edged her way toward the next table, order pad ready.

Kurt took a drink of his beer and grimaced. *Flat. Damn.* He started to signal the waitress when he saw *her* step into the club's entryway, red hair shimmering in the lights like a flame. It had to be her. The description was too perfect to be anyone else. He smiled.

Showtime.

"I can't believe it took us so long to get here," Susan shouted over the music.

She dragged Midge through the crush of people toward the bar overlooking the dance floor below.

"I never should have let you talk me into getting a cab. He took as long to come to your house as you did getting dressed. Look at this fucking crowd."

"Cinder-Midge was almost late getting to the ball," Jeremy quipped behind them. "Should have brought your vehicle. We could always catch a cab back later."

Midge stumbled, wishing she could tell them both to go to hell and stay there. "Will you slow down? You know I can't see well."

Jeremy groped her ass.

She swung her fist around, stopping short of his chin. "Pull a stunt like that again and you'll be shitting your teeth."

He snickered. "Hey, don't blame me for trying."

They pushed their way forward. Susan kept waving at people Midge couldn't see clearly. The dim light didn't help. It felt like being in a walk-in closet with four hundred strangers.

She silently cursed Susan for convincing her to leave the house without her glasses — and herself for allowing it to happen. Maybe it was time to revise her stand on contacts. She could wear them off-duty. Getting LASIK surgery sounded even better. She stepped over a pair of long male legs that threatened her progress and glanced up at their bearded owner, ready to offer an apology. Her heart skipped a beat or two as he pulled his legs back and leaned into her space. He was close enough to see, and the look in his dark eyes — something between surprise and curiosity — mesmerized her. He reached for her arm, lips parted to speak.

"Over here." Jeremy motioned them to a nearby table overlooking the dance floor.

Susan hooked her arm and tugged. "Come on."

Midge stumbled. The man's quick reflexes caught her before she could fall. She stared up at him, absorbing the feel of his arm around her waist. He was warm and hard in all the right places. He had that look again, probably a match to her own. His hair was brown and appeared soft. His short, neat beard added sophistication. The urge to kiss him overwhelmed her. It didn't help that his gaze was on her lips — or that he wore the same sandalwood aftershave as Davidson. Her body came alive, lost in those nightly fantasies where he had a starring role.

"Come *on*," Susan shouted.

Midge longed to tell her to go fuck herself. Instead, she thanked her hero.

"My pleasure."

He released her little by little, as if he hated to let her go. His smile devastated her senses. She missed his touch. He'd said the words as if he meant them, not as an attempt to get into her panties. Here was a real gentleman, a nice man, who made her hotter than hell.

"Midge!" Susan shouted.

"Sorry," she mumbled to him.

"The night's young," he said. "I'm not going anywhere for a while."

His smile sank into her veins. Reluctantly, she joined her associates, squinting until she reached them. All the chairs were taken. The high heels were killing her feet. Her toes throbbed with every beat of her pounding heart.

"Where do we sit?"

"I'll snag some chairs after I get us drinks." Jeremy's fading voice indicated he was already aiming for the bar.

"Isn't the music great?" Susan danced around the edge of the table and leaned over the railing that separated the bar from the short drop to the dance floor. "I can't wait to get out there."

She jiggled her bottom to the music, drawing heads their way. The tight jumpsuit highlighted every bounce. Embarrassment overwhelmed Midge.

"Here we go." Jeremy set an overloaded tray on the table. Shot glasses brimmed with gold liquid. "Drink up, ladies. A toast to our birthday girl—wishing her a successful evening."

Midge hated tequila. "Didn't they have any red wine?"

"It's a celebration. Live outside your box for once." He threw the contents of the shot glass into his throat then slapped the empty glass down on the table. "Aaah. Tequila." He leaned too close and gave her a stupid grin. "Happy birthday, Midge."

Susan raised her shot glass. "To adventure, and to men who'll keep us in the style to which we'd like to become accustomed."

Midge glared at the vile liquid. *Just leave. Get up, call a cab and leave.* "You were going to get us some chairs?"

The DJ chose that time to crank up the volume.

"Let's dance."

Susan hooked Jeremy's arm. He stumbled, knocking Midge's purse off the table. She squatted to pick it up. When she stood again, purse in hand, Jeremy and Susan were halfway to the dance floor and the growing crescendo of the new set.

"Excuse me." A Texas drawl drifted over her shoulder. "Since your friends left you, would you like to come over to the bar and sit with us?"

Midge stared up at him, unnerved with how near the man stood. His close-cut hair identified him as a Marine with an unfortunate taste in clothes. He was wearing a godawful shirt in clashing colors of red, purple and yellow that had palm trees patterned all over it. Nothing like the mysterious and alluring stranger two tables away.

"Come on over and sit with us." He tugged at her elbow. "My buddy and me are saving a seat just for you."

She wavered. Sitting down sounded like heaven. Her feet were really starting to complain. Calling that cab sounded even better.

"Thanks. I'd love to sit." Midge flashed him a tentative smile.

This guy wouldn't be any different from the Marines she worked with every day. Most of them were good guys, all in all. When he grabbed her hand in his hot, sweaty palm and yanked her through the tables, she regretted her decision. All her efforts to pull free were in vain. His grip threatened to crush her fingers. Finally, they reached their goal. There was indeed a stool waiting for her there, but it was surrounded by a crowd of Marines playing a game of quarters with jiggers of rum.

"Here she is, guys," her escort crowed. "Told you I could get her to come with me. Pony up the ten-spot you owe me, Clark."

Midge stopped dead in her tracks. She should have stayed where she was or, better yet, left as her instinct demanded.

I can't believe this.

"You don't get the cash until she sits on your lap, McConnell," one of the men shouted. "I'll double it if she sits astride you."

"C'mon, baby." McConnell clamped his hand over her wrist. "Come sit on daddy's lap and I'll show you how it's done."

The group whistled and catcalled, urging McConnell to pick her up.

"Where I'm from, a girl like you needs a strong man to keep her in line." Her captor tugged on her wrist.

She set her jaw, braced her heels and yanked free. "No way, jerk."

Midge spun away, weaving through the fuzzy blur of tables and people. McConnell shouted after her. She hastened her step, praying he wouldn't catch her. A rail and flashing lights told her she'd reached the steps leading down to the dance floor. Another glance revealed their table had been taken.

Enough is enough. I'm going home.

Susan and Jeremy were lost in the swarm below. Midge had no choice but to dive in. She couldn't leave without telling them. Hand grasping the rail, Midge descended into the mass of gyrating dancers.

The DJ had the bass cranked high. Each thud reverberated through her to the point of pain. Her eyes watered from the bitter stench of cigarette smoke. *Where's a health inspector when you need one?* She was going to report this first thing in the morning. A thousand different perfumes and colognes underlaid the smoke, each one vying for dominance, all blending together in a heady mix that reeked of sex and sweat. Panic threatened to overtake her.

"Susan!"

Shouting over the noise was impossible. She turned left, right. Faces and bodies pressed up against her, each one an indistinct mass. Irritation crawled over her skin. *I'm going to fucking kill her.*

A warm, gentle hand curled around her upper arm. She took a giant step away from the male heat surrounding her. The stilettos refused to cooperate. She found herself falling backward for the second time that evening.

The man grabbed her waist and clamped her firmly against his hard thighs. She recognized the body — her long-legged savior. A glance up confirmed it. She clutched his massive shoulders, stunned by the speed at which he'd moved and his devastating smile. His aftershave cut through the haze of smoke and booze, igniting fires down below.

Her heart raced in time with the beat of drums, her body trembled, but overlying everything was a deep twist of desire. The man brushed against her and he was anything but disinterested.

"Are you all right?" He skimmed his thumb over her lower back.

"Hey, buddy, she's with me." McConnell and his pal, Clark, loomed up behind her rescuer. Even without her glasses, she could see they were spoiling for a fight. Body posture didn't lie.

The man straightened, rising to his full height, which was considerably above that of the two Marines. He turned toward them, keeping Midge clasped to his chest.

"I think this lady has had enough of you and your drinking games." His words were calm, measured and blunt.

"Listen, baby," McConnell pleaded above the ear-shattering music, "we were only kidding. Come back to the bar with us and we can get to know each other. Hands off, I promise. No more fooling around." He swayed, a victim of his excesses.

"Not interested." Midge prayed her voice was firm and no telltale quiver gave away her concern. "Go away."

"You heard her, Marines. Leave."

Something in the man's no-nonsense posture and the tone of his voice made the men pause rather than force the issue. Giving each other a look, they turned and left.

The muscles beneath her fingertips shifted as her bearded hero faced her. "We'll have to keep an eye out for those two. They don't seem like they give up easily. Are you all right?"

"I am, thanks to you. I only wanted to sit down. My feet are killing me in these blasted heels. I didn't realize the Marines were messing with me. I feel stupid."

"Not stupid...in pain. And not having a good time, from what I've seen tonight."

She gave him points for being so observant. "Thank you for your help…again."

He smiled. "And again, my pleasure. Let's find you a chair."

"I'd love that."

She eased her hands from his broad shoulders. Her fingertips tingled, branded with the feel of warm, taut muscles. Cupping her back, he led her to the steps.

"I'm Ku…" He coughed. "Sorry, dry throat. It's all this smoke. I'm Orin Davis, by the way." His voice was soft against her ear. Shivers of delight raised over her skin.

She smiled up at him. "I'm Midge, but you already know that."

His laughter rose above the noise, lifting her spirits. She loved the sound and regretted the disguise.

Susan, with Jeremy in tow, cut them off. "We can't leave you alone for one dance. I can see you're going to have to be watched every second. You *are* helpless as a newborn kitten. What the hell happened with those guys?"

"Nothing you need to worry about now," Orin replied. "They won't bother her anymore. I'll see to that."

"Good. We wanna dance. I didn't expect to have to babysit tonight." She grabbed Jeremy's hand and dragged him back into the crowd of writhing bodies.

"Some friends," Orin said.

"I can't call them friends," Midge replied. "More like pests I don't know how to get rid of."

"Telling them to get out works."

"If only it were that simple." Thinking that made her sad. She was hating this new version of herself more and more.

"Life's too short to be miserable. You always have a choice where your happiness is concerned."

Knowing he was right didn't make her feel any braver. Confrontation still tied her gut in knots, even when it was for her own happiness.

"Come on. Let's sit and have a drink." He led her up the steps.

"Not tequila," she said.

Orin laughed. "Definitely not. It always tastes like cleaning fluid to me. Wine?"

"Red, please."

"And a quieter spot so we can talk without yelling." He held out his hand when they reached the upper floor.

Midge hesitated for a moment before slipping her fingers into his. "That would be really nice. Thanks."

She loved the way he interlaced their fingers as he escorted her to a dark corner booth for two. They ordered wine and talked about everyday things…safe things. All the while she built fantasies of hot, heavy, never-ending sex with him, not Kurt Davidson. She felt comfortable being with Orin, as if they were a couple.

Midge remembered those days — and the heartbreak of being dumped. Not that she blamed Brian… Had their situations been reversed, she might have left as well. Reporting a colonel for sexual harassment had put a target on her, big time. Too many people had been ready to take *her* down and not the high-ranking prick at fault. It was much easier to try to shut up and intimidate a sergeant than to prosecute a colonel. She'd had two attorneys on her side. It had been a big risk for them also — two captains going against a colonel. She was forever grateful to them both and glad they'd reconnected here in Twentynine Palms. Funny how they'd all found themselves here. Fate, some would say. Midge wasn't sure she was a believer.

Thinking about the past dragged all the horror to the surface, re-traumatizing her and pulling her into the pit of despair. She tried to shake off the feeling and turned her attention to the dance floor.

"Feet up to a dance?" Orin asked.

Midge forced herself to smile and chase the dark memories away. The music had segued into a slow song. Couples drew together. The unattached returned to their drinks.

"I'm willing if you are," she told him.

Taking her hand, Orin led her to the center of the dance floor, directly under the largest twirling globe. Reflections from a thousand multicolored lights flowed over them like a rainbow of fire.

He gathered her close, his strong hands at the small of her back. She felt their heat through her silk top. It called to her, stoking warmth throughout her body. Hesitating for a moment, she slid her hands up his chest and rested her fingers on his shoulders. His eyes were dark in the pale shadow of his face and he focused on her.

Her heels put them near the same level and she loved the intimacy of dancing with someone close in height. She relaxed against his chest. The music rolled over them in waves of sensuous longing. Each movement of his hips brought them together, sending sharp awareness through her. Their bodies fit as if he'd been made for her. Her mind wandered to how that might translate to the bedroom, skin to skin. She tightened with want yet again. Slickness pooled between her legs. She felt his erection against her—hot and hard. Midge bit her lip, trying not to shiver with the force of her lust.

Say something. Say anything, before you burn up in a puff of wanton desire. Damn, I've been reading too much romance.

"You're an excellent dancer." Smooth, with no hesitation.

"Thanks to my sister." There was humor in his voice.

"How so?" She glanced up. The beard cloaked his face in darkness.

"She insisted I learn how to dance. She said men who danced well were true gentlemen. Mom agreed that women couldn't resist a man who danced." A hint of laughter edged his tone.

She wasn't wrong. Midge kept that thought to herself. "She must be proud of how well you dance now." Midge offered another smile. "Does she live around here?"

"No." His response was short and flat, indicating no more questions.

Midge stared over his shoulder, wondering if she should apologize, then she realized she'd done nothing wrong. She had buttons of her own that were off-limits. Had Orin touched on one of those, her reaction would have been the same. She felt the whisper of his breath over her cheek and glanced up. He'd maneuvered them to the edge of the dance floor and stopped.

"I'm sorry. That was rude of me." He brushed his thumb over her cheek.

"I—"

His lips cut off the words and stole her breath. It was a simple kiss—the mere press of his mouth on hers—yet it devastated her senses and activated all her erogenous zones. When he eased away, she tightened her hold on his shoulders and prayed he couldn't feel her trembling.

"Ready to head back to the table?" He skimmed his hand down to her waist and slipped his arm around her. "I'm sure your feet are feeling it." A devilish gleam lit up his eyes. "Want me to carry you?"

A dozen responses ran through her head, all underlined, bolded and fear-based. She tensed, ready to bolt. Orin drew back a little, no doubt feeling her unease. She struggled to pick out logical words to cover her reaction.

"I don't like to draw attention to myself."

"Sweetheart, you drew attention to yourself the second you walked into the building."

Midge didn't know whether to head for the hills or melt at his feet.

"Come on. Let's sit."

Orin tucked her under his arm and led her back to their table. It looked like melting was going to win.

She *was* strikingly beautiful. Those Marines hadn't exaggerated. But if half of what Kurt had heard about her was true, she had the soul of a viper, and she'd done an excellent job of mesmerizing him. There was a familiarity about her that he couldn't place. Yet if they'd met before, he was sure he'd remember. The red hair alone—

A wig?

The dim light made it impossible to tell. Even if it was, her beauty still stood out. This was a memorable woman, one who drew attention her way, whose sensuality was front and center. On the surface, nothing about her was hidden. Alone with him in this corner, she was different, somewhat shy even. It was quite a contradiction.

He loved women with a bit of mystery about them. It was what had drawn him to his little court reporter. *No. Not* your *court reporter.*

He tried to shake away thoughts of the unattainable Staff Sergeant Ellis, but the damage was already done. He imagined an impossible scenario where she'd release her hair from that stark bun and it would tumble over her bared, full breasts. She'd slip her glasses off, perch the stem between her lips and give him a come-fuck-me look he wouldn't be able to refuse. His dick had been locked and loaded from the second he'd rescued Midge on the dance floor, and he'd imagined it was his staff sergeant in his arms.

Again…not yours. And you know nothing about her.

Kurt told his conscience to shut the fuck up. He *didn't* know anything else about her, other than her first name was Michelle. It was all part of the getting-to-know-each-other stage, part of the allure of being with someone. Doing a background check on a potential date was not only bad form, it was also creepy and an invasion of privacy. Ellis wasn't interested, period. He had to let it go. He had to stop feeding himself fantasies of her night after night, *especially* tonight. His focus had to be on the job.

He had to admit that at some point he'd forgotten this wasn't a date. Their conversation, the feel of her in his arms, her *everything* wove a spell around him. Then he'd done what he shouldn't have. He'd made the first move and kissed her. Her response had been so innocent, like that expression on her heart-shaped face—too similar to the shape of Ellis's face. He was beginning to wonder if he had the right woman. There was nothing predatory about Midge. He wondered if that was part of her allure. Yet all her victims had indicated she'd pursued them with relentless determination. None had been strong enough to refuse.

Kurt could see that. Under normal circumstances, if Midge had made a move on him, he would have gone with it. The difference between him and her victims was that he was single and diligent about using protection. All the hot moves in the world wouldn't make him deviate. As for sex... It had been a while. His cock didn't care that she was an extortionist. He wanted her with a single-minded determination that had nothing to do with the case, and he blamed his lapse on fantasies of Staff Sergeant Ellis.

In the dark you can pretend it's her.

Kurt mentally rolled his eyes. Already he'd screwed up with that kiss and had almost messed up by giving his real name. He had to calm down and let her make the first move. No way would he allow her to scream entrapment.

He ordered Midge another glass of wine when they passed the server. Midge refused it, laughing.

"I've had my limit for tonight."

She glanced up at him with smiling eyes. They were gray like a fog in the night, begging to be explored.

"I was ready to leave the minute I got here. Now I'm glad I didn't," she told him.

"Me, too." Odd that it wasn't his special agent voice talking.

When they reached their table, Midge slid across the booth. Her tiny skirt creeped up, revealing black lace grazing the top of her shapely leg. His mouth went dry. He'd always loved the accessibility of thigh-high stockings and he lost his focus wanting to explore what lay in the dark shadow above the lace. His hand itched for contact. Had her action been a deliberate ploy to draw his attention? Her body language screamed innocence again. That made him want to dive in and taste her from head to toe.

At this rate, he was going to cave long before she made any move. He had to subtly nudge her in the direction he wanted.

Kurt pulled her hand into his and traced the outline of her slender fingers with his thumb. She flushed and fanned her free hand against the hollow of her slim throat.

"Would you like to step outside for a few minutes?" he asked.

He studied her face, all curves and shadows in the half-light of the bar. There was that familiarity again. He chalked it up to having read the repeated descriptions of her. "The smoke is getting to me, and I wouldn't mind getting some fresh air," he added.

She surprised him by not jumping at the opportunity. He questioned again if he had the right woman. The wig was right, but she wasn't wearing the boots and she wasn't aggressively pursuing him, though she did seem interested. Kurt decided to play it out. It was possible she suspected a trap.

He laced his fingers through hers and brought her hand to his lips for a kiss. "We can stand next to the door if you feel uncomfortable being alone with me. I promise I won't ask you to sit astride my lap."

She laughed, relaxed and nodded. It was a nice laugh—strong and clear—and it sank deep into his veins.

"I could use some fresh air," she replied.

After retrieving their jackets from the coat check, he escorted her to the exit where they had their hands stamped with the Oasis palm tree logo that permitted reentry. Stepping outside into the cool desert air, they walked toward the row of concrete benches down from the entrance. The air was crisp and smelled of spicy desert creosote. The crescent moon rode high, a thin icy sliver in the air. All in all, a perfect night. It'd be even more perfect if he could close this case.

They sat side by side, leaving room between them. Kurt tried to keep the conversation easy while he ferreted out information about her. He asked about her likes and dislikes in movies and food, asked if she had any pets and feigned interest in her cat. Though he tried to keep a professional distance, each minute he spent with her made him want more. Telling himself this was how she entrapped men didn't cool his libido. He wanted her, plain and simple. He racked his brain, trying to determine if she'd somehow managed to put something in his drink. Nothing came to mind. He'd kept his drink close.

And her closer?

The words rattled him. He was supposed to be a professional. There was *nothing* professional in how he felt about her. She might be just the woman to rid him of his unrelenting want of Staff Sergeant Ellis, even if doing so was for the case. What-ifs rolled through his head. *What if I pull her to my lap? What if I drag her back inside to the nearest restroom? What if I take her to my car and —*

"You'd make a great reporter." Her light laugh punctuated the sentence.

Kurt dipped his head to one side. "Why do you say that?"

Midge averted her gaze, looking shy. More doubts about her resurfaced.

"You're very good at putting people at ease and getting them to talk with you. I'm not much of a talker. I prefer to keep to myself."

"And yet you're with them." He jerked his head toward the building.

"They're more a nuisance than friends. They came into my life one day and I haven't figured out a graceful way to get rid of them, although I came pretty close to showing them the door tonight." She shrugged one shoulder. "I let myself be talked into coming here and was hating every second…until I met you."

Midge turned his way, sliding her hand over his chest. His cock hardened and heartbeat accelerated.

"I so want to kiss you," she whispered, leaning in.

Kurt slipped his hand around her waist and met her halfway. He dusted his lips across hers. The warmth of her breath against his mouth felt like a caress. She closed her eyes with her sharp intake of breath. He waited, not moving. Her small sigh sifted through him. They eased into the kiss. She tasted of warm wine and sweetness. His brain shut down with every curl of her tongue over his. His body demanded full contact. That small sound of pleasure deep in her throat didn't help. He dragged her astride his lap, cupped her fine ass and pulled her close.

"There are much more comfortable places to do this." She cupped his face and rubbed her thumb through his fake beard. He prayed the sucker would stay in place.

"I agree."

He kneaded her ass, torn between thrusting against her and pulling her off so they could leave. She tossed her head back on a gasp, exposing the long column of her neck. He traced his tongue from the well of her throat back to her lips. She turned her head, avoiding his kiss. "I need to let my companions know I'm leaving."

Midge kissed him again, slow and sweet, then pulled away and pressed her forehead against his.

Belowdecks, his body throbbed in time with his racing pulse. Here was the come-on he'd expected. The woman was a skilled tease. None of his past liaisons had ever managed to pull this type of response from him. She had to be his target. He had her right where he wanted.

Really? His conscience chortled.

He concurred that she was the one in control, but what better way to get the goods on her? They'd share a bed, she'd make her standard blackmail move and they'd have her dead to rights. With the lights off, he could obscure his use of a condom. Though disposal would be tricky, he always carried a plastic bag with him.

By the end of this night, he'd know her full name and address, something her victims claimed they didn't know. The best description they could give was it was a house like all the rest around it and sparsely decorated inside. Sometimes she took them to a motel. A search of her purse should get him what he needed. She'd have to go to the bathroom at some point.

Kurt slipped his hands from her panties and eased her back, tugging her skirt into place. "Why don't you wait here? I'll go inside and tell your pests that you're leaving." He brushed his hands down her thighs. "You shouldn't have to go back into that mob. It'll just take me a minute or two, okay?"

Relief softened her face. "Thank you. The smoke was really getting to me. Don't be too long. I'm starting to get cold without your hot body against mine."

She was killing him, because Kurt was fairly certain that if he didn't get inside her soon, he'd die. He blamed it on his long dry period, blamed it on the elusive Michelle Ellis. He was primed and ready now, more invested in the sex than in catching his prey. *Not good*. He had to gain some perspective and objectivity here.

"I can take care of that."

He pulled his key fob from his pocket and aimed it toward the white Camry belonging to NCIS—a match to his own. One press of the button flashed the lights and opened the door. Midge's bright smile blessed him.

"I'll be right back." He gave her a quick kiss and headed for the entrance while she walked to his car.

At the door, he showed his hand stamp to the bouncer, who acknowledged him with a nod. Kurt couldn't risk finding Midge's companions. They might decide she was better off with them and get her to stay. He waited in the men's room until enough time had passed to make it plausible that he had searched the club for them. Then he walked to his car, shaking his head as he formed an apology for her.

Midge kept her gaze forward as he slipped behind the wheel. Her body language didn't bode well for him. Her arms were crossed and her posture stiff. He never should have left her alone. It was a rookie move that had given her too much time to think. Kurt thrust his key into the ignition.

"I couldn't find them anywhere. I think they may have left. Let's get you home."

Midge tightened her arms when he started the engine. "I can call a cab. You've been drinking."

"I only had one glass of wine. I'm good."

"I don't want to put you out."

She was taking giant steps away from him. It was another new move. None of her victims had indicated she'd changed her mind once she'd targeted them. That seemed to be clear evidence he'd been made. Kurt had to find a way to salvage things and get them back on track.

"It really isn't any trouble," he assured her. "I don't mind. If you want to make sure I'm not a serial killer, you can go ask Dougie the bouncer over there. He knows who I am and will vouch for me."

He was taking a huge risk. The chances of Dougie recognizing him in disguise were zero. Kurt was counting on Midge not doing what he'd suggested and that the offer alone would ease her concerns. Then he took another chance.

"It's just a ride home and me walking you to your door like any gentleman should do. It doesn't have to be anything more than that. You're the boss. You're in control."

When she didn't respond, he pulled out his burner phone. "Or I can call you a cab."

She stared at the device he offered. After a few breath-holding seconds, she smiled at him. "You really are a gentleman. It's been so long that I'd forgotten what one looked like. How did I get so lucky to have met you?"

Luck had nothing to do with it, sweetheart.

He shrugged and put the phone away. "Funny. I've been thinking the same thing. We good?"

"More than good." The tension in her rigid posture faded. "My place isn't far, about two miles away. It's easy to find."

Kurt wondered if it was a ruse. Her victims indicated a drive of at least fifteen minutes. If she were suspicious of him, she could direct him to any house where she could allow him to see her to the door, then take off once he left.

On foot? In killer heels? Barefoot?

He tossed the notion aside and followed her directions. Within minutes they were in front of a two-story structure that stood out among the single-storied houses around it.

"It's an awfully big house for one person," he said.

"It's two houses. I live in the left one. We share the garage between them," she replied.

No cars in the driveway probably meant all the vehicles were in there. The idea of running her plates was off the table. He pulled to a stop at the curb and cut the engine.

"I'll get your door," he said, opening his own.

"Not necessary."

She was out before Kurt could stop her. He hurried to her side before she started for the door.

"You're not making it easy for me to put my gentleman moves on you."

She pressed her palm to his chest. "There are moves then there's overkill. I'm not a fairy princess who needs sit in place to have her carriage door opened."

He slipped his hands around her waist. "Ah, so you're a warrior queen. I've met a few of those." *And loved them all.*

Midge's gaze dropped to his throat. "Maybe I was back in the day, but not now."

The sadness in her voice tweaked his heart. Curiosity begged him to ask what she meant. Duty required him to keep his mouth shut.

"It's getting cold. Let's get you inside" — he tucked her against him — "because I *am* walking you to the door."

After that, it was all up to her. Kurt couldn't press to enter the house, couldn't entreat her into sex, couldn't do anything that made it appear as though he'd tried to entrap her, despite the fact he wanted to do all of those things.

She cuddled close and somewhat led the way. He committed her address to memory. The house numbers were clearly visible. No other details leaped out at him.

"Who lives in the other unit?" he asked.

"My busybody landlady. The woman knows no boundaries," she replied. "I'd leave, but I really love the place."

He heard the jingle of keys as they reached the front stoop.

"Have you tried setting some boundaries?"

"I…" Midge paused, key poised to unlock the door. "Not yet."

Warmth curled around them when she pushed open the door. She stepped over the threshold then turned his way.

"Would you like to come in?"

"I would very much like that."

So it *was* her place. What did that mean? Wrong woman or new moves? Kurt wasn't sure what to do. He'd never been this conflicted before. Night-lights here and there gave Kurt enough illumination to do a visual sweep of the place. There was nothing sparse about it.

Bookshelves lined the room, packed neatly with books of various ages, mostly old. There was the overstuffed leather couch with a coffee table facing a flat-screen television on an entertainment console. Two armchairs with end tables pointed toward the fireplace but could be easily turned toward the couch. A multi-colored Oriental rug was in front of the fireplace. There was no computer or laptop that he could see, but there was a tablet and an e-book reader on the coffee table among some magazines.

The walls had two pictures, one a numbered Picasso serigraph at the foot of the staircase above a polished oak sideboard, and the other, a still-life depicting a wooden bowl filled with water-beaded lemons above the fireplace.

"Nice place." *Expensive things.*

"Thanks. I buy secondhand and restore. I find it challenging and calming."

All right, so not expensive. A pair of golden eyes staring from one of the chairs jolted him. "Is that the infamous Hades?"

Midge laughed lightly. "It is. I'd caution you about making friends. He's persnickety."

More doubts. She wasn't fitting the profile, or rather, she fit the profile sometimes but not others. The cat was one more example of how she might not be his target. Pets and kids were always a good way to break the ice, though. Did he want to break the ice? If she wasn't the woman he was looking for, he needed to leave.

"I've never been able to resist cats and dogs." He walked toward the cat.

She snorted. "Don't come crying to me if you draw back a bloody stump."

"Heaven forbid."

Hades sat up at Kurt's slow approach. The cat's tail was flicking and Kurt got the feeling he was being sized up for the kill. No growl or purr greeted him, just those unblinking eyes.

"Hey, buddy. You are a handsome guy. With that glossy black fur, you've got great camouflage to stalk the night, panther-like."

Hades stood, stretched his back and kneaded his paws into the cushion. Kurt avoided eye contact and offered his hand, knuckles first, as he sat on the arm of the chair. Hades took a tentative sniff, then head-butted him with a purr. Kurt rubbed his cheeks and continued his scan of the place. All was neat and orderly. A landline phone was on one end table. The message light was flashing like crazy.

Hades meowed and rolled to his back. Smiling, Kurt rubbed his ears, earning a rumbling purr. He turned his attention away from the cat and back to her. She stood beside her long couch, watching him through wide eyes.

She was a looker. His body fully appreciated that. If she was the perp, he had to keep emotional distance, no matter how great the sex might be. If she wasn't... *Fuck.* If she wasn't, Kurt would want more. He'd want to know her, be with her. How could he do that when he sat there in disguise? Would he have a shot at her without it? Come clean now? *And what if she is this blackmailer?*

Leave.

That seemed his best option. If only he could make himself get up and go. *Screw Ellis. If she doesn't want me, I don't want her.* But he did. He wanted her more than he could bear, despite her rejection. Right now, contemplating a relationship with Midge, if she wasn't the suspect, felt like cheating on his nonexistent girlfriend.

"Looks like you have a lot of messages." He jerked his chin toward the answering machine.

Midge shrugged. "They can wait."

"Not even curious?"

"Not really. Anyone important to me has my cell phone number."

"Would it be ballsy of me to ask for that number?"

"Why?" Suspicion laced her tone.

"Maybe I'd like to take you out to dinner. I don't want to be swallowed up in the mass of messages."

She studied him for too long before she pulled her phone from her purse. "Give me yours first."

Midge flipped it open. It was yet another discrepancy in her methodology. His target had a state-of-the-art smartphone, not a flip phone. *Who has a flip phone in this day and age?* He rattled off the number to his burner phone, not his real number. She punched it in with record speed then tossed the phone back into her purse.

He watched her studying him. 'Sizing him up' was a better term. Kurt could see the wheels turning in her head. It worried him. This whole night had him second-guessing himself. Right now, he didn't know what to do. The awkward silence was killing him.

"Not decorating for Christmas?" he asked.

"I'm saving that for the weekend. I would have started today, but I was overtaken by events."

"The undynamic duo?"

She snickered. "They wouldn't take no, and I didn't feel like arguing the point."

It hadn't been the first time she'd said something similar. *Leave now. Fuck. Give me some sign of what to do.*

"I'm giving you points for the clever superhero reference." Midge kicked her heels off. Their *thunk* on the wooden floor pulled Kurt to his feet. Hades hopped down beside him.

"What was so special about today?" He walked toward her, Hades by his side.

"Today is my birthday."

Her slow steady pace as she started toward him mirrored a feline stalking prey. His cock rose up to meet her.

"Happy birthday." Kurt hoped he managed to sound cool and collected, because he was anything but.

"It will be in a few seconds." In front of him now, she slid her hands up his chest and around his neck. "I'm making you my birthday present."

She covered his lips in a tongue-tangling kiss that shut his brain down and set his cock on high alert for action. *This* was how *she* lured men in, though her victims had indicated she'd enticed them until they made the first move. It didn't matter. He'd have her and her schemes dead to rights now. She couldn't accuse him of being the aggressor. She was clearly in charge and, God help him, all he could think about, dream about, pretend about…was a buttoned-up court reporter who wouldn't give him the time of day.

Oh, damn, this man can kiss.

Midge went melty in some parts, hard and wet in others. She wanted to climb Orin's body until she could wrap her legs around his waist and rub against that delicious hard-on.

She hadn't needed to have her glasses on to see — to *feel* — Orin's interaction with Hades. In the two years since she'd adopted him from that godawful shelter, Hades had never taken to anyone at first sight. Ninety-nine percent of people got a hiss and growl from him or the rare claws-out swat. But Orin had known how to approach him, and Hades clearly loved every second, evidenced by his deep purrs and the need to rub all over Orin. Midge understood *that* feeling all too well. In that moment, he'd won her body and maybe a little of her heart.

She craved him against hers, to be pressed so tight atoms couldn't get between them, to fall into his embrace and drown in his kisses, to fuck him right here and right now. Midge could have blamed it on the wine or her too-long abstinence, and maybe she would in the morning, but all she wanted was him. Hunger, need and an attraction she couldn't deny drove her to make the first move, something she hadn't done in years. It felt liberating to have her old self resurface.

Too many times tonight she'd heard herself thinking or saying how she didn't like conflict. She was sick of hearing the words roll through her head or come from her lips. Enough was enough. She'd let that awful incident years ago define who she was now. She'd stopped living and hidden away, afraid of... *Of what?* She'd done nothing wrong. God, how she wanted her old self back for good—starting now. She prayed the wig stayed put.

Guilt seeped in past her horniness. Orin had talked about them going out to dinner. Was it a come-on or the real deal? Wasn't having sex with him now under false pretenses? It wasn't her he'd be fucking. It was a fake—

Oh God, yes.

He'd curled his hand around her breast. One squeeze had sent her libido into overdrive. She broke the kiss and arched her neck. Orin dragged his lips down her exposed throat.

"Please, tell me you have condoms," she said in a rush a breath.

He stopped moving for a second before he said, "I do." The rumble of his voice against her neck speared downward. "But I'm thinking two might not be enough tonight."

"Some men say it with flowers. But you? Damn."

Stretching to her toes, she tried and failed to hook one leg around his waist. He was so much taller than she was without the killer heels. Orin cupped her ass and hoisted her to the back of her couch. When she locked her ankles around his waist, he pressed into her. Midge let a moan speak for her. Then his lips were on hers again, delving deeper with every flash of his tongue. She writhed against the ridge of his cock. Denim had never felt so good.

He braced one hand on her back, the other kneading her breast in time with her gyrations. His low groan rumbled down her throat. Her body clenched at the sound. Then he ground into her pussy. She broke off the kiss with a gasp, offering her throat once more. Orin nibbled his way downward, shoving her tank top up and her bra down. She fumbled for the hem, dragged the garment over her head and threw it aside.

Hades will love making a nest of that.

A flick of Orin's thumb released the hook on her bra. The straps fell. Before she could pull her arms free, he captured his prize, sucking one nipple hard while he twirled the other between his thumb and forefinger. Midge fisted the back of his shirt and pulled it up. He stopped long enough to yank it off. She placed her hands over his pecs, loving the strength she felt and damning the semi-darkness that kept her from seeing him clearly.

But she could feel, and he did nothing to stop her from doing so, emitting soft sighs and grunts of pleasure with every sweep of her hands. She brushed her fingers through his chest hair, palmed his hard nipples, traced the contours over, down, around and up to his shoulders. Puckered flesh halted her exploration.

"What's this?"

Orin caught her wrists, thumbs poised over her pulse. "It's nothing, really."

Another topic off the table. How many more did he have? It really killed the mood. Maybe she'd be wise to set a few ground rules of her own.

He sighed and dropped his hand to her waist. There wasn't anything turned-on about the sound this time.

"It's a bullet wound," he said. "I got it in the line of duty last year."

That spawned a lot of questions, none of which she was going to ask.

"And you don't want to talk about it."

"I don't," he replied. "At the risk of sounding crass, I like you enough to want to have crazy sex with you. But I don't know you well enough to share my life stories with you…yet."

It was lovely to know they were on the same page. "I appreciate that and concur. Shall we take this up to my bedroom?" She brought her lips a breath away from his. "I want your body on me."

He slipped his hands around her back. "And I want my body in yours."

Before she could realize what he was going to do, Orin scooped her into his arms. "I'm presuming up the stairs?"

"Yes."

She wanted to protest, wanted to tell him to put her down, but his alpha male tactics made her heart tumble a little bit more. Midge draped her arms around his neck.

"Don't kill us."

Orin's smile and the gleam in his eyes devastated her senses. "Stop distracting me by being so hot."

She laughed. "Oh my, I do love having my ego stroked."

"Is that all you like stroked?" He kissed her quick and started up the stairs, halting halfway up.

"What's wrong?"

"It's hard to walk with a cat curling through your legs." Orin put Midge down and scowled at Hades. "I have to admit this is the first time I've been cock-blocked by a cat. If you cut it out, I'll let you watch. You might learn a few things about the ladies."

Hades meowed.

"Neutered, huh?" Orin replied. "Pity. Still, I'll let you watch and you can dream of things you'll never have."

Hades actually managed to sound mournful.

"I hear you, buddy."

Midge laughed. "His pain is real. He has a love interest who won't give him the time of day."

"Been there, done that."

Orin scooped him up in one arm and draped the other around Midge's shoulder. There went her heart again. She was liking Orin more with every second. That dinner out he'd suggested sounded awesome. This could be the start of a new relationship. Yet here she was in disguise, walking up the stairs toward her bedroom for that crazy sex he'd mentioned. And, really, wasn't that all he wanted? He'd said as much minutes ago. She'd leave the wig on.

He set Hades on his feet when they reached the second floor. The cat flicked his tail and trotted into her bedroom, most likely to his favored spot on the windowsill. Midge laced her fingers through Orin's as she led the way those last few feet.

"We need a few ground rules," she told him. "I don't want the momentum shattered by any false moves."

He pulled her into his arms when they crossed the threshold. "'No' works very well for me. It doesn't matter how far along we are at the moment. If you say 'no', I stop. But I agree knowing what's off-limits first might be good."

She pulled in a breath and released it slowly. "It freaks me out when someone starts running their fingers through my hair. I'm very tender-headed."

Midge hated herself for the lie. Having a man dig his fingers in her hair was a major turn-on…when done right. Her instincts told her Orin would be that person. He'd start at her nape, then slowly crawl his fingers up. A shiver ran through her. She hoped he didn't notice.

"I'm with you on that. I don't like people messing with my hair or my beard."

"And I prefer sex in the dark. Night-lights notwithstanding." *Liar, liar.*

"Me, too. Now, for what I do like." He pulled her against him, cupped her ass and walked them toward her bed. When the mattress hit her legs, he unzipped her skirt. Midge wiggled free of it and sat down. Kneeling, he tossed the garment aside.

"I love undressing a woman." He brushed his hands up her legs, stopping when he reached the lace at the top of her stockings.

"Taking my time."

The barest touch of his thumbs over her exposed skin made her body sizzle. She curled her fingers over the edge of mattress, frozen in place and waiting for his next move.

Orin toyed with the lace, running his index finger under one band then the other. He was close enough that her arousal had to be obvious. Her panties were damp with want and her clit was swollen. She'd never been with a man who'd taken his time with seduction. While her body screamed for relief, she was more than content to let that need build, to let Orin have his way with her. Who knew when she'd have the opportunity again?

He slowly peeled one stocking down, pausing at her knee. His breath danced over her thigh. She parted her legs, giving him better access. The feel of his lips on her skin took her breath away. Eyes closed, she basked in the tremors ignited by his slow crawl upward. Once he reached the top, Orin skipped to her other thigh, peeling her stocking away, kissing what he'd exposed all the way to her ankle.

"You're shaking." He reached for the remaining hosiery, feathering his fingers down her leg.

"I can't ever recall being this turned on before." *And, by the way, I want to clamp your head between my thighs while you trace your tongue through my lady parts.*

"Talk about an ego-stroker. That really puffs up my...chest."

Midge giggled and traced her toes over his cock. "Did you know I can pick up a roll of quarters with my toes?"

"Now *I'm* more turned on than I've ever been."

He chuckled and reached for her panties. The slither of microfiber had never felt more sensual. When that last impediment was gone, Orin stood and shoved his hand into his pocket to retrieve a condom.

"Uh-uh. My turn. You aren't the only one who likes to unwrap presents."

She hooked her finger through his belt loop and pulled him against the bed. He started to reach for her head, then yanked his arms to his sides. The little package crinkled in the crush of his fist.

Midge thumbed open the fly button as she traced her tongue over his six-pack. The musky scent of his arousal coiled around her, stirring her juices.

"Excuse me if I'm not as patient as you are." The telltale quiver of anticipation wiggled through him, much to her delight.

She caught the tab of his zipper between her teeth and pulled down. Heat basked her face. Grabbing the waistbands of jeans and boxer briefs, she yanked them down. His cock bounced free, hitting her cheek and leaving precum behind. She flicked it away with her finger, then slowly sucked the digit clean. Hard breaths lifted his shoulders. The tension in his fists doubled.

Midge pushed the clothing to his ankles, but his shoes kept her from removing them. Orin wasted little time pulling free, taking shoes and socks with him. When he reached for her, she pressed her breasts against his thighs, tickled her fingers up the backs and raised herself until his cock was cradled between her breasts.

"You realize I'm about a breath away from coming," he told her.

"So if I dig my nails into your ass, you're toast?"

He chuckled. "Oh, yeah."

"Hmm."

It thrilled her to know she'd turned him on that much—again, something no other man had ever admitted to before. She eased away and crawled backward on the bed, pushing the covers down as she went. Orin took his sweet time putting on the condom—gathering his control, she'd bet.

We'll see about that.

Midge toyed with her nipples. His sharp intake of breath speared through her. The mattress dipped with his weight. She parted her legs ever so slightingly, inviting him in. Orin took his time about it, kissing and licking his way up her body and setting little fires in his wake. She reached for him when he hovered over her, wrapping her arms around his steely torso. He brushed his fingertips over her cheek, kissed her nice and slow then sank his cock deep inside.

Her brain shut down, lost not only in the feel of his possession but the swirl of emotions that engulfed her. At some point she realized Orin hadn't moved—not even his lips. It was as if they were frozen in this moment. They ended the kiss at the same time. Orin released a hard breath and pressed his forehead to hers. She tightened her hold on him, never wanting to let go. He made her feel…whole.

"Afraid to move?" she asked him.

"Not afraid to. I just don't want to. You feel like…" He lifted his head, gaze locked on her. "There are no words."

He slipped his hand between them, nestling his thumb on her clit. "I love that you're as hard as me. Come with me. I want to feel your muscles clamped tight around my cock."

Then he moved—a slow glide in and out that invited her to join him. She coiled her legs over his calves, catching his rhythm, loving the rise in momentum and speed that matched the flick of his thumb. Orgasm raced over her. She relished the feel of him coming with her. The sensation hovered, demanding and getting more from them both. By far, it was the best orgasm she'd ever had.

Their hard breaths mingled in the aftermath. She basked in his kisses and caresses. No flopping over in bed for this guy. Another first, as was never having come at the same time as her lover. Now that she'd experienced how delicious it felt with him hot and hard inside her, Midge hungered for more.

"We are *so* doing this again," he murmured against her lips.

"I totally agree." She grinned. "And if it's just as good as the first time, I might be willing to break into *my* stash of condoms."

"I love a challenge. Allow me to show you my moves."

He rolled to his back, taking her with him.

Chapter Three

"Michelle!"

Bernadette McFee's shrill voice reverberated from the living room below, piercing Midge's dreams.

"I need to borrow your iPod, but I can't find it in all this debris. This is most untidy of you."

Kill me now. Better yet, she could kill her intrusive landlady. Any jury in the world would consider it justifiable homicide.

"It's in your lease that the unit be kept in peak order."

Midge groaned. Sated from a long night of sex, she hadn't bothered to pick up once Orin had left at four. She hadn't done anything except yank off the wig and throw it aside before going back to sleep.

"This is a great inconvenience for me. I know you're still here. I saw that huge vehicle of yours in the garage. I do wish you'd park it outside."

Only because she wanted to park her blasted Cadillac dead center. Midge wasn't going to budge on that issue. Her lease indicated she could park in the garage and that was where her SUV was going.

Midge heard footsteps stomp her way. Bernadette was coming up the stairs. Nothing was sacred. Privacy was a foreign word to her.

Hades' snarl told her that Bernadette had entered the room. Midge cracked open her gummy lids. The chubby little blonde dangled last night's attire on the tip of her finger as if afraid mere contact would soil her expensive chartreuse linen suit and fuchsia silk blouse.

"It's on the dresser. Leave me alone."

She groaned, glanced at the bedside clock and tried to turtle back under the warm bedclothes. Being around her neighboring landlady was a painful experience under the best of circumstances, but especially so at seven-forty in the morning when she had a pounding headache.

Seven-forty in the morning? Oh, crap, I'm late for work.

She tossed back the covers, scattering pillows in her leap from bed, realizing too late that she was naked. Bernadette gasped and averted her eyes. Ignoring her dramatics, Midge grabbed her glasses from the nightstand and dashed into the walk-in closet.

There wasn't time for a shower. If she wasn't in the courtroom in twenty minutes, the judge would crucify her. She was never late. *Never.* She'd either slept through her alarm or forgotten to set it.

"This hideous costume smells like a filthy ashtray." Bernadette's screech filtered into the closet. "If this carpeting absorbs the odor, I'm going to have to charge you for a cleaning service."

Midge grabbed a clean pair of panties and bra, then fumbled around on the floor for an olive-drab T-shirt. Her shapeless camouflage uniform was hanging on a hook, waiting to be ironed. She wrinkled her nose in disgust. The T-shirt wasn't clean and her uniform was creased. She'd planned to do laundry before Susan and Jeremy had arrived last night. *Then there was Orin.*

A shiver coursed through her. He'd kissed her senseless before he left, trying to coerce her phone numbers from her. Midge had placated him with a promise to call him tonight by nine and the reminder that he knew where she lived.

"Michelle, you aren't paying attention."

Will her tirade ever cease? Just take the iPod and leave, bitch.

Midge longed to let loose and give the woman a piece of her mind. That whole confrontation thing reared its ugly head. That—and the lack of time.

"I said I was looking for your iPod. I know you have one. You wear it when you run. I desperately need it."

"I told you it's on the dresser," she shouted back.

She burst from the closet, buttoning her cammie blouse with one hand, carrying her heavy black military boots in the other. At least they were clean and polished, one positive thing in her favor. She sank to the edge of the bed to put them on.

"You got in late last night. What is this, pray tell?" She dropped the red wig next to Midge on the bed.

Her mind raced for an answer. Time was a bigger enemy than Bernadette and Midge had had enough.

"Not that it's any of your business, but it belongs to a friend." After she twisted her unruly dark curls into a tight bun at the nape of her neck, she snagged a tote bag from the closet then grabbed her keys off the dresser.

"I have to go. You can let yourself out."

"I saw you with a man last night." Bernadette remained rooted to her spot, blocking the exit. "You've never mentioned having a brother. Are you *seeing* anyone? What is the polite term for that sort of activity these days? I noticed he stayed rather late."

Interfering bitch. One day, she was going to get up the guts to really tell Miss Priss where to go. If only she had time to unleash her inner warrior queen. Shoving past her was the best Midge could do. She dashed into the bathroom, randomly tossing bath accessories into the tote. If luck was with her, she could take a fast shower when the judge called recess.

Bernadette hovered by the door, arms crossed. Midge darted past her and ran down the stairs. Bernie dogged her steps.

"Late nights really don't agree with you, dear. You're being quite rude."

With that remark, the bitch made her exit, without the iPod. She'd probably never wanted it in the first place and had been fishing for information about Orin. Bernadette's idea of exercise was an all-day shopping spree down in Palm Springs. Even then, she selected high-end boutiques where clerks brought the clothing to her while she sipped champagne and ate chocolates.

She loved the house and the rent was reasonable, but the fact that Bernadette used her pass key to come in whenever she needed something—a bottle of wine, a magazine, food—rightfully pissed Midge off. She valued her privacy above all things.

Seven-forty-five. Damn, damn, damn.

Snagging her purse from the couch, she dashed into her kitchen, grabbed the box of cat chow from the pantry and shook a cupful into Hades' bowl, ignoring his this-won't-do snort.

"Don't start with me, mister," she muttered. "I'm having a very bad morning."

She darted through the side door. The garage she shared with Bernadette's adjoining home was quiet, no sign of her nosy neighbor. *Thank goodness for small favors.* Bernadette was probably calling one of her cronies to report the encounter.

Midge punched the button for the garage door opener, started up her silver SUV and backed out with a roar, careful not to get too near Bernadette's cherry-red Cadillac. One scratch and she'd be in small claims court for sure.

This had to stop, but she hated the thought of having to move. Living close to work was a blessing — especially today — and the condo was snug and homey with lots of room for her books and window ledges for Hades to perch upon. It was time to draw that line in the sand and order Bernadette not to cross it.

What if she'd walked in on me and Orin?

The thought made Midge laugh. It'd be worth it to see the horror on old Bernie's face. She let images from the night before sink into her veins and couldn't wait to do it all over again. She ached thinking of him filling her, of him making her come, of the way their bodies moved in perfect synchronicity. Her nipples tightened with her clit. She shut down the fantasy train and focused on her anger at herself for letting others walk all over her. Doing so was her fault, no matter what her justification. *No more.* It was time to fully resurrect the Midge who wasn't afraid to back down.

Her SUV's tires squealed around a corner she took too fast. She checked the dash clock. *Seven-fifty-five.* No way was she going to make it. She turned onto the main thoroughfare leading straight to the Marine Corps base. At this rate, she'd be lucky if a cop didn't pull her over. She accelerated to the guard gate, breaking hard at the last second. The armed military policeman on duty extended one hand for her ID card. He looked at her photo then squinted at her.

"Doesn't look much like you. Rough night?" He snickered and waved her through the gate.

Shocked and confused, Midge eased into the base traffic. At the stoplight she turned the rearview mirror toward herself to see what the sentry was talking about. Her hair looked like a bird's nest, her eyes were bloodshot and puffy from the club's smoky air and she still had remnants of last night's makeup smudged on her face.

"I look like a train wreck."

Steering with one hand, she tried to wipe the mess away with a tissue. It was hopeless. There weren't enough tissues in the world to clean her face. She turned the mirror to its correct position and tried not to think about her less-than-stellar appearance. At eight on the dot, she skidded into a parking spot at the Office of the Staff Judge Advocate, grabbed her things and sprinted for the door.

It was a busy Friday morning. Marine clerks crisscrossed the long hallway, ducking between offices, carrying paperwork and delivering case files. Two civilian defense attorneys, preparing to meet with their military clients, paced impatiently in the reception area, waiting for the military police to deliver them.

Midge raced down the corridor, ignoring gaping coworkers hovering around the communal coffee urn. She threw her tote and purse at her desk as she passed her office and headed straight for the courtroom at the end of the long building.

One minute past eight. Late.

Maybe they hadn't started on time. Maybe the judge was still in his chambers. She opened the door and cringed.

Lieutenant Colonel Epstein sat in the judge's chair, twirling his silver pen between two fingers. He glared as she hurried to the court reporter's station located directly in front of and below the judge's box and slid into place.

"Staff Sergeant Ellis, so nice of you to join us." Judge Epstein's voice carried through the courtroom with quiet, deadly precision.

She forced emotion from her face as she readied her closed microphone equipment. "Sorry, sir."

From the corner of her eye, she saw the prosecutor and the defense counsel had broken off their chatter with Special Agent Davidson to watch the interplay between her and the judge. Embarrassment overwhelmed her to have Davidson see her this way, not that he'd ever been interested. She had Orin now. What did she care what he thought? But she did and, despite the killer sex last night, she still craved him.

"Thank you for gracing us with your presence this morning. If it isn't too much of an imposition on your time, I'd like to commence with the court-martial," the judge said.

"Yes, sir. Sorry, sir." Were her cheeks as red as they felt? "I apologize to you and to the rest of the courtroom for my lapse."

He eyed her for a moment before he nodded. "This tardiness hasn't happened before. Make sure it doesn't happen again." His mouth tightened as he looked her up and down. "Also, Staff Sergeant, next time you're in here, I expect you to be looking like a Marine, not a bag lady."

"Yes, sir."

Blind with shame, she double-checked her equipment. Faint snickers drifted from the bailiff and from the first sergeant, who attended the proceedings as a representative from the accused's command. She gritted her teeth and began recording. She had no one to blame but herself. It had been pure carelessness on her part not to have prepared her uniform the night before and double-checked her alarm. She wasn't a raw recruit and prided herself on being on top of things. Plus, she'd worked hard these last three years to not bring attention to herself — to keep her head down and do her job. She'd failed miserably this morning, all because of a hot guy.

Midge fought to keep her smile inside. No way would she regret last night.

The testimony dragged on. The accused made his plea for leniency in the face of the larceny charges brought against him by the government prosecutor. The young man had been caught pilfering gift cards from the convenience store on base. It was a slam-dunk case that didn't need all these witnesses and didn't require the presence of NCIS. At the one-hour mark, Lieutenant Colonel Epstein called for a fifteen-minute recess. Her bladder cheered.

"I expect you to use that time to clean up, Staff Sergeant," he told her.

Heat burned her face. She was never going to live this down. To make matters worse, her stomach complained about the lack of food and the growling drew more looks her way. She counted the seconds until the judge's chamber door closed behind him. There was a controlled surge to the exit — everyone heading for the coffee urn. She shoved her sliding glasses up her nose. She had fifteen minutes and knew she could get cleaned up in five — *if* everyone got out of her way. In her haste, she cut in front of First Sergeant Yost and Special Agent Davidson.

"Hold up there, Ellis," Yost said.

She reluctantly turned to face him. Yost's weathered face was sunburned from a recent training exercise out in the desert with his tank battalion.

"You all fired up to get back to the Oasis?" He gestured at the distinctive ink stamp still visible on her hand. "I wouldn't have thought it was your type of place. Did you wander in there by mistake?" His loud bray turned heads.

Midge said nothing, hoping Yost would shut the hell up and not keep reminding her of her public embarrassment. He was the type of man who continued to joke about other people's humiliating moments ad nauseum. She could only hope he got transferred to a remote location where she wouldn't have to deal with him ever again. The moon sounded great.

His Southern drawl continued as she hurried on.

"She's a fine court reporter but odd as all get out. Y'all know what I mean? Keeps to herself and walks around like she's trying to hide all the time. God, did you smell her?"

The reply from Davidson was low but audible. "The entire courtroom could smell her."

Yost snorted. "She reeks of something, that's for sure. I'm surprised the judge didn't order her to report to the shower the minute she walked in. Another court reporter could have filled in."

Davidson snickered. "I'm surprised the accused didn't change his plea to guilty just to get the hell out of there. She also needs to lose the bun hair."

Midge jerked to a stop outside her office. Coworkers paused in the corridor and stood wide-eyed, waiting for her response. She'd had enough. Sometimes a woman had to make a stand. That started here and now. Yost's comment was typical, but Davidson's comment was unexpected and hurtful. To think this was the man she'd spent her nights lusting after. His unnecessary cruelty fueled the simmering anger inside.

She whipped around to face the men, halting them in their tracks. Long strides put her five feet from them, though she longed to stick her face up close and personal—nose-to-nose, drill instructor mode—so they'd really get the message.

"With all due respect, *gentlemen*, I may not be a fashion model, but I have manners enough not to bad mouth someone behind their back. If you've got something to say, say it to my face."

Arms stiff at her sides, fists balled, she glared at Yost then turned her stare on Davidson. It was the first time she'd ever been so close to him. She already knew he was an extraordinarily attractive man. This close, he looked even better. That hint of a dimple in his left cheek begged to be licked. A flush covered his cheeks. At least he had the courtesy to be embarrassed.

He waited, head tilted ever so slightly. His nostrils twitched and she swore he took a deeper breath. She hoped he had the sense to keep his mouth shut. All she needed was one more straw and she'd explode. She longed to tell them that the elusive scent Yost couldn't identify was the smell of sex—hours and hours of hot, body-grinding sex. That if he'd had any, he would have recognized it. If she gave in to that urge, Midge was certain a charge of insubordination would be leveled against her. Was she brave enough to counter-attack with a charge of harassment? Maybe, but she doubted anyone would back her up. She'd learned that the hard way.

She stood her ground, daring one of them to say something. As precious seconds ticked away, the hint of sandalwood drifted her way. Her body took notice—

heart racing, nipples tightening, clit hard and ready for action. Midge swallowed and took a closer look at Davidson, appreciating his good looks and hating herself for it. She had a man, a hot man. *Why give this guy the time of day?* Again, her body disagreed.

"Is there a problem here?"

Judge Epstein came up behind Davidson and Yost. An empty coffee cup dangled from his finger and they were between him and his target — the coffee urn down the hall.

"You've got" — he glanced at his watch — "thirteen minutes. Move it. Clock's ticking, Staff Sergeant."

Midge didn't have to be told twice. Her beef with Yost and Davidson would keep until she had time to plan a proper rebuttal, and the more distance she put between herself and Davidson, the better. She spun around and saw Major Zach Taylor standing behind her, and he was pissed. Dread crawled up her spine, until she saw his ire was directed toward Davidson.

"I'd like a word with you."

"Right there," Davidson replied.

His voice struck her, so much like Orin's that it added to her dilemma.

Zach turned, clearly expecting Davidson to follow. Why wouldn't he? They were friends and running partners at lunch. Once she'd realized that, Midge had put a stop to the occasional dinners at the Taylor and Stuart homes. She couldn't risk anyone finding out she was fraternizing with senior officers, despite their history as friends. It wasn't a big deal to hang out with Phillip Stuart since he'd left the Marine Corps. But Zach Taylor? She owed both men more than she could ever repay and loved their wives, but not at the risk of losing all she'd worked to hide. As much as she missed their company, it was over, and she didn't have time to dwell on friendships lost. A hot shower called her name. She grabbed her tote and aimed for the women's head, daring a parting shot of Davidson's fine ass as he followed Zach.

Goosebumps rose on her arms, making her shiver. He was memorable, all right, but in the same category as a caged leopard—beautiful, but dangerous, and quite capable of great bodily harm.

* * * *

Kurt followed Zach to his office in the building next door, wondering what the hell was wrong. Zach's body posture screamed upset. Kurt worried if something had happened to Claudia. She was due to deliver their son within the next two weeks. Anything could have gone wrong.

Zach whirled on him the instant the door closed them in privacy. His dark eyes shot lasers at Kurt. He jammed his fists on his hips. Kurt had seen this stance before. He hadn't liked it then and didn't now. This had nothing to do with Claudia. Zach was mad at him.

"What the fuck is wrong with you? That was uncalled for."

He'd heard the exchange with Ellis and was rightfully pissed. Kurt had no defense. He wished he could take the words back. She didn't deserve to be treated with disrespect. She was a top-notch court reporter who always did one hell of a job. He admired her work ethic and her dedication. So what if she wasn't interested in him? It wouldn't be the first time a woman had shut him down. But he couldn't get her out of his mind or his fantasies, even after last night with Midge. Hell, he'd pretended it *was* her and not Midge he'd been with. He ached to see what was behind the mask Ellis showed the world, wanted to pull her hair from that bun, to open her uniform one button at a time to see the woman beneath the façade. Yet she remained prickly and standoffish. Her doing so only fired his fantasies.

Then she'd charged up to him and Yost, putting them in their places. Fire and outrage spat from her and she'd been close enough to burn them both. Very close. Too close. Close enough for Kurt to identify the scent exuding from her pores. She reeked of sex. Jealousy strangled his gut. His cock had filled to bursting before he could blink. Worry over Claudia had helped subdue him. He wasn't in the mood for a lecture from Zach on his behavior.

"You're no better than Yost. Worse, in fact." Zach stabbed a finger at him. "You've complained about her from the minute she arrived here. I don't understand why you dislike her. You barely know her."

Kurt rubbed at the headache blooming behind his eyes. "I don't dislike her. I just don't understand her."

Zach snorted. "Welcome to the club. I've yet to meet a man who understands a woman."

He straightened his shoulders, taking offense. "I understand women just fine."

"Being able to dress up like one for an undercover assignment doesn't make you an expert."

Kurt's irritation grew. *What the hell business is it of Zach's?* Yeah, Kurt may have crossed a line with Ellis and he shouldn't have engaged in good-ole-boy talk with Yost, but Zach was more than pissed. He was furious, and Kurt couldn't figure out why. He pulled in a breath that did little to calm him.

"Allow me to clarify. I don't understand *her*. She looks like she could be a beautiful woman if she'd fix herself up a bit." He cursed himself for the lie. There was beauty there waiting for him to discover bit by bit.

Zach's eyes widened. "She *is* a beautiful woman. What the hell is wrong with you? It's not like you to judge someone based on what you see on the surface, especially when *you* look like shit this morning."

"I was working last night." Had he stumbled over those words? Because it'd felt like anything but work being with Midge, and that was causing him all manner of angst.

"Whatever. You were an ass back there. In fact, you've been a jerk about her since she arrived two months ago. I want to know why."

Fine. "If you must know, she shut me down."

His eyebrows inched closer. "Shut you down?"

"I flirted with her and she ignored me."

Zach burst out laughing. "Oh my God. I've seen your sad attempts at flirting. You probably did something innocuous like offered her a stick of gum or a candy. She didn't fall at your feet and you considered yourself kicked to the curb."

He'd almost nailed it. Anger flushed Kurt head to toe. He couldn't find words to defend himself. She hadn't said no. She'd said *nothing.*

"This from the king of bad courting?" Kurt shot back. "How long did you pursue Claudia?" He stared into the corner as if the answer were there. "Five years, I believe."

"Don't try to change the subject," Zach replied. "I get it now. I should have seen it before. She's bothered you too much not to mean something to you."

Kurt wanted to deny it, but the images of having her in his arms, slowly removing her clothing a piece at a time, swam through his head.

"In any event, you owe Staff Sergeant Ellis an apology."

He wasn't wrong, but he'd be damned if he'd let Zach know that. "I'll think about it."

"No. You'll do it. You were wrong. Instead of putting on your good-ole-boy persona for Yost, you should have worn your knight-in-rusted-armor one and defended her. *That* would have gotten her attention."

He hated that Zach was right—hated himself more that he'd missed that opportunity.

"And if I don't?"

Zach smirked. "I'll tell Claudia."

Fuck. Score to Zach. Claudia would tear Kurt to shreds with that sharp tongue of hers if she knew he'd disrespected a woman. It didn't help that Kurt knew he was out of line and stupid on top of it all. Why hadn't he seen the incident as a chance to win Ellis' favor? He'd been too focused on how she'd ignored him to figure out how to correct it and too dumbstruck by the smell of sex that clung to her.

"Fine," he snapped, and whipped open the door.

"I'll know if you don't," Zach said behind his back.

Kurt flipped him off and kept walking.

* * * *

Midge hurried through her shower in record time, returning to her desk to find an oatmeal-raisin energy bar, iced coffee with cream and a box of alcohol wipes waiting for her. She blessed whoever had taken pity on her—someone who knew she loved cold brew and the perfect proportion of coffee to cream. It had to be Zach. She'd thank him later. Midge wolfed down the treat, used the wipes to get the blasted club stamp off her hand and was back at her station with two minutes to spare. Yost and Davidson were gone—another blessing.

The court-martial zipped along. By the time lunch rolled around, the guilty verdict and sentencing were announced — brig time, forfeiture of pay, demotion to private. The Marine had the nerve to look outraged. Midge bet he'd be back in court shortly after he was returned to duty. He had 'career criminal' written all over his expression.

She gathered her work, looking forward to lunch, during which she might recover some of her reputation by working through the ninety minutes. That hope was dashed when she saw Zach coming down the hallway dressed in PT gear.

"Good. You're here." He motioned to her. "I've lost my running partner."

"Lucky me," she mumbled.

He grinned. "Glad you feel that way. Let's go, Staff Sergeant."

Instinct told her that he had an ulterior motive, but Midge had little choice. He was her superior officer. She dressed to run and met him outside. After a quick warm-up, they hit the pavement.

"That was a new low for you this morning," he said.

Midge stifled a groan. *Always trust your instinct.* She braced herself for his lecture.

"I get that you don't want to draw attention to yourself, even though I don't much like that you've chosen to hide. But that —"

"Would it help if I told you it wasn't intentional?"

"It wouldn't hurt. Want to talk about it? You know you can tell me and Phillip — and our wives — anything."

That was very true, and she hated the regulations that made her keep her distance. She missed their company. She told Zach everything — the disguise and her decision to go with it, not having her glasses, Orin coming to her rescue, how hot the sex was and missing the alarm. By the time she was finished, they'd run their two-mile course and were nearly back to the office.

"Sounds like quite the man," Zach told her. "I'm guessing you're going to see him again?"

"I told him I'd call him tonight. He said something about us going out to dinner. I'm still not ready to give him my phone numbers."

"I don't see why not? He already knows where you live and can find you if he wants."

"That was my feeling, as well. I guess I want him to work a little more for the numbers." She smiled. "I can't give him everything all in one night."

Zach laughed. "That's it, my friend. Make him work for it. What's his name?"

"Orin Davis."

He stumbled in mid-stride, quickly recovering.

"Are you all right?" she asked.

"Tripped over a stupid crack. I'm okay. Embarrassed, but okay."

They picked up the pace, sprinting the last fifty yards to the office.

"Good run." He fist-bumped her shoulder. "Gotta stay in shape for when Claudia's able to jog again. The woman can run me into the ground."

Midge laughed and prayed no one made an issue of them running together. "My pleasure, and thanks for the energy bar and cold brew this morning. I was starving."

"Wasn't me."

Her thoughts went to his earlier demand to talk to Davidson. "You told him to apologize."

"I did indeed." He winked and aimed for the men's shower.

She wasn't sure how she felt about that. Take the olive branch extended or beat Davidson over the head with it?

He was wearing sandalwood aftershave.

Midge ordered her subconscious to shut up and hurried to the women's head for what was going to be a cold shower.

* * * *

Jess Alderman reached into his shirt pocket and took out a toothpick. He slid off its cellophane wrapper then deftly placed it between his teeth at the corner of his mouth. Leaning forward over his battered old desk, he laced his big hands together. It was a deliberate pose that made his lanky frame seem unthreatening and approachable.

Kurt had seen his boss use the trick many times when interrogating witnesses. The real Jess could be as approachable as a great white shark circling its prey.

"So, you went to the club in search of our blackmailer with the idea you could gain her trust and get some valuable information, and you ended up driving her home where you subsequently engaged in sexual intercourse. Am I getting this straight?"

It wasn't sexual intercourse. It was sex and we fucked each other senseless.

It was the best sex he'd ever had and though he shouldn't, he wanted more. Telling himself this was how she roped in her victims didn't help. He blamed his lust on his dry spell and those fantasies of Ellis that had run through his head while he screwed Midge.

"She made a move on me. I ran with it. It's how she operates. We play her game and let her trap herself."

Jess grunted and pushed the toothpick to the other corner of his mouth. "What next? Dinner and a movie? Or will you keep fornicating with her for the duration?"

"Don't start with me, Jess. I've had one bad run-in today, and I'm not in the mood for any more crap."

"A bad run-in with who?"

Jess was baiting him, but Kurt wasn't interested in playing games, and he sure as hell wasn't going to tell his boss that he'd made an ass of himself.

He couldn't stop thinking about Ellis this afternoon. The erection from hell had returned with a vengeance. He cursed himself for the thousandth time for not seeing his golden chance.

Jess cleared his throat. "A bad run-in with *who*?"

"Doesn't matter," he mumbled. "I just owe someone a personal apology."

The treat he'd left on her desk wouldn't suffice. He hoped she didn't realize it had come from him. He'd been too fearful of rejection to leave a note. Her knowing that the food and drink were from him might make her question how he knew her likes. Kurt was wondering that himself. Clearly, he'd been paying more attention to her than he'd realized.

It worried yet intrigued him that she'd been at the Lost Oasis the night before. Why hadn't he noticed her? Surely he would have seen her walk in. He'd been lying in wait for his target a good hour before she'd arrive. He'd seen everyone who'd walked into the place, watched it fill to capacity. Ellis would have stuck out. Had she seen him and avoided contact? He mentally shook his head. That was impossible. He'd been in disguise.

She reeked of sex.

All he could think about was how she'd be in bed and wonder who the lucky man was who had opened that prize. Would she be better than Midge? *Oh hell, do 'em both.* He willed the fantasy away and waited for Jess to make his next move.

They eyed each other for a minute, then Jess broke the tension.

"Okay, slick, let me remind you about the last time you went a little too far with your investigation. You ended up getting shot and spending a lot of quality time healing and in rehab, remember?"

Kurt's shoulder and thigh twinged with half-remembered pain. His recovery had been long, involving months of rehabilitation. He refused to argue with Jess about old cases so said nothing.

"You've got to stop getting obsessed with these parts you play." Jess shook a finger at him and put on his lecture face.

"I'll do my best to stay as uninvolved as possible." Kurt mustered his most earnest expression. "It's a blackmailing case, nothing too difficult."

That seemed to appease Jess, so Kurt changed the subject. "In any event, that's where I am with that case. I was unable to get her phone numbers. The place she's renting is owned by a Bernadette McFee, who lives in the adjacent house."

"In all your shenanigans, did you bother to get her name?"

Kurt resented his snide tone. "Midge. No last name…yet."

Jess snorted and rolled the toothpick to its original position. "Another new investigation has come up. I want you and Vic to start looking into the specifics."

"Can't the new guy do it? I've got enough to handle as it is."

Jess smirked. "Indeed you do. Stop calling Anders 'the new guy'. He's been here a month already."

"And hasn't done shit," Kurt snapped.

"He doesn't like it any more than you do, but he's got to keep a low profile until that federal trial is over. At the moment, he's got a huge target on his back."

Drug cartel bosses didn't take kindly to being taken down. Kurt appreciated Anders' situation and his frustration.

"This one's important, Kurt."

Aren't they all?

Jess looked tired. His lean face had developed a score of new lines in the two days since they'd started the Lost Oasis case. The blue eyes that normally snapped and sparked with life were dimmed with worry.

"This is about ketamine." Jess leaned back, reached into a battered metal file drawer and brought out a thick manila folder.

Ketamine had become popular with the club crowd because in small doses it produced a fast high. In larger doses it was a date-rape drug. Anders' past experience with drug cases made him the perfect guy for this investigation. It would also put him at great risk should someone see him.

Jess opened his folder and flipped through the papers. He pulled out a page marked with the logo of the Drug Enforcement Administration and slid it across the desktop to Kurt.

"Take a look at this."

Kurt scanned the DEA memo that had been distributed to the law enforcement agencies and military installations throughout Southern California. A large shipment of liquid ketamine, destined for veterinary laboratories in Mexico, had been diverted to the United States and tracked as far as the Riverside area.

At that point, the agents had lost track of the shipment but suspected the bulk of the contraband had made its way up to the high desert area surrounding Twentynine Palms and the Marine Corps base.

Jess' chair creaked as he leaned back again. "There have been several vials of the ketamine confiscated by recent DEA sting operations in the Palm Springs area. Testing confirms it's from the original Mexican shipment. Unfortunately, the bulk of the shipment is still unaccounted for."

Palm Springs was an hour away and a popular weekend destination for the Marines. Hooking up with the stuff would be easy.

"Any hits on our Marines?" he asked.

Jess flicked his now-decimated toothpick into the metal trash can next to his desk. "My sources confirm someone has been distributing powdered ketamine locally, a lot of which is making its way onto the base." He sighed. "That means someone purchased the liquid, cooked it down and packaged it for resale. We need to find out who's selling the stuff and where they got it from."

"Any idea of where to start?"

"DEA is sending one of their regional agents up to meet with me tonight. After that, we'll get started, and I'll bring you and Vic in to meet whoever they send." Jess squinted at Kurt. "I was a little uneasy about having to work so closely with the DEA, but we don't have much choice."

"Why do you say that?" Kurt asked.

"We think the dealer is a Marine."

Saying the words seemed to weigh Jess down more. Kurt understood how he felt. After over thirty years in the business, he knew Jess was tired of always hearing the military was involved, even if that was the job. Retirement might be looking better and better to him.

Kurt leaned forward, ready to suggest it once more.

The office door flew open and crashed against the plaster wall before he got the chance. Kurt jumped up, reaching for the pistol at his side. Streams of dust filtered down from the cracked white ceiling tiles above the desk.

"What the hell?" Coughing, Jess waved his hand in front of his face and shoved to his feet.

Kurt frowned when he recognized the intruder.

Lieutenant Lee Parsons was stocky and built like a boxer. He filled the opening to the hallway as he gripped the doorjamb in a white-knuckled hold that threatened to demolish the wood. The man's dark eyes were wide and bloodshot, flicking between Jess and Kurt, as if he didn't know who to go after first. He quivered with rage and his short blond hair was spiked in disarray rather than combed.

Kurt positioned himself between Parsons and Jess. He balanced on the balls of his feet, ready to intercept any sudden moves from their unannounced visitor. Parsons was big, but Kurt had the martial arts training to bring him down.

"Ease up, both of you," Jess told them. "Sit down, Lieutenant." Jess' chair sighed as he sat.

Kurt lowered himself onto the edge of his chair, keeping one eye on the agitated Marine. He didn't trust the twitchy bastard.

"Lieutenant" — Jess laced his fingers before him on the desk — "what can we do for you? Are you here to break my door or provide us with more information related to your case? As I told you yesterday, Special Agent Davidson has things well in hand."

"He's taking his damn sweet time about it, too." Parsons' anger turned his deep voice into a growl.

Jess flicked Kurt a narrow glare but continued to placate Parsons. "I assure you, Lieutenant, Agent Davidson is working for your best interests. He needs to gather more information about this woman, perhaps entice her to become more involved with him in order to thoroughly expose her blackmailing schemes. He's not taking this lightly. We have to have sufficient evidence to prosecute. You don't want her to get a slap on the wrist and time served for misdemeanor crimes."

"He's too damn slow. She's already working her next victim. I saw some civilian last night with that blackmailing bitch's tit in his hand."

"You were at the club last night?" Kurt didn't bother to keep the annoyance out of his voice. "We asked you to let us handle this and to keep away from her."

Parsons shifted on his chair and twisted his military cover between his paw-like hands. The cap was going to look like something he'd pulled from the trash by the time he was done with it. He focused his gaze everywhere but on them. "I was sitting in my car in the parking lot, waiting for her. I've been there most nights for the past couple of weeks, hoping she'd show up."

Patches of red spread from his thick neck up to his cheeks. "My wife thinks I'm working late on a special project. I patch my desk phone through to my cell phone so if she calls me at work, I can pick up right away."

"Clever you." Kurt didn't bother to hide his sarcasm or his contempt.

"What did you see last night?" Jess asked.

Parsons' jaw clenched. "I saw that whore arrive around twenty-one hundred with a man and another woman. I was parked pretty far back in the lot, and by the time I got out of my car and ran up to the door, they'd gone inside."

Kurt was curious. "Why didn't you go in? Confront her in front of everyone?"

Another flush. Another glance away. "The last time I was in the club I caused a little bit of a ruckus, and now that fuckin' bouncer won't let me in. If the other guy had been on duty, I would have gone after her."

He pounded his clenched fist against Jess' metal desk, knocking paperclips from their bowl. "I swear to God, I'm going to kill her. She thinks she has me by the balls because of one quick hop in the sack. Well, I'm not going to let her do it. Do you hear me?"

"Are you sure it was her?" Kurt asked.

Parsons whipped around. "Of course it was her. No one else has red hair like that."

"Calm down, Lieutenant. We're only trying to make sure we have the right woman," Jess said. "Are you one-hundred percent positive?"

"She's put on some pounds since I was with her. She's curvier than I recall but it's her. I saw her outside last with her new target. He drove off with her. God help the fool."

"Has she asked for more money or tried to contact you in any way?" Jess asked.

He shook his head.

"Then, at this point, you have two weeks to come up with the money before she delivers copies of her video to your wife and your command. That gives us fourteen days to gather enough evidence to solidly convict her. Between now and then, I suggest you stop lurking around in parking lots and spend more time with your wife and children. It's almost Christmas, remember?"

Parsons bobbed his head.

"Are you sure you can't remember where she took you the night you had sex?" Kurt asked for what had to be the tenth time.

The lieutenant stared at the worn carpet and shook his head. "I already told you…some house. It was too dark and I was too drunk. Everything was a blur that night." He glared at Kurt. "Believe me. If I could remember, I'd take care of this problem myself."

Jess gestured toward the door. "Leave the investigating to us, Lieutenant. We don't need any screwups at this point, okay?"

Parsons glanced from man to man. Faced with Jess' implacable reserve and Kurt's glowering stare, he had no choice but to leave, albeit more quietly than he had arrived. The door closed softly behind him.

"Asshole." Kurt slumped into his chair. "So much for happily-ever-after married life. What happened to fidelity? Jerk. I hate men like that. Probably not the first time he screwed around on his wife, and I'd bet it won't be the last."

Jess rubbed his temples. "She knows her targets well, from all the reports that have come in."

"You'd think the men would be too embarrassed to admit they'd been screwing around on their wives. They've risked being brought up on adultery charges by their commanding officers."

"I'd bet she's been counting on that, as well. Parsons still maintains he was too drunk to know what he was doing."

Kurt snorted. "If you believe that, I've got some beachfront property to sell you here in the desert. This isn't the type of woman you can keep your hands off of."

He regretted the words the instant they left his lips.

Jess raised his eyebrows. "What I'm more concerned with right now is your method of information gathering." He nailed Kurt in place with a glance. "Don't screw this up by getting too involved with the suspect."

"Don't worry, Jess." Kurt stretched and yawned. The late night and early morning were catching up to him. "I've got everything well in hand." He grinned. "No pun intended."

"I'm sure."

It seemed Jess wasn't above a little sarcasm himself.

Chapter Four

Midge paused outside of Bakkman's Boutique. The clothing in the window was fashionable but not too outrageous. They were outfits real women might actually wear, not the ragged shreds of polyester and leather waif-like models touted in magazines.

She glanced at her reflection in the store window and sighed. She'd exchange military cammies for a comfortable plaid wool skirt paired with a soft sweater and her winter coat. She'd raked her unruly hair into a ponytail, yet wayward strands refused to be tamed. Wisps of curls framed her face. Off-duty also meant letting her guard down a little. Mascara darkened her lashes and the kiss of blush accentuated her cheeks, but the glasses remained.

She had time to browse through the clothing before heading over to the bookstore for her shift. Though she hated shopping, it was time to cast off a bit of her shell and return to the living. Also, she did need something nice for her potential dinner date with Orin. Squaring her shoulders, she pulled open the glass door. A little bell announced her arrival. The shop was small and scented with pine potpourri that she presumed was in honor of the holiday season, since Christmas decorations were up.

"Welcome. I'm Mrs. Bakkman. May I help you?"

The regal British tones of an older woman suddenly at her elbow so startled Midge that she spun around and knocked into a rack of forest-green silk blouses. The display tipped over, scattering the garments over the floor like leaves blown from a tree.

"I'm so sorry." Midge stooped to pick up the blouses.

"Don't mind those. Stacy will get them." She cupped Midge's elbow and gently urged her to stand. Turning her head toward the back of the tiny store, she called out, "Stacy, I have a job for you. Please come here."

Seconds later a young woman scurried from the back room.

"Tidy up these tops, will you, please?" Mrs. Bakkman waved her bony fingers over the pile.

Without pause, Stacy gathered the blouses from the floor.

"Now for you." Mrs. Bakkman clasped her hands and gave Midge her full attention. "May I help you find something specific?"

"It's time to upgrade my wardrobe." She loved the confidence and determination that came from her voice. The move felt right and perfect.

Mrs. Bakkman dissected Midge's appearance with careful precision. "Anything particular?"

"A mix of casual and something nice I could wear on a date."

"Hmmm," she murmured. "I like a challenge of matching people to the perfect clothing. What size? Ten, if I'm guessing correctly. With all this bulky clothing you've got on, it's difficult to see you have a shape at all. But I think there's more to you than meets the eye." She clapped her hands. "I think we might have a few items that will do nicely. Stacy, when you're done with those, please pull out the wine velvet and the charcoal satin suit, size ten."

"Right, Mrs. B." The girl straightened the last blouse, then bounced off toward the display racks to Midge's right.

Mrs. Bakkman guided Midge to the left where a curtained dressing room awaited. "Undress and I'll pass the outfits through."

Midge complied. As she got down to her underwear and bra, Mrs. Bakkman thrust two hangers through the curtain. Midge hung them up and examined each outfit.

The first was a velvet dress with a scalloped neck and long, fitted sleeves. The color was a beautiful shade of burgundy. Midge stroked the soft material, admiring its classic lines. It was dressier than she wanted but lovely.

The second outfit was a black, two-piece suit. The lapels and cuffs were satin, and the neckline plunged in a deep V that ended at one glittering onyx button. She searched the hanger for a blouse but found none. Midge stuck her head outside the curtain and located Stacy rearranging skirts on a nearby rack.

"Excuse me. I'm missing the blouse that goes under the satin jacket."

She smiled. "There isn't any. The only thing that goes underneath is you." Stacy wagged a finger over her chest.

"Oh." Her lack of fashion acumen was definitely noticeable. Midge ducked back inside and pulled on the burgundy velvet dress. It hugged her curves, kissed her knees and accentuated her breasts.

"Are you doing all right in there?" Mrs. Bakkman's called out. "Once you've got one on, step out so I can assess you."

Midge stepped through the curtain. Mrs. Bakkman stared, one hand cupped to her face, mouth pursed in thought.

"What do you think?" Midge asked hesitantly.

"Could we lose the ponytail, dear?"

Midge slid off the scrunchie. Her curls sprang forth in a riotous tumble and cascaded halfway down her back. A few more errant twists curved around her face. Her mother had always nagged her to get it cut short so it could be more manageable — 'tidy' was the word she used — but Midge refused. She liked long hair.

"Gorgeous." Mrs. Bakkman flicked a hand toward her. "That dress, combined with your deep brown hair, is glorious. I love the red-and-gold highlights. Absolutely beautiful. I don't see why you keep those curls all wadded up at the back of your head like that. If I'd had hair like that at your age, I'd make sure everyone could see it. And your figure... See for yourself." Her voice was sincerely complimentary.

Midge turned to face a three-way mirror on the wall next to the dressing room. The ghost of Midge's past was reflected back to her. This was who she'd been before *it* had happened and Midge wanted that person back again something fierce.

"You've got a lovely figure. It's a shame to cover it up with frumpy clothing. Didn't your mother ever take you shopping?"

Midge's smile froze. Her mother had never had the time to take Midge anywhere, let alone shopping. All her waking hours had been spent slaving away at her administrative job in order to maintain a home and put food on the table for them—something she never let Midge forget. Her parents' divorce had been bitter. It had tainted her mother's attitude about everything reminiscent of her former husband, including her daughter.

She smiled at Mrs. Bakkman in the mirror. "I'll try on the black suit. I'd also like to try one of those forest-green blouses with gray slacks."

"I'll get those for you. By the way, what is your name?"

"Midge Ellis." She extended her hand.

Mrs. Bakkman's handshake was firm and dry. "I'll only be a minute, back in time to see the next outfit."

Midge changed into the tuxedo-style suit, which left quite a bit of her cleavage exposed. Air from the store's heating vents slithered down the V-neck like a cold finger. *Or a hot tongue.* Suppressing a shiver, she stepped out of the changing room.

"Marvelous." Mrs. Bakkman clapped her hands and walked around Midge while she eyed her with a proprietary stare. "Well, you can see what I mean."

Again, Midge turned to the mirror. "Holy cow." She was shocked by the amount of creamy bosom that surged between the black satin borders of the lapel. "I couldn't wear this in public." She laughed at the thought.

"Pishposh." Mrs. Bakkman waved the notion aside with a toss of her fingers. "You've certainly got the bosom for it. So many women come in here who don't have enough to fill up a teacup, let alone a sophisticated little number like this." She sniffed. "Then they have the nerve to suggest alterations. Imagine the ruin. If they would stop drinking diet soda and eating lettuce for breakfast, lunch and dinner, they might have something to put into that jacket."

Midge laughed again as Mrs. Bakkman placed the blouse and slacks in the dressing room.

"You realize you wouldn't wear a bra underneath that, don't you? Otherwise, the front of the bra would show."

Midge cocked her head to one side as she studied her reflection. *No bra?* That sounded sinfully delicious. "It's beautiful. They're great. I'd like both. Now let me try on—"

"Midge, look at you!"

She cringed at the sound of Susan's voice.

"I thought that was your SUV outside, but I didn't think you'd actually be shopping *here* for clothes. I thought you lived for Walmart." She walked toward Midge, looking chic in a pair of black knit trousers and a fitted black cashmere sweater.

Irritation crawled up her spine. "Did you need something, Susan? I don't have a lot a time before my shift at the bookstore."

"Judging from your selection there, you're the one who needs something." Susan perused her through narrowed eyes. "I think it's a little bit much for someone like you. How about this one?" She grabbed an electric blue dress with dolman sleeves off a nearby rack. The neck was an unadorned scoop and the bias-cut hemline would skim at mid-thigh.

"That dress is totally inappropriate for this young woman's hair color and aura," Mrs. Bakkman sputtered.

Susan leaned close to Midge and whispered, "Perfect for red hair though, right?"

Midge winced. *Damn.* She'd forgotten about the stupid wig and the charade she'd gotten herself into. Susan was right. With the crimson wig, the dress would be fine, and it certainly was eye-catching. But she wasn't about to spend money on something that wouldn't look good on her real self.

Susan checked the size of the blue dress. "This will fit you. Listen... I'm parked next to a hydrant out front, and I don't want my car to get towed. I'm going out back to see if there's another space available."

"No." Midge returned the dress to the rack. "I'm good with my choices. I don't want your help."

She crossed her arms and jutted out one hip. "Awfully snotty all of a sudden. You ditched us last night. We didn't really appreciate it. So now that you've gotten laid, we're too good for you?"

She had some nerve. Resurrected Midge wasn't putting up with it. "You need to leave. Now. I'll see your things are returned to you."

"Fine." She turned and walked out. The tinkle of the shop door heralded her exit.

Mrs. Bakkman mouth puckered as if she were sucking lemons. "That one is definitely no lady."

Midge sighed. "You're right about that."

"Good riddance," Mrs. Bakkman added.

"But she did draw my attention to this lovely evergreen number." Midge pulled a feather-soft shift with long sleeves from the rack. Her encounter with Susan had cost her time. She wouldn't be able to try anything else on. "I'd like all four outfits, please."

Mrs. Bakkman applauded her choices and lost no time getting Midge's purchases on their hangers and hung in a black garment bag that had the Bakkman's

Boutique logo emblazoned across the front in spidery gold script.

"I hope you enjoy these," she said as she handed Midge the receipt. "I know you'll do justice to them all. You are a strikingly beautiful young woman. We hope to see you again." The lines at the corners of her eyes deepened with her smile.

"I'm sure you will."

Midge waved goodbye as she exited the store. A few minutes later, she pulled into the Book Nook's parking lot. After a moment's hesitation, she picked up the garment bag. She wanted to share with someone and there was no one more perfect than Vera Livretti.

The Book Nook was in an old adobe house that had been converted into a bookstore. Emma Alderman was the proud owner and had wasted no time hiring Midge part-time. Vera was the manager, display designer and resident palm reader, although Midge wasn't sure how many of Vera's prophesies were geared toward encouraging book purchases and how many were genuine portents. Midge had loved the bookstore from the second she'd walked in. Its maze of rooms promised surprises at every twist, as did the chimes attached to the front door.

"I'll be right out. Feel free to browse," Vera called from the back.

"It's me."

Midge wound her way through the rooms. Vera had spent considerable time transforming the shop into a winter wonderland for the holidays. A few customers stood here and there, absorbed in their browsing. Most of them were regulars who came in for the conversation as much as anything else.

She finally found Vera in the children's section, struggling to set up an end cap filled with DVDs of the latest Disney movies.

"Let me give you a hand with that." She laid her purchases on a reading table and grabbed the other side of the unit.

They shuffled the end cap into place near the chapter books and took a step back to admire the display. Vera had used papier-mâché and paint to make an ice castle.

"The kids are going to love that." They doted on the attention Vera gave them.

"Goddess, I hope so." Vera sighed and stretched her back. "It took me hours to get those silly turrets just right."

Somehow Midge didn't think Vera minded all that much. She had a zest for life and an appreciation for detail not too many people could match. She was a vivacious woman in her early forties with long black hair worn in a single plait down her back.

Creative and eccentric, she dressed to entertain herself as well as the customers. Today she must be in an exotic mood, as she wore a mango-colored sari with matching brocade slippers. Her arms were piled with brass and copper bracelets that clinked as she moved, and her braid was decorated with strands of yellow and orange beads looped in and out through her hair, ending at a small bell that tinkled with each twitch of her head.

"Nice outfit," Midge told her.

"Thanks," replied Vera. "I did a *Jungle Book*-themed story time for the kids today. They each pretended to be a different animal while I narrated. We may have gone off book." She laughed—a bright sound—then she studied Midge. "You're looking especially lovely and bright-eyed today." Vera raised one delicate eyebrow. "Do I sense a man entering your sphere of influence?"

Midge didn't want to go into any details right now but knew that once she showed Vera the Bakkman's bags, more questions would come. Vera was a good listener. She might be able to give some good advice about the wig and what to do about the charade.

Midge sighed and picked up her bags. "Let's put these away in the coffee room then I'll spill the whole sordid tale once we close."

Two hours later, the last customer left and Vera turned the 'Closed' sign around on the front window. Between book buyers, Midge had managed to share her recent exploits, and now they were finally alone, so she could get Vera's opinion.

"What do you think I should do? Wear the wig again or not?"

Vera opened her mouth to reply when a hard rap at the door interrupted her. "Who could that be?" She peeked through the Venetian blind then unlocked the door and pushed it open.

"I'm so sorry, Jess. I'd forgotten you were coming by tonight."

Midge's breath caught. It wasn't the tall, lean man with the gray hair who'd caught her attention. It was the younger man with the killer looks who trailed Jess into the store.

Davidson stared at her as if seeing her for the first time. She wished he'd stop because the flame in his eyes had found a target between her legs.

Ellis stared a hole through him. Not that he didn't deserve it. A wave of annoyance tinged with embarrassment rushed over Kurt.

Stay calm and pull it together. Apologize.

He would, but not in front of an audience. He forced a smile and tried to ignore the curl of shame twisting in his gut. Something about the woman always pushed his buttons, and he was damned if he knew what it was that had her front and center every night in his masturbatory fantasies. And *fuck,* he was hard again — in full view of anyone who looked.

Look, baby.

Why should she after the way he'd behaved that morning? Why the hell did he want her to see what he was packing?

"I presume you two know each other from work?" Jess' question hung in the air.

Kurt pulled the door shut, waiting for her to answer.

"We do." Her tight voice dripped acid. "Special Agent Davidson considers himself a fashion consultant for women Marines."

"Just the ones who need a lot of help," he snapped back.

He got that she was angry. She had every right to be. But he wouldn't stand there and take her barbs. A man needed to defend himself.

"I don't need your help with anything, buster."

She stepped toward him, fists balled at her sides. Her hair drew his attention. Free of its usual confining bun, it cascaded in a waterfall of curls down her back and around her face. It was a rich brown and shone with mahogany highlights. There was a familiarity about her that he couldn't pinpoint — hair down, her heart-shaped face, full lips.

Of course she'd be familiar. He saw her often at work. It was the hair. There was so much of it, it had to weigh a ton, and it looked silky. He had the urge to reach out and stroke the one soft curl kissing her cheek. Kurt plunged his hands into his jeans pockets.

"Children, children." Jess followed up with a fatherly *tsk-tsk*. "How was business today, Vera?"

Jess moved between him and Ellis, blocking whatever current coursed between them. His cock could still feel her presence. Kurt took the opportunity to pull it to a more comfortable position while he was hidden from view.

"We had a great day." Vera shuffled a stack of bookmarks into place beside the register. "Lots of sales."

"Good. Emma asked me to get a trunk from the attic. Apparently, it can't wait until she comes home on Monday. Frankly, neither can I."

Neither could Kurt. Jess had been out of sorts while his wife visited college friends in San Diego. He chanced another peek at Ellis. Her ivory cheeks glowed pink and her gray eyes narrowed behind the glasses balanced on her cute little nose. He envisioned drawing her glasses off, leaning in to —

Stop it.

The mental reprimand fell on deaf body parts.

"I brought along muscle to help with the lifting." Jess jerked his thumb at Kurt, scattering his wayward thoughts.

A twinkle lit Vera's eyes, making her appear ten years younger. The little bell at the end of her braid emitted a small peal as she turned.

"Come on and help me pull down the ladder. There's a lot up in that attic. It might take a bit to find the trunk.

The previous owner left a treasure trove. We'll call your muscle when we need him."

Vera tossed back, "Play nice, kids," as they left and suddenly Kurt found himself alone with a very hostile yet beyond desirable woman.

"Why are you here?" His question cut the long silence.

"Are you surprised to know I can read?" She shot back.

Kurt took a deep breath and tried to remain calm. "I know you can read. I've seen you with a book or tablet during lunch on many occasions. I was making small talk. That's all."

She studied his face as if trying to decide what his motive might be. All Kurt wanted was to apologize and get out of there in one piece. Since they were alone, now would be a good time to do so.

"I started working here part-time about a month ago. I fill in whenever they need an extra pair of hands."

She pushed her glasses up again. He knew the gesture was unconscious and automatic. It was also sexy as hell.

"Have you ever considered getting contact lenses?" Kurt blurted out before he could stop himself.

Anger flared in her eyes.

"I'm sorry. That was rude of me." He had to salvage something here or he'd be up all night, caught between obsessing over Ellis and wanting Midge so he could pretend it was her. The investigation was his priority. Once it was over, he'd be free to... *Shit, am I really thinking of hooking up with Ellis?* "You know, we really got off on the wrong foot this morning. I was having a bad day, and I took it out on you. I'm sorry. I wanted to tell you at work, but you were in court. I did leave you something to eat and drink, and the wipes to clean off the stamp."

He watched her weigh his words as she scanned his face. Finally, she nodded. "I appreciated everything. I accept your apology, and you're right. You were a real asshole."

He stiffened. "I didn't say I was an asshole."

Jess' shout from the back of the bookstore interrupted further sparring. Kurt edged past his antagonist and stalked back to the modified kitchen that served as a small break room for the staff. A pull-down ladder greeted him. The light was on in the attic and he could hear Vera chattering up there.

He scaled the ladder and poked his head through the trap door. A space the size of the building was packed with neatly labeled boxes and several trunks. In the far corner, he saw an old black steamer trunk with brass trim and a small padlock. It was battered and scratched, looking as if it had been hauled around the world and back. Jess removed boxes stored on top of it and stacked them to the side. When it was cleared off, he grabbed one handle and dragged it to the opening.

"Vera, you remember Kurt Davidson." Jess shuffled the end of the trunk within Kurt's grasp. "He works with me on base."

"I do. He's been in one more than one occasion." Flashing another of her glowing smiles, Vera continued to rearrange boxes that were in Jess' way.

Once the trunk was near the trap door, Jess stood up and rubbed the small of his back. "Would someone explain to me why vintage Christmas decorations have to be so damn heavy?"

"Because they're the real deal," Kurt replied. "Claudia and Rowan are going to love them."

"Claudia and Rowan?" Ellis asked.

He started a little, not realizing she'd followed him. "Good friends of mine and each other's sister-in-law. Claudia's pregnant and due soon." Kurt knew he was babbling but couldn't help it. He was beyond excited about the baby.

When she didn't respond, he glanced down at her, ready for battle. The wonder on her face stopped him cold and fired up the beast in his jeans.

"Claudia and Zach Taylor are my best friends. I get to be Uncle Kurt." Joy and pride swelled his chest. "When Claudia let me feel the baby move…" Love poured over him. "I can't wait to hold him. I get to be in the birthing room."

Her expression softened more and that urge to kiss her overwhelmed him again. He turned away, breaking eye contact.

Jess squatted down as he angled the trunk toward the door. "I don't know why Emma wants the women to go through everything now, but I've learned it's best to go with it when she gets a notion." Jess sighed and shook his head.

Kurt backed down the ladder, balancing the end of the trunk against his chest with one hand while grabbing the ladder with the other. "I still think you should have made Phillip and Zach come get the thing."

Jess slowly backed down the ladder, maintaining a tight grip on the handle in order to keep the weight from smashing down on Kurt's head. "Emma forbade the two of them to come bumbling up here. Didn't want them hurt. Me? I'm just the work-horse. The things I do for the woman I love." He chuckled.

Kurt laughed as he eased his way down the last few rungs. "So I've been warned. I'm prepared." He took the last step to the floor and held the trunk steady so Jess could finish his descent.

"Nothing in the world can ever prepare you for falling in love." Jess set his end of the enormous trunk down on the kitchen linoleum.

Ellis replaced them at the bottom of the ladder. "I'm leaving, Vera. See you Monday evening."

Vera swung onto the ladder, kicking dust before her. Ellis winced and backed up, blinking rapidly.

"You all right?" he asked.

She peeled off her glasses and wiped at the corners of her eyes. "Just a little something in my eye. I can't—"

"Here. In the light. Let me see."

Kurt gently pulled her around the ladder and over to the sink light. She came without hesitation. He yanked a paper towel off the roll, wet it and lifted her chin for a better look.

"I see it. Right in the corner." He dabbed at the particle, drawing it away.

"Thank you," she said. "I'm blind without my glasses."

What?

"Not literally, of course," she added.

Her smile turned his insides upside down.

"Midge, are you all right?" Vera asked.

No fucking way. It was a crazy coincidence. That was all. His heart went wild, as did other parts of his anatomy.

"I am." She shoved the glasses back on, turned and breezed from the kitchen.

The skirt flared out to reveal her shapely calves and trim ankles. Like the ones wrapped around his waist the night before? He ordered his cock to stand down, but the thing had a mind of its own. For the life of him, Kurt didn't believe it—or want to believe it.

She reeked of sex.

Fuck.

Why hadn't Jess said anything when Kurt told him the woman's name was Midge? Midge worked for his wife. No way Jess wouldn't have checked her out first. He'd know Midge's address. But hadn't he snorted when Kurt had told him the woman's name was Midge and given Jess her address? He'd known and he'd said nothing. *Why?* Because it was too impossible to believe Ellis could be the femme fatale? Then there was Jess' last-minute request to help him with this trunk. He'd known she would be working tonight. Was Jess fucking with him? Maybe Kurt was wrong about all this. But how many times did a person hear the name Midge—and now there were two?

"Well, you two certainly hit it off." Vera released the ladder, closing the attic. "What's next, pistols at dawn? Mud wrestling?"

The last suggestion hit too close to home. The very image drained the blood from his brain and landed below the belt.

He rubbed his neck and glanced over Vera's shoulder to the far wall. "I was rude earlier and was trying to apologize."

He knew where she lived. If he hurried, he might be able to get there before her to see if both Midges were one. No, that wouldn't work. If he went over as himself and Midge wasn't Ellis, he would have blown his cover. She'd promised to call him tonight. He had to convince her to let him come over. Pleading his want for her should do it. It wasn't a lie. He did want the sex...in the dark...pretending it was... He was driving himself insane. If she agreed, then what? Pull off her wig? It had to be a wig. It was why she'd insisted on sex in the dark. He couldn't fault her for that. He'd readily agreed, to keep his own disguise intact. In any event, he had to get home and get ready, because no matter what, he *was* going to see her tonight.

Kurt aimed for the door.

"Where the hell are you going?"

He snapped his attention to the smug expression on Jess' craggy face.

"Sorry, distracted. Let's get this monstrosity in your truck. I'm presuming Phillip can help you unload it? I need to take care of something."

"No sense you driving all the way out there." Jess glanced at his watch. "We'll catch up over an early breakfast."

That sounded like a plan to Kurt. He might even be able to tie this case up tonight. Other images swirled through his head.

Chapter Five

The buzz tingling through Midge's body was at odds with her brain. She wished to hell her nipples weren't so tight. It didn't help that her clit was growing harder by the second.

Why did Davidson have to be so nice to her? He loved kids as she did and was devoted to Zach and Claudia. Joy had danced in his eyes when he'd talked about the baby. Though the breeze outside had ruffled his hair, it had still managed to look great. The urge to comb her fingers through it had overwhelmed her. Balling her hands into fists had helped keep them to herself. She'd watched the muscles flex under his blue shirt as he'd maneuvered the trunk from the attic. His tight ass had begged her to take a nip.

Her heart had triple-timed when he'd helped clear her eye. There was a familiarity in his touch that dredged up more want, as well as suspicion. Then there his damn aftershave.

What were the odds of two men wearing the same aftershave? *Probably good.* She racked her brain, trying to recall if Davidson had ever used his full name in courtroom testimony. He hadn't. *Orin Davis. Kurt Davidson. One and the same?*

Midge stopped for a red light. She couldn't get the possibility out of her head. It would certainly explain why she'd been attracted to him the previous night. Some part of her might have realized it was the man she'd been craving for months.

"No." She shook her head. Their coloring was different.

Hello? Contacts, wigs, false beard.

She pursed her lips and eased through the green light. Orin was a little taller. Or was he? They'd spent most of their time sitting...or horizontal.

She slowly shook her head. Orin *was* Davidson. She could tell by the tone of his voice when it softened as he'd cared for her. The way he touched her and looked at her told on him as well. They were close enough that she'd seen puzzlement change to recognition when he'd realized who she was. So why hadn't he said something?

Midge laughed. *That* would have made for an awkward situation. She could see the expressions on Vera's and Jess' faces, not to mention the fact that Jess and Emma were protective of her. Talk about awkward. Jess was Davidson's boss.

Maybe Davidson wasn't sure and was tearing identities apart right now. If he'd been at the Lost Oasis in disguise, he would have been working a case. He couldn't very well divulge that information. That made her wonder why he'd hooked up with her. She'd been in disguise too. He'd have to think she was part of whatever he was investigating. He'd be pissed now that she'd inadvertently screwed that up.

Worse yet, he'd think *she* was involved in the criminal activity. Well, she'd straighten that out first thing Monday morning. That meant swallowing her pride and telling him that she'd gone out in disguise because she didn't want anyone recognizing her. Then he'd want to know why, though if he dug into her background, he'd find the answer. Was that the reason he'd gone after her? Had someone seen her with the Taylors and was getting ready to charge her for fraternization?

She shook her head. No, she had been in disguise the previous night. Davidson couldn't have recognized her.

Midge told herself to calm down. It didn't help. She'd told him she would call tonight. It'd be the perfect time to address the issue. She'd rather do this over the phone than in person.

Damn, she'd had sex with Davidson. Great sex. Hot sex. Sex that made her want more. How could they look at each other now without thinking about that? Hell, he was a man. It'd probably been another day-in-the-life moment for him. She prayed her face didn't go red every time she saw him. First Sergeant Yost would have a field day with that.

She blew out a frustrated breath as she pulled into her driveway. A click of the remote opened the garage door. Dread crawled up her spine at the sight of Bernadette's Cadillac. She prayed she could get inside without running into her, not that it mattered with Bernadette's open-house policy.

Midge pulled inside and turned off her SUV as the garage door shut behind her. Somehow, she managed to gather her packages in one fell swoop and got into her house. With a sigh of relief, she hung the new clothes on a hook behind the door and put two grocery bags on the countertop. She'd have to hide the two bottles of malbec from Bernadette later, perhaps in the living room behind some of her books. Since Bernadette didn't read, it'd be the perfect spot.

The desert wind had started to gust, raking the limbs of the mesquite tree against the building like fingernails on a blackboard. A winter storm was sliding into the area, and that usually meant high winds and power outages. Sometimes there was snow — or so she'd been told. She was glad she'd stopped at the grocery store after work and picked up some staples.

Hades strolled into the kitchen and wound himself through her legs.

"I missed you, too."

She laughed and bent down to pick him up, digging her fingers into his soft, silky fur. His deep purr rewarded her attentions. He headbutted her chin then squirmed for his freedom. Midge put him down.

After brewing a cup of chamomile tea, she retrieved her flip phone from her purse and went into the living room to call Orin. She would have preferred wine but needed her head clear when she talked to him. Midge practiced her speech, grateful she wouldn't have to do this in person, yet sad she had to do this at all. She should have known last night had been too good to be true. Even Hades had liked him. That should have warned her something was off. Hades didn't take well to strangers. He still hated Susan and Jeremy, weeks after meeting them — a feeling she echoed.

Midge daydreamed a scenario where Kurt-Orin confessed all then revealed that last night had been special — that *she* was special and he couldn't let her go. They'd start over, more or less. The sex was too great to put on the back burner.

The minutes ticked by. Making the call was harder than she'd anticipated. If Orin was Kurt, he could have gotten her number from Jess or Vera and called to straighten this out. Maybe she was wrong. Maybe she *was* the one in trouble. Was that why Zach had called Kurt into his office? If so, why hadn't Zach warned her when they'd gone on their run? Better yet, why hadn't he said something when she'd told him her date's name? Under these circumstances, his stumble was suspicious. Something wasn't right.

Sitting still was impossible. She paced the rug in front of the fireplace, checking the clock and sipping her tea. Hades watched from his favorite perch on the bench seat beneath the big bay window, tail flicking in time with her steps.

The landline blasted a ring. Midge jumped, spilling her tea. She snatched up the receiver before it rang again.

"Hello?" Her voice came out a choked whisper.

"Where have you been?" her mother screeched. "I've tried to get you all afternoon. I thought having a reliable cell phone would make you more reachable. I should've known better. I'm tired of being left to the mercy of that infernal device."

Midge glanced toward the answering machine and saw the light flashing ten messages. "I just walked in. I thought it was too late to return your calls. You left me *ten* messages?"

Her mother sniffed. "What else could I do? I could only imagine what had happened to you. God only knows what all those randy Marines out there do when they've been living in an isolated area with few women around. They could get desperate and go after you for sexual favors. It wouldn't be the first time you were put in that situation."

That much was true. It was the 'desperate' part Midge had a problem with, among other things. She tried to remain calm. "Mother, I can't talk right now. I have to make a very important telephone call."

"Are you hustling me off the phone so you can take a call from your father?" Her antiquated Mid-Atlantic accent became more pronounced in her fury. Few knew she was Georgia-born-and-raised. "That son of a bitch can drive three hours and see you any time he pleases, but does he let me have one uninterrupted telephone call? No."

"It's not Daddy." Damn, she was tired of this age-old tug of war for her emotions.

"Don't you lie to me, young lady. I bought you a top-of-the-line phone for your birthday and I expect—"

Midge hung up. She couldn't take the shrill accusations any longer. There'd be hell to pay later. Her mother wasn't the type of woman who took rejection lightly—from anyone. Midge couldn't believe she'd actually gotten up the nerve to hang up on her mother mid-tirade.

Oh, the power.

Pleased with herself, she wandered over to her answering machine and deleted all ten messages. A burst from the phone startled her. *Mother simply won't give up.*

Midge yanked up the receiver. "What."

"It's me...Jeremy."

He had that whipped-puppy sound in his voice that she hated.

"Can I come over? I need someone to talk to."

No way. She was ending this association now. "No. I haven't felt good about my relationship with you and Susan from the start. Last night made me realize that it's time we all went our separate ways."

"I really need to come over. It's important. You're the only one I can talk to about this. I'm in trouble."

When isn't he?

"I'm done," Midge told him. "Call Susan."

"She's the last person I'd be calling right now," he replied.

Probably another breakup. Each girlfriend was 'it' for Jeremy, and he'd had a lot of them in their short association. Each time he was dumped, it was a tragedy of epic proportions. Susan was never sympathetic. Frankly, neither was she.

"I meant what I said. I don't want to see either of you again. I'm hanging up now. Goodbye." She put the receiver down.

Hades warbled his opinion from his cozy nest on the window seat.

"I agree with you, pal. This is getting ridiculous."

He jumped down and wandered to the kitchen. Seconds later, she heard him picking morsels from his bowl. By the frequency of the sounds, she'd bet he was arranging them on the floor, either for later consumption or to complain that his bowl was empty.

Emboldened by her actions, Midge sank into the couch and called Orin. At the first ring, her heart pounded and her body hummed.

"Hi. I've been hoping you'd call soon. I miss you and have been tempted to come over but didn't want you to feel pressured." His deep, smooth tone caressed her ear. Now she wasn't so certain Orin and Kurt were one and the same.

"I appreciate your consideration." The quiver in her voice betrayed her nerves. She hoped he didn't notice.

His low chuckle sent shivers up the back of her neck.

"I'd really love to see you tonight. I miss you."

No, definitely not Kurt. He would have gotten to the point and explained the misunderstanding. She drained her mug.

"That sounds wonderful. I'll make sure to leave the porch light on for you. It's hard to find the sidewalk in the dark."

"See you soon. I'm looking forward to it. I was too occupied by the feel of you against me last night that I didn't even think to ask your last name. That's beyond rude and I'm sorry for that."

A crash and a scream from the kitchen kept her from replying. Bernadette's furious screech soared over Hades' high-pitched snarl.

"I've got to go. My cat has gotten into a fight with my landlady."

"What?"

"I'll see you soon," she said in a rush of breath, and for the third time that evening, hung up on someone.

"Michelle, get in here and help me. This wretched beast of yours won't let me down." Bernadette's voice crackled with anger and fear.

Midge ran into the kitchen. The woman stood on one of Midge's ladder-back kitchen chairs. Her pink, ostrich-hide ankle boots scuffed the seat's polished surface as she teetered back-and-forth, trying to evade Hades' swiping paws.

The furious tom crouched, hissing. Claws extended, he swiped Bernadette's leg, ripping her purple tights and leaving behind bleeding furrows. She wailed and shuffled backward on the seat.

"Get off my chair. You're going to break it or fall and hurt yourself." Midge scooped up Hades from his attack position. "What happened?"

"He scratched me." Bernadette jabbed a manicured finger at the cat.

Midge bit her lip and fought hard not to smile as she cuddled him. It served Bernadette right since she persisted in using her pass key to come in without permission.

Bernadette huffed. "Your mother called and asked me to come over and check up on you. When I walked in, this beast attacked me for no good reason."

Hades had more than enough reasons to take down Bernadette, but she kept her opinion to herself. The other news churned her stomach.

"My mother called *you*?"

That was an all-time low, even for her mother. Midge trembled with rage. "So you entered my house again, *without my permission*, because my mother asked you to check up on me?"

Bernadette slowly descended from the chair, keeping one eye on the growling cat in Midge's arms.

"She's worried you're getting involved with some unsavory elements." Bernadette had her composure back, and with it, her venom. "Since Mona and I chat occasionally, she felt confident I'd be able to assess the situation and see what kind of trouble you've gotten yourself into. You're not pregnant, are you?"

Of all the nerve. "For your information, I'm not in any type of trouble nor am I pregnant. Furthermore, any elements I'm involved with are my business — not yours or my mother's."

Bernadette's sharp-eyed gaze zeroed in on the Bakkman's garment bags hanging from the hook on the back of the door.

"Shopping at Bakkman's and you didn't ask me for my advice on what to buy? You know I'm well-known in the best circles for my exquisite fashion sense." She sniffed. "I find it very difficult to believe you actually found anything that would fit you at Bakkman's, given your awkward bosom." She paused and smiled. "They usually cater to the more petite sizes."

Midge tightened her hold on Hades, causing him to squirm. "I think he's getting away from me. I'm going to have to put him down."

She bent over as if to set him on Bernadette's dainty boots. Hades yowled and struggled. Loose hairs flew around the kitchen. Most of them clung to Bernadette's clothes.

She scooted toward the kitchen door, brushing cat fur from her sky-blue suede jacket, one eye on the cat. "We'll talk about this tomorrow. Try to keep that thing locked up in the bathroom when I come over. If I need a rabies shot after being mauled by your mangy beast, I'll be sure Animal Control comes to have him taken away and put down."

With that, she slipped into the garage and slammed the door behind her, but not before she'd eyeballed the two bottles of wine on the counter.

Midge stroked Hades' soft fur. "Good boy. You're an excellent judge of character and that earns you a special treat." She reached into the pantry, brought out a small can of tuna and scooped it into Hades' emptied bowl ringed with dry food. He dissolved into raptures, purring with pleasure as he gulped down the rich treat.

"Next time, take her leg off at the knee," Midge said as she watched him eat.

Here was more evidence she was headed down the right path by making a stand for herself. This insanity would end.

Midge hid the wine behind her first edition copy of *Sense and Sensibility*, closed the front drapes then trotted up the stairs. Dealing with Bernadette had left her little time to prepare for Orin's arrival. It'd taken forever to get the blasted wig on with Susan's help. Now she had ten minutes at the most to transform.

She stopped inside her bedroom. The crimson beast lay on her dresser. No way could she pull this off in the bright light of her home. Darkening the place was ridiculous, as was this entire charade. A relationship couldn't exist on a lie. If all he wanted was sex, Orin wouldn't have suggested a date.

She bit at her cuticle. Maybe it was just sex for him and she was making it more than what it was. In that case, he wouldn't care about the wig. If he wanted more, the lie had to stop now.

Midge drew in a breath and trudged down the stairs. The doorbell rang the instant her toes hit the first floor. She started to remove her glasses, then dropped her hand. Nope, he needed to see the real her.

She looked through the peephole. Arms crossed, he stared at the ground. It *was* Kurt Davidson. She'd spent too much time ogling him these last months not to recognize him now, even in disguise. Confront him or play along?

No games. No lies.

She scrunched up her nose. There was that sex thing again nibbling at the corners of her mind, demanding to be appeased. The doorbell shut off her rambling. Shoulders back, she opened the door.

His smile froze and his eyes widened when he saw her disguise-free. In the light, wearing glasses, she could see the false hair. Hell, she could smell the fresh spirit gum. His expression turned to one of resignation. He *knew* she knew.

Without a word, she motioned him inside. Kurt kicked off his shoes as soon as he stepped inside.

"Sorry. The lifts are killing my feet. I'd rather wear stilettos than lifts."

"*Have* you worn stilettos?"

"Yes." He pulled off the wig and cap.

Midge curled her fingers at her sides, fighting the urge to ruffle his sandy blond hair into place.

"Bathroom?"

"Same place it was last night."

"Makeup remover?"

"Medicine cabinet."

She followed when he started up the stairs. Hades shoved past her to catch up to him.

"Did you recognize me at the bookstore?" she asked.

"Eventually."

He stopped to pick up Hades. Deep purrs drifted her way as Hades butted his head against Kurt's chin over and over again.

"And you?" he asked.

"I've been debating the possibility you were one and the same. What does it really matter at this point?" she snapped. "What's going on? Was this a ploy to get me into bed?"

He turned so fast she nearly ran into him.

"Seriously? I didn't know it was you last night. Also, you came on to me first."

He stared at her, continuing to indulge Hades' demand for petting. Midge understood that well. She hadn't been able to get enough of his touch the previous night.

"My reaction should be answer enough." He set the cat on the landing and walked to the bathroom.

"If you'd known it was me, would you have still done it?"

"Yes."

She didn't believe him. "Why?"

Kurt sighed and braced his hands on the vanity. "It's...complicated." He opened the cabinet and retrieved the remover.

She sat on the closed toilet to watch. The contacts were the first thing he took out, placing them in a case he'd had in his jeans pocket. Getting the beard and mustache off was going to take a while.

"Why the getup last night?" he asked.

"It was Susan's idea. Her birthday present to me. I didn't much like it, but it was easier to go with the flow than fight her."

"Why no wig now?"

She was embarrassed to tell him. "I'd convinced myself you and he were the same person. When you called, I told myself I was wrong. I thought there might be some relationship developing and I didn't want the lie to continue. Then I saw you as him and I knew it was you. Your turn. If you recognized me, why the disguise now?"

Another sigh was followed by a wince as he pulled off the mustache. "All right. Don't be mad."

Midge cringed, taking his warning to heart. She wasn't going to like this. "Go on."

He started on the beard. "It was part of an investigation."

Rage coupled with heart-rending despair welled up in her chest. This was never going to die. She'd been threatened with retaliation 'if it takes forever' and it had followed her wherever she went. But take down Zach, too? Midge willed tears away and hiked her chin.

"I can more or less understand why you'd go after me, but to hunt Zach? I thought he and Claudia were your best friends? If this is how you treat your friends, God help your enemies."

She darted for the door. Zach needed to be warned so he could defend himself. Kurt hooked her arm before she could make an exit.

"Whoa, whoa, whoa. What in the world are you talking about? I would *never* do anything to hurt them. And what reason would I have to investigate *you*?"

She frowned. "Then what were you investigating that drew you to me?"

Kurt relinquished his hold on her and turned back to the mirror to remove his beard.

"We've had several reports of a stunning redhead luring Marines into bed then blackmailing them. I was at the Lost Oasis to find her. You were the only gorgeous redhead there and the description matched. Your actions after we met more or less followed hers, including you coming on to me."

Midge sank to the toilet seat. She tried to focus on her upset rather than the joy that he'd thought she was gorgeous. He hadn't wanted her at all. It was all in the line of duty. She tucked her arms tight to keep the pain from showing.

"You fucked me last night to trap the woman you thought I was?"

"Yes, but—"

"Don't insult me by saying you liked it. It was sex. What man has ever hated sex? I can't believe Jess would sanction an action like that."

"He didn't know until after the fact and he wasn't pleased."

Good.

"If you realized I was her...me...whatever, why not say something when you called? Why come here in disguise?"

He paused, and in that brief time, Midge had her answer. She vaulted to her feet.

"You *still* thought I was this woman?"

He cupped her shoulders, looking ridiculous with the top of the beard peeling down.

"I was doing my job. Find this woman and establish contact. I honestly didn't know until you opened the door. If you'd been her, the red hair would have remained. She's never been seen otherwise."

She scowled up at him. "Your logic is flawed. I could have realized who you were—which I did—and decided to throw you off."

"If that were the case, you never would have agreed to see me again when we talked on the phone. You would have ended it."

He had a point. "Does Jess think I'm this woman?" Midge didn't think she could bear it if he did.

"All he knows is that I hooked up with a redhead named Midge. He said nothing about you, even after I told him where you lived. I think he was setting me up to look like an idiot." He brushed his thumbs over her shoulders. "Please don't respond to that." He turned back to the mirror.

"I'm guessing this woman has given a different name each time?"

"Yes." He winced as he pulled. "I'd never heard anyone call you Midge. I don't think I've ever heard the name and I didn't associate it with Michelle."

"It's a nickname because my half brother couldn't say Michelle—which I hate, by the way. And while we're on the subject… Orin?"

He sighed. "Kurt Orin Davidson."

She grunted. "That explains Zach's reaction when I told him your name was Orin Davis." She had some strong words for him the next time she saw him. "You'd think she'd use a different hair color, too. Red hair really sticks out. Surely the word would have gotten out about her." Men liked to brag about their conquests. Women, too, for that matter. "What's she blackmailing them over?"

"Telling their wives, if they're married. Saying she's pregnant and needs money to take care of the problem, if they're single. Cash operation."

"God, I need a drink." She aimed for the door.

"Bring me one, too?"

She liked that he'd asked rather than ordered. "Sure."

"Midge?"

"Yeah?" She turned, meeting his gaze in the mirror.

"I'm really glad you aren't her. I liked last night a lot. Then today…"

Tilting her head, she waited for him to finish. The hunger in his eyes matched the gnawing ache inside her.

"Ah hell." He grabbed the edges of the beard and yanked it off. "Fuck, that hurt."

She snickered. "Then why did you do it?"

"I had my reasons."

"Care to share what those are?"

He issued yet another sigh, then turned to face her. His face was red where he'd ripped off the beard. He'd be feeling the burn for a while.

"I'm trying to have a calm discussion with you and being with you makes me hard as hell."

"Really? I hadn't noticed." *This time.* He didn't need to know she'd seen his erection at the bookstore. She bit back the urge to say there were much better ways to quell a hard-on.

"Apparently that's a common affliction for you. You were hard last night for her."

"Her *is* you." His voice raised several decibels.

Midge crossed her arms. "You didn't know that last night."

"No, but you were on my mind. It's the only way I could get through it."

"Seriously?" She cocked out her hip and braced her hands on her hips. "You're telling me that the only way you could have sex with me last night was because you were fantasizing about me?"

"Yes." He drew in a breath and released it slowly. "I've wanted you from the first time I laid eyes on you."

"Oh puleese." She rolled her eyes. Her want for him dissipated. She might have been out of the game for a while, but she knew a come-on when she heard it. "Yet not once have you ever given any indication of interest."

Would you have reciprocated if he had? Midge knew that answer too well—no. Her rules forbade it. Now? Hell yeah, but at the moment she refused to let him have that level of control over her.

A flush crawled over his cheeks. "It's been recently brought to my attention that I suck at flirting, so my attempts to seduce you may not have been apparent."

"I find that very difficult to believe after last night."

He shrugged. "I was playing a role."

"Goodness, the sacrifices you'll make to get the job done." She hoped she'd framed the words with enough sarcasm.

"I had a job to do." He slipped his hand over her shoulder. "You have to admit the sex was damn fine."

"It was okay." Midge shrugged off his touch. "I'll see you downstairs."

That would give her the distance she needed for now. With every second she spent with him, her resolve crumbled a little more.

"Right behind you," he replied.

He meant it, too. She'd just pulled a bottle of malbec from its hiding place when he trotted down the stairs.

"Unusual place to store wine," he said.

"My landlady helps herself to my things, especially when I'm not here." She headed for the kitchen.

He followed. "Same person Hades was battling?"

"I only have one landlady." Midge pulled a corkscrew from the drawer.

"I can get that for you."

When Kurt reached for it, she blocked him.

"I'm perfectly capable of popping my own cork."

He could take that anyway he wanted. She divided the bottle between her two largest wineglasses and handed him one.

"You do realize that if I drink this, I'll have to stay over."

"I'll call you a cab." She brushed his shoulder as she made her way to the living room. "Coming?"

"Apparently not any time soon."

Midge fought a smirk behind a sip of wine and curled into the corner of her couch. Kurt took the opposite end. · "I wasn't aware you were friends with Zach and Claudia," he said.

Midge's heart warmed to know they hadn't confided in Kurt. They'd guaranteed no one would hear of their relationship. The Taylors and the Stuarts were true to their word, as always.

Kurt sampled his drink, gaze locked on her as he waited for her reply.

"I know Phillip and Rowan Stuart, too."

"I'm presuming you were stationed together elsewhere?" He arched his eyebrow with the question.

"Yes. We lived together, too."

His eyes widened then narrowed. His lips thinned to a taut line. She knew jealousy when she saw it. That it came from Kurt stirred up her lust. She was tempted to lie and tell him they'd had a hot and heavy ménage but decided to give him a pass.

"It's not what you think," she told him.

"How do you know what I'm thinking?" His gaze drifted to the cushions between him as he drank.

"The tic in your jaw gives you away."

His attention was back on her, but the tight jaw remained. "What was the story? Or do I have to call Zach and Phillip for the information?"

Midge brushed her thumb over the bowl of her glass. "They'd never tell you. But I'll save you the trouble of investigating."

"I'm listening." He draped his arm over the back of the couch.

"You first. Do you even have a sister — or was that part of your cover?"

"I have two sisters and a brother."

"Where does your family live?"

"Los Angeles. Yours?" His smile did a number on her insides.

"San Diego. I have a half brother and sister. How did you get the scar on your shoulder?"

His humor faded. "Line of duty. I was trying to keep Claudia from being killed. I was shot in the shoulder and thigh."

In the midst of taking a sip, Midge froze as alarm trickled through her.

Kurt took a healthy drink. "It still scares me to think about how close we all came to death. I met Claudia and Zach last fall. I can't believe we've only known each other for a little over a year. It feels like forever. I'm not looking forward to the day they get orders." He slowly shook his head. "Anyway, they'd gone undercover to try to catch a killer. I was assigned to keep Claudia safe. Since she didn't trust strange men, I met her as Kiki, a crossdresser."

"Ah…stilettoes." His dedication to his job impressed her, though she did admit to wanting to see his skills as Kiki.

"I'm presuming you caught the killer?"

He nodded. "We did. Your turn." He lifted his glass her way. "You were living with Zach and Phillip…?"

Midge couldn't look at him. Though she'd done nothing wrong, the incident still haunted her.

"It was about three years ago. I was a sergeant. Zach and Phillip were captains. The military judge, a colonel… Don't ask his name because I won't tell you."

He could research it if he wanted to. Knowing Kurt, he probably would, though it wouldn't surprise her to hear the record had been destroyed.

"I was constantly fending off his advances. I was scared to death to say anything because of his rank. He said he'd ruin me, that he had the power to do so and that I needed to get with the program. I did everything I could to avoid him. One evening I'd returned to the office because I'd forgotten my phone. He caught me and forced himself on me. Zach and Phillip had also returned to the office to shower after playing basketball before heading out for a drink at the Officers' Club. They saved me from being raped."

Talking about it made her sick inside. It made her feel dirty, too. Her wine suddenly had little appeal. She set the glass on the table behind her and hugged herself. Kurt closed the gap between them, wrapping his arms around her. Midge tensed then eased into the comfort of his embrace. He stretched out, pulling her with him until she was draped along his body. She rested her cheek against his chest.

"You don't have to tell me anything more." He rubbed his hand over her back.

"No. I want you to understand," she replied, then continued.

"They stood by me when I filed a formal complaint and backed me up one-hundred percent. Battle lines had been drawn—the three of us against the might of higher-ups. Friends deserted me to stay out of the fallout. My boyfriend was one of them. Alone, I became a target to take down. Threats against me escalated. I moved in with Zach and Phillip for my own safety. In the end we won, sort of. The colonel wasn't court-martialed. Instead, he was *invited* to retire. He threatened to take me down with him, if it took forever. I've been somewhat hiding ever since, doing my job and trying to keep as low a profile as possible. I was thrilled to discover Zach was stationed here and that Phillip had resigned his commission. But I've also been scared to death someone would find out I'd been to their houses for dinner and that I'd be charged with fraternization. They didn't like it, but I refused further invites."

Kurt slowly nodded. "It's why you downplay your beauty and keep yourself isolated."

He really thinks I'm beautiful? Her heart skipped a beat. "It's what drew the colonel's attention in the first place. I've been afraid ever since."

He slid his hand under hers. A lifeline against the world... That was what it felt like. Midge looped her thumb around his.

"That's no way to live, baby."

"I've recently come to that conclusion as well," she admitted. "Maybe it was the birthday. Maybe it was Susan and Jeremy forcing themselves into my life. Maybe it's my busybody landlady. Maybe it's because I was too fearful to go out last night without a disguise. Maybe the loneliness and isolation took its toll."

"Or maybe it was all of the above."

He was right. It was everything all piled up at once.

"I'm fed up with the person I've become. I'm so damn tired of hiding. I hit the wall last night. The disguise, allowing myself to be dragged to the club..."

It still shocked her at how far she'd fallen from the person she'd once been. In hiding from the world, she'd let herself become a doormat, taking what people dished out because she'd been too afraid of confrontation.

"I'm glad you let yourself be dragged to the club last night." He brushed his thumb over hers. Heat crawled up her arm. "I meant what I said. I've wanted you from the first day I met you."

Frowning, she turned her gaze his way. "When did you flirt with me?" Surely, she would have noticed.

He scrunched his nose. "I'm embarrassed to admit it was pretty lame, now that I think about it. During the Duran murder trial, I spent a week offering you gum, mints and hard candy. I couldn't even get a smile out of you."

Midge tried not to laugh. "You'd rendered me speechless. I couldn't believe a man like you was interested. Then I realized I couldn't act on it because my rules forbid office relationships."

"I expect a written statement from you, notarized, to the effect that I don't suck at flirting."

"For Zach?"

"You bet."

Smiling, he twisted a length of her hair around his finger. "Despite the sting of what I presumed was your rejection, I couldn't get you out of my head. How else would I know how you liked your coffee and your go-to treat? Or that you read at lunch every day? Then today you hit me hard when you came at me and Yost—deservedly so. The fire in your eyes… I love strong women. Women with a little mystery to them waiting to be revealed, layer by layer."

He released her hair and slid his hand down her arm. Her nipples tightened and her breath quickened. His cock swelled against her stomach. Images of pulling up her skirt and riding him filled her head.

"I didn't lie. It was you I fantasized about last night. In the dark I could pretend it was you. I've been conflicted and torn between duty and want all day. I'm beyond relieved to discover the Midges on my mind are the same person. Because the sex? It was damn good, even more so now that I know it was you."

Midge wanted to lie and tell him it had meant nothing. Her heart and her hopes refused to let her. Here was her chance to have the relationship she'd longed for — one built on honesty and truth, even if it hadn't started out that way. She slid her fingers down his abs, loving how the muscle quivered under her touch, wanting his body on hers...in hers.

"I wanted you badly," she admitted. "I wasn't about to let you leave last night without having a taste of you. The only regret was the disguise. Because the sex? It *was* damn good. Granted, it's been some time since I've had sex, but it's never been that fine."

"It's been a bit for me as well." He traced his finger down her spine. "When I'm inside you, I felt as if I'd put my dick in a dragon."

Midge tugged his shirt from his jeans and slipped her hand under it. "How could you have possibly wanted me all this time? I did everything I could to be unappealing."

"Maybe to other men." A grin split his face and lit up his eyes. "I love discovering what's beneath all the layers."

Which was probably one of the reasons he was a good investigator. He'd be determined to get the answer.

"I've been known to drive my family insane with how long it takes me to open a present. And I do recall telling you last night that I like to take my time, to undress a woman nice and slow."

He cupped her breast and thumbed her nipple through the material. A furrow formed between his eyebrows. "I'm beyond furious over what you went through. I'm sad you've lived in fear all this time. I want to track his bastard down and make sure he never hurts anyone ever again. It wouldn't be the first time I've helped take down a colonel."

Kurt in hero-mode was a powerful aphrodisiac. Her body thrummed with want, keeping time with her racing heart.

"Right now, all I want is you," she told him.

"With the lights on this time, yes?" He cupped her bottom and rolled them forward until she was flat on the couch and he was on top.

Hot damn, that killer smile of his.

"Oh yes." She rubbed her foot down his calf. "I want to see every part of you that I could only feel last night."

"Aw, baby, I loved how you touched me last night. Your hands set me on fire."

"I hated having the lights off." She skimmed her palms over his abs, loving the catch in his breath.

"I hated not being able to do everything I wanted with you."

"For example?"

His grin deepened the devilish glint in his eyes. "I'm so glad you asked. Allow me to demonstrate."

Before he could do so, Hades meowed from his new perch on the back of the couch.

"Not tonight, tuna breath." Kurt hopped to his feet, then helped Midge to hers, pulling her flush against his hard body. "I'll grab the wine, you get the lights down here and we'll take this upstairs."

"Excellent plan."

Smiling, she teased her fingers over his taut nipples. He reciprocated by grabbing her ass and grinding his pelvis over her stomach. Midge traced her tongue up his Adam's apple and over his chin, pausing at his lips. He fisted her skirt and dragged it to her waist. Cool air raised goosebumps on her bottom — or maybe that was a result of his determination to undress her. Clutching the skirt in one hand, he eased her panties down her legs nice and slow. His smoldering gaze never left her face.

"Allow me to assist?" she asked.

Fire lit his eyes. "By all means. I love audience participation."

Midge pulled free, kicking the panties aside. Kurt unzipped her skirt, pushed it past her hips, then lifted her from it and into his arms. Want beamed from his eyes. His intent was clear. He was going to carry her up the stairs. She wanted to tell him that she was much too heavy, that he'd trip and they'd fall. The truth came out instead.

"You make me feel treasured."

"You are. I've waited months for this moment. Kiss me, Midge."

She ran her fingers up his neck into his hair and kissed him — hard, slow, deep. His arms trembled and she prayed it was from the force of her kiss, not her weight. The bullet wound to his thigh came to mind. Had he recovered enough to do this? Midge wouldn't ask, wouldn't take this moment from him. She eased her lips from his and brushed her thumb over his hard nipple.

"I'm still waiting to see what you were going to do to me now that you couldn't do last night. Or is this it? While it is impressive, I'm not as wowed as I anticipated."

"Impatient, aren't you?"

She raked her fingers into his hair. "Especially when I know the pleasure that's coming. Or should I say the pleasure *in* coming."

"You're making it very hard for me to take my time."

"I look forward to being ravished."

"In that case…"

He set her down and braced her against the couch. Midge tried to hook her legs around his waist. He dodged the effort by kneeling at her feet. He wedged his shoulders between her legs, then brushed his hands up her thighs, pausing right below her pussy. Kurt glanced up. She quivered from the intensity in his gaze, unable to determine if he was waiting for permission or drawing out the pleasure. She dropped one hand to his head, deciding to play this her way.

"Permission granted."

A growl rumbled from his throat, setting off tremors deep inside her. His smoldering gaze shifted to her pussy. He stroked his fingers through the hair.

"Damn, see how wet you are for me," he whispered.

She wanted to reply, '*only for you*.' "You say the sweetest things."

"I have my moments."

Still staring up at her, he licked around her clit. Midge closed her eyes on a hard moan, fighting the urge to clamp his head in place. She snapped her hands over the back of the couch and rocked with every sweep of his tongue. He took his time, as if he were savoring the taste of her. Up and around. Over and down. In and out. Pleasure banked, waiting for release, and still he played. Her groans turned to pleas that he make her come, but Kurt took his own sweet time.

Time to take charge.

"Are you as hard as me?" she asked.

Kurt laughed as he pulled away. "What do you think? Nice try, by the way. It won't work."

"Won't it?"

She tried to slip down next to him. He wedged his shoulders behind her legs, keeping her in place, and dived back in. There was nothing subtle about his caresses this time. He kneaded her labia between his lips, then lashed his tongue over her clit. Each time Midge neared the peak, he moved away then started all over again. She writhed into his face, so desperate to come she wanted to weep, yet loving every single second. No man had ever been so meticulous.

"You just wait. Your turn's coming," she managed to say.

Kurt responded with a deep groan and sucked her clit. Orgasm quaked through her. The aftermath left her spent and gasping for breath. He scooped her into his arms and carried her up the stairs, eyes locked with hers the whole way. When he reached her bedroom, he draped her in the center of her bed then stepped away. One by one he turned on all the lights. Midge shoved the bedcovers down and removed her sweater and bra.

Now standing at the foot of the bed, he passed a slow gaze down her body, licking his lips as he undressed. She soaked in the sight of him — lean muscle marred with those awful scars that tugged her heart again. Here was a man devoted to his job — and most especially his friends. A man who was all hers...for now.

She set her glasses on the nightstand and reached for him after he'd donned the condom and knelt on the bed. Kurt cupped her breasts and thumbed her nipples, seemingly mesmerized by what he held in his hands. She expected him to suck one. He kissed her instead, pulling at one lip then the other before slipping his tongue around hers. His dick was hot and hard between them. She locked her ankles around his waist and rolled her pelvis until his erection rested against her pussy.

Kurt moaned and slid one hand under her ass. He squeezed her breast and butt cheek at the same time and sank in deep. Midge broke the kiss and rocked with his slow thrusts. He wedged his hand between them and pressed her clit against his cock. She stole another kiss from him. He deepened it and moved faster. She clutched his shoulders, never wanting to let go, never wanting this moment to end, yet needing the release as much as she had mere moments ago.

He broke the kiss. "Come with me, baby. Come with me now."

Midge didn't think it was possible. She never had before. Yet there she was, reaching for the top with him, coming with him. And her heart. Oh damn, her heart.

Chapter Six

"What the hell happened to your face?"

Kurt slipped into the booth across from Jess. A steaming mug of coffee awaited him.

"I was out of spirit gum remover and had to pull off the beard."

No way in hell was he telling Jess that he'd yanked it off in a desperate attempt to lose a hard-on. It hadn't helped. Relief only came when he fucked Midge, and even then, it was temporary. He was beyond addicted to her. Leaving her warm body curled against him this morning hadn't been easy. It'd been a night filled with the hottest sex of his life. He couldn't wait to get back to her and do it all over again.

"I ordered your usual for you," Jess told him.

Kurt muttered his thanks and stirred cream into his coffee. Real cream. After adding ice from his water glass, he drained the mug. Wanda was there with a refill before it hit the table. Her teenaged grandson trailed her with the best damn breakfast in the world.

The mom-and-pop operation was Jess' go-to place for meetings. He always chose early morning to avoid the crowd. Although, judging from the dark circles under his reddened eyes, Kurt wondered if he'd pulled an all-nighter and was regretting the hour.

Wanda filled their cups with a smile, leaving the carafe for them. Jess dug into his ham and cheese omelet while Kurt attacked the pile of steaming hash browns. Emma would have a fit if she knew about the cholesterol-laden treats Jess pumped into his body whenever she was gone. Kurt wasn't about to enlighten her.

"Midge isn't the woman we're looking for."

Jess peered at him from under his eyebrows. "Ya think?"

"You could have said something when I told you the woman's name and address." He stirred cream into his fresh cup.

"And spoil the fun?" Jess grinned.

"Zach called you. That's why you suddenly needed my help with the trunk."

Jess' answer was to shrug. It was all part of the family connection. They'd probably been laughing their asses off over the whole thing.

"How did you finally come to your revelation?" Jess carved off a bite of omelet. "Don't spare the details."

"Because everyone's waiting for the full report?"

Jess laughed. "You *are* smart." He shoved his food in his mouth.

Kurt told him everything while they ate. Well, almost everything. He kept the sex to himself. Jess could fill in the blanks, and judging from his silence, Jess wasn't happy. Whether that was because they'd lost time or because of Kurt's developing relationship with Midge, he didn't know. Being with her compromised his initial assignment. Kurt couldn't pursue this femme fatale with the same vigor now. He wouldn't cheat on Midge, not even for the job. They were doing this — trying to be a couple. Phone numbers had been exchanged and all that — the real numbers, not burners. Making that clear to Jess wasn't going to earn him points.

"I put Anders on this blackmailing case. I want you focused on the ketamine."

Kurt sighed with relief and prayed Jess didn't catch it. "Anders has been chomping at the bit to do something."

"He's new enough to the area and knows disguises as well as you do. He should be able to keep a low profile."

If not, Jamison Anders was a dead man.

Decision made, they could move beyond the silence as they finished eating.

"What's the latest word from the DEA on the ketamine shipment?" he asked.

"Not good. They know the bulk of the stuff is in the Twentynine Palms area, and it's only a matter of time until it hits the streets." Jess turned his coffee spoon over and over on the tabletop as he spoke, an unconscious movement that revealed his inner worries. "DEA agents don't have the access we do to move around subtly on a military base. That's why they're depending on us to work with their local contact and determine if the shipment has reached here or not."

"They believe it'll be distributed soon," Kurt said, more to himself than to Jess. "That means we're rushed for time."

"You'll be able to hit the ground running on this come Monday. DEA's man will meet with you and Vic around noon or so." His gaze caught Kurt's. "His name is Everest. Anders had worked with him in the past."

Jess paused to allow Wanda to leave the bill on the edge of their table. He picked up the tab, examined it, then left it and a pile of cash next to the salt shaker.

"This is our priority. I don't want your burgeoning romance getting in the way. Got it?"

"Loud and clear."

Kurt swallowed the rest of his now-tepid coffee. Though he meant what he'd just said to Jess, all he could think about getting back to Midge. He had two days before Monday and he intended to take full advantage of them.

* * * *

Midge missed Kurt the minute he'd left the bed — his warmth, his scent, the way he curled around her as he slept. She hugged his pillow, hoping to drift back to sleep, but she was too excited to see him again. They'd planned to spend the day decorating their respective homes for Christmas before they headed off for a night in Palm Springs. The shackles from her past were off, and with them, the weight she'd carried on her shoulders. There'd be no more hiding from the world. Her reward was the man she'd been craving for two long months.

Giddiness welled up inside her. It was time to put her nervous energy to good use. She tossed the covers aside and leaped from the bed. As much as she disliked running, a jog in the crisp morning air was what she needed. If she timed it correctly, she could be home and showered before Kurt returned.

She pulled her hair into a ponytail, then tugged on black sweatpants and a red USMC sweatshirt. *Ooo-rah*. She strapped on her watch, laced up her running shoes and trotted down the stairs, hoping the thuds woke Bernadette.

The wind was brisk, pushing the predicted storm into position. As she stretched her muscles, she debated her options and decided to risk it. A three-mile run wouldn't take all that long. After setting the timer on her watch, she started down the street — the sole inhabitant this early morning. She'd mapped out a series of challenging runs that kept her from being too bored yet helped improved her endurance.

Midge cut across the isolated desert road and turned onto the paved street, something she wouldn't have risked on a busy weekday. Traffic and the inattentive drivers that went with it were too dangerous. But on Saturday morning it was mostly deserted. If she ran this road for two miles, she could cut over to another dirt road that swung around on the three-mile loop back to her own street. It would also take her past the Lost Oasis, a couple of blocks ahead.

She wrinkled her nose. She'd had more than her fill of that place for the time being. The only good thing that had come from that night was Kurt. Her body tightened at the thought of him and everything they'd done since. It felt like ages ago yet had only been two days. As she neared the building, she saw a man splayed out on one of the concrete benches, arm dangling.

She slowed to a stop, running in place, undecided. Was he a homeless person? If so, where was his shopping cart? Stolen? That would have been cruel. It might have been one of the club's last customers, too drunk to make it to his car. But there were no cars in the parking lot, so that couldn't be the case.

He could be dangerous. Maybe armed.

For pity's sake, you're a Marine and fully capable of defending yourself.

If he gave her trouble, she'd just break his legs — or run like hell.

"Okay, here we go."

She trotted along the edge of the parking lot, trying to get a better view of him. He was facedown. The hand that dangled to the ground was battered and bruised and the knuckles torn and bloody. His white-blond hair was matted with blood.

Midge paused. Few had hair that color. *Jeremy.*

She sprinted the remaining distance to his side. "Jeremy, it's Midge." When he remained unresponsive, she gently rolled him over.

A gasp lodged in her throat. His face was a mask of dried blood, cheeks battered and bruised, lips split. Someone had thoroughly and methodically beaten the hell out of him. She didn't know if he was alive or dead. Fresh sweat broke out on her forehead.

She touched the side of his neck, ignoring the stickiness, and tried to feel for his carotid artery. After fumbling past his blood-soaked shirt collar, she found a weak pulse.

Thank God. "Jeremy, you need to wake up."

He groaned and coughed up blood before curling into a fetal position with his arms wrapped around his stomach. He opened his eyes a crack. They flickered back and forth until they lit upon her face.

"Midge," he whispered pitifully. He hacked again, bringing up more blood, then passed out.

She had to get him to a hospital and she'd left her cell phone at home. That habit had to change. Midge spied a pay phone on the side of the building but didn't have any change with her. A pat-down of Jeremy's jean pockets came up empty—no wallet, no cell phone, no money. The only thing she found was a matchbook-sized baggie. It had a grayish, flaky substance inside. *Ketamine.* She'd seen enough of it in evidence bags to recognize it.

Jeremy moaned softly. Midge slipped the packet into the waistband of her sweatpants. Could she call 9-1-1 without money? Run back to her house?

The sound of tires crunching on the driveway drew her attention to the white sedan coming to a stop in the parking lot. Midge froze, fearful. Relief poured through her when she realized it was Kurt. He shoved the door open and hurried her way. His gaze cut to Jeremy's limp form.

"Any idea what happened to him?" He squatted beside them, reaching for Jeremy's pulse as she had.

"I don't know. I was on a run and found him. He regained consciousness long enough say my name. I don't have my phone with me. No change, either. I was trying to figure out what to do."

He checked Jeremy's face, then lifted his shirt. Jeremy's ribs were tattooed with deep purple bruises and red welts.

"Probably has a few broken ribs, but we can't be sure there's not more internal damage. He'd be dead weight to move and doing so might hurt him more. I'll call 9-1-1."

He did more than that, in her opinion. He flexed his NCIS muscles as well. It might not get the paramedics here any quicker, but it did alert local law enforcement of a potential conflict of interest—a Marine had been attacked in the civilian community.

"This could be a while and the sky's about to open up any second. Why don't you take my car and go home? I'll call you when we're done or walk over. It's not that far. I might even be able to get the deputy to give me a ride. He'll want to get your statement."

Guilt and indecision warred in her head. "Jeremy called last night before you got there, wanting to come over to talk about something. I gaffed him off. I was so damned tired of his and Susan's crap. If I'd agreed—"

"You could be lying somewhere beaten half to death...or worse."

Kurt had a point.

"I feel like I deserted him."

He cupped her shoulder. "You're leaving him in good hands, sweetheart. Help is on the way. Go home. Clean up."

She glanced at her bloody hands. "I'll get your car messed up."

He moved his hand to her cheek. "I carry a bottle of water with me at all times. Use it to wash the blood off."

Sirens reached them. Help would be here at any minute. There wasn't anything else she could do. "His name is Jeremy Forton. He's a private first class with Tanks."

"I know."

Of course he'd know. Jeremy wasn't known for staying out of trouble.

"At least sit in my car," Kurt asked. "It's getting colder by the second."

She glanced at the gathering clouds and a snowflake kissed her nose. A shiver rattled through her. Kurt cupped her elbow and stood, taking her with him. She clutched her stomach, trying to hold in her fear and shock. Her watch beeped twice, indicating her workout was over. If she left Kurt, he'd be without protection from the storm. If she sat in his car until this was over, she'd drive herself insane with anxiety.

"I think I need to run home," she said.

"I understand completely." He dropped a kiss to her lips. "I'll be there as soon as possible."

After a nod, she trotted toward the road, then broke into a hard run, taking a shortcut home. She hit her door ten minutes later, no better than she'd been before. After washing the blood from her hands, she chugged a glass a water, debating whether or not to call Susan. Common courtesy decreed she should, but it was the last thing she wanted to do. Manners won out.

Midge leaned against the kitchen counter and called. Susan picked up midway through the fourth ring.

"This better be good," she grumbled. "It's not even close to noon. I'm barely awake."

That was sadly too true. Susan's late nights took a toll. Midge tamped down her irritation and told her about Jeremy.

"I'm sure he had it coming. Is that all?"

Her lack of compassion hit a nerve. Midge was done with her nonsense. It was definitely time for new friends.

"No, it isn't. The presumed friendship between us isn't really working for me. It's time we parted ways."

"You little bitch," she snarled. "*You're* kicking *me* to the curb? You wouldn't have gotten laid if it weren't for me."

Midge hated that she was right. "I'll return your things to you on Monday."

Susan snorted. "You'll never keep him without it."

Excuse me? "For your information, Kurt likes me the way I am."

Laughter exploded through the phone. "He's only saying that for the sex. You are so fucking naïve."

"You know what, Susan? We're done."

Midge ended the call and aimed for the shower, stripping as she walked up the stairs. Kurt could return at any moment and she didn't want him to have to wait outside. Leaving the door unlocked was out of the question.

Something crunched under her foot when she hit the second floor. *The packet of ketamine.* She'd forgotten all about it. She picked it up by the corner and held it up

"What the hell were you thinking, Jeremy?"

The answer was clear—he hadn't been thinking. In any event, Kurt needed to know about this. She returned downstairs to call him. The sound of Bernadette's engine roaring in the garage stopped Midge in her tracks. It might still be some time before Kurt could get here. She couldn't risk Bernadette barging in and finding it. If she even suspected Midge had a packet containing an illegal substance…

Midge didn't want to think about those ramifications. She'd hide it with the wine until Kurt arrived.

Handling the bag by its corner, she slipped it snugly into the center of *Sense and Sensibility*. When closed, the pages only showed the slightest gap. It would have to do.

She showered in record time and found Hades sitting outside the bathroom door waiting with that half-lidded gaze indicating he'd been napping. A big yawn backed up her theory. Midge rubbed his ears and walked on to her bedroom. Hades trotted ahead and jumped to his perch on the window. His lazy meow and the flick of his tail drew her attention. The snow was really coming down.

"No birds and squirrels today, big guy."

As she brushed her hand down his back, the electricity flicked off, on, off and, thankfully, back on. She hurried to dry her hair, then dressed in the warmest clothes she could find — dark green sweater, jeans and thick wool socks. Contacts were next. Wearing them empowered her. It felt good to be alive again.

"Makeup later. I need coffee." Before the electricity went out. She'd fill her thermos bottles.

A fire would have been nice, too, but she had no wood for the fireplace.

Midge grabbed her phone on the way to the kitchen and sent Kurt a text.

Could you bring wood with you?

She realized the double entendre the instant she hit Send. Kurt's response was quick.

I won't be a smart ass. It's too damn cold. I'll hit the grocery store. Almost done. Paramedics just took him to base hospital. They'll stabilize him then most likely send him down to Desert Regional in Palm Springs.

Relief sighed through her. She hoped he made it and that they could find out who'd done this to him. Hunger rumbled her stomach as she set the coffee to brew. Kurt had already eaten, so there was no sense in waiting for him. Midge grabbed a raisin bagel and returned to her bedroom to put on a little makeup. She'd just put the finishing touches on her mascara when the doorbell rang.

"That's probably Kurt."

Hades perked up at the news and shot from the room. Laughing, she followed. His hiss reached her seconds before she found him sitting in the window, back arched, fur bristled out.

Not Kurt.

Heart pounding, she crept to the peephole. A muscular man bundled in a black leather jacket stared back. He'd hunched his shoulders in what she guessed was a vain attempt to shield himself from the wind whipping his dark brown hair in all directions. He had a bright red clipboard tucked under his left arm and clutched a pen in his gloved hand. After ensuring the chain lock was in place, she opened the door a crack. Snowfall slanted her way, carried on the wind.

"Can I help you?"

The man offered a wide smile that didn't translate to his brown eyes. "Yes, ma'am. I'm with the city checking on an application for vacation rentals."

On a Saturday? Her apprehension tripled.

"Are you Bernadette McFee?" He tapped his clipboard with his pen.

"She lives in the other house." Midge jerked her head toward it.

The man's brow furrowed. "Are you a tenant or renting as a vacation home?"

"Tenant."

He made a slow, careful mark on his clipboard. She stretched her neck to see the form, but he guarded it too well.

"And your name is?"

"Michelle Ellis." Gusts blew a flurry of snow through the door and shot cold through her clothing.

"No one else lives here with you?" He craned his neck and peered over her shoulder. "It's freezing out here, ma'am. Perhaps I could come in and ask you some more questions?"

"Do I look crazy?" she snapped. "Go away before I call the sheriff's office."

She shut the door and secured the deadbolt. She watched through the peephole and saw him get into a silver sedan. He sat there scribbling notes into a small booklet.

"I should have asked for a business card, Hades. I ought to go out there and get his license plate."

Hades meowed.

"Yeah, I know. That would make me too stupid to live."

He responded with another small mew.

"Cold, too. I hate being cold."

His *brreow* made her smile. It was her favorite sound of his. She stepped away from the door.

"Coffee's done. Time for a cup. Need food in your bowl?"

That normally got his attention. Instead, his ear perked and he stretched his neck. Anticipation widened his eyes.

"Ah...your boyfriend's home."

Hades quivered.

"I know that feeling well."

Midge returned to the peephole. Kurt had a bundle of wood in each hand and a glower directed at the departing sedan. She opened the door.

"He said he was from the city and tried to worm his way into the house."

His frown deepened. "Bastard. I've got his license plate now."

"Need help? I can put on some shoes."

"I've got it."

He trudged through the snow, nowhere close to the sidewalk. She couldn't even find it under the blanket of white.

"Deputy sheriffs are right behind me. The grade is closed. We won't be going down to Palm Springs tonight."

"I'm good with that." She stood to one side to let him in. "Someone is all aquiver to see you."

"Is it you?" He kissed her.

Before she could reply, Hades jumped in front of them and announced his presence.

Kurt smiled, set the wood aside and indulged his new BFF. "I missed you, too, buddy." The cat arched into Kurt's petting. "Come help me get a fire going before the electricity decides to go out."

He grabbed the wood and headed for the fireplace, faithful companion by his side. A deputy sheriff's vehicle pulled to a stop behind Kurt's car as she was shutting the door. She kept the door closed, monitoring two deputies' progress toward her house.

"Sheriff's deputies are here."

Kurt glanced up. "I love the contacts, by the way. I'm not sure how I feel about them seeing how beautiful you are, though. They're both single and not afraid to move in on another man's—"

"Don't even say 'territory' or 'turf' or 'property'."

His eyes widened in feigned shock. "I wouldn't dare."

"Good. You're pretty safe...for now." She grinned and swung open the door. "Come in, deputies. I've got hot coffee."

"That'd be great, ma'am," the older one replied. "Black for both of us."

"Creamer," Kurt called out.

"Sit and be comfortable, gentlemen."

By the time she returned with a tray of mugs, Kurt had a nice blaze going and a contented cat in his lap. Midge envied Hades.

"We'll try not to be long," the older deputy told her.

"Take your time." She sank to the couch next to Kurt. "Get warm and enjoy the coffee."

"Thanks, ma'am," the younger one replied, taking a cautious sip from his mug. "It's going to be a long day for us. Snow makes people crazy. Tell us your name and what happened."

Midge tried to be precise, hesitating only when it came to the packet she'd pulled from Jeremy's pocket. She wished she'd had time to tell Kurt first. In the end, what did it matter? They were all law enforcement. They could sort out jurisdiction later. She sure as hell didn't want to be found with a controlled substance in her possession.

"I found something in his pocket when I was looking for change. It was the only thing he had on him. His wallet and cell phone were gone."

She felt their gazes on her as she retrieved the ketamine. When she turned around, packet extended, the men tracked the movement the way Hades would a toy. The older deputy pulled a nitrile glove from his pocket to accept it. Midge cursed herself for not thinking about that. Her fingerprints would be all over it. A criminal investigator, she was not.

"Ketamine," the men replied in unison.

"I'll get an evidence bag from the car." The younger deputy strode toward the door.

"We're going to need your fingerprints at some point for exclusion, Miss Ellis." He older one kept staring at the substance, shaking his head.

Kurt looked pissed.

"I can't pass this on to you," the deputy told him. "It's our case for the moment."

"I know," Kurt replied. "Doesn't mean I have to like it. Jurisdictional matters aren't for me to determine."

"Me either. I'm only following procedure."

Hades offered his belly to Kurt and batted his paw against Kurt's chin. Eyes still locked on the drug, Kurt gently rubbed the cat's chest. Purrs of contentment filled the room. Hades was the only one happy at the moment. With each minute that passed, the tension and awkwardness increased. The men exchanged no handshakes upon departure. Kurt made certain of that by not relinquishing his hold on the cat.

Midge accepted the deputies' business cards and saw them to the door. When she closed it, she turned around to find Kurt on his feet and reaching for his coat.

"I have to go to work."

She suspected as much. "Take my SUV. It has four-wheel drive and a higher profile than your car."

She pulled the keys from her purse and handed them to him. He didn't argue.

"I'll try not to be long. Keep your door locked. Don't open it to anyone." He leaned in to kiss her.

Midge drew back. "Is it bad?"

"It's not good." He kissed her and left.

Chapter Seven

Kurt was beyond mad and edging into fury by the time he made it to the NCIS office. He hadn't bothered to see if Jess was in. He knew he would be. With his wife away, Jess was in full workaholic mode. Kurt ordered himself to calm down until he got the full story. It didn't help. Jamison Anders had been spying on Midge, and he wanted to know why. Yes, he'd been given the blackmailing case, but she wasn't a part of that. He and Jess had already established that—Jess well before him—and the report would reflect it.

He parked next to Anders' silver Stratus. A check of the license plate confirmed it had been the vehicle at Midge's house—not that he had any doubt. He'd seen Anders with that leather jacket slung over his shoulder too many times.

Turning his collar up, Kurt stomped through the building snow toward the entrance, blessing Midge's consideration in allowing him to use her SUV. His car might have made it here, but with the storm getting worse by the second, he couldn't guarantee it would have made it back to her place. He'd then have been forced to walk, because there was no way he wasn't going to be with her tonight. Even with the higher profile vehicle, it had still taken him twice as long to reach the Marine Corps base because of the treacherous roads.

Kurt paused for a deep, calming breath. Charging in full bore would only make a bad situation worse. He had to present this as the wronged party, guilt Anders into admitting he'd crossed a line. The door to Anders' office was open — so was Jess'. He swung in to Anders', knowing Jess wouldn't be far behind once he heard the conversation.

"You want to tell me why the fuck you were at my girlfriend's house?" *So much for calm.* He stabbed his finger in Anders' direction. "You tried to push your way into her house."

Anders leaned backed, wiggling a pen between his fingers. His nose twitched. Kurt recognized an attempt to hide a sneer when he saw it.

"What's going on?" Jess stepped in beside him. "Why were you at Midge Ellis's house?"

Anders tossed his pen to the desk and stood. "You gave me a job to do. I was doing it."

"Midge isn't part of the blackmailing case," Kurt told him.

Anders snorted. "How the hell do you know? She's got you by the balls." He jerked his chin toward Kurt, then toward Jess. "And you're fooled with her cutie pie looks and sunshine smile."

The jerk wasn't winning points by admitting he'd noticed Midge's good looks. Anders motioned to his computer monitor. "This isn't the first time she's been the focus of an investigation."

"She's not the focus of an investigation now," Kurt shouted.

"She should be." Anders snickered. "First, you cross paths with her in the club where's she's dressed in full regalia—a perfect match to this woman blackmailing servicemembers. Second, she's keeping company with a Marine who's gathered himself quite the record. I'm shocked he hasn't been given a bad conduct discharge. Third, she's found with his beaten body this morning and the first thing she does is search his pockets."

"Wrong." Kurt snapped his finger at him. "She rolled him face up, checked his pulse *then* checked his pockets for change for the pay phone because she didn't have her cell."

Anders splayed his palms up. "What idiot goes running without a cell phone?"

"She doesn't like cell phones," he and Jess replied.

"In this day and age?" Anders tossed back a laugh. "Open your eyes. What person—what *woman* doesn't live by her phone constantly texting and messaging?"

My woman. Kurt left that unsaid.

Anders crossed his arms, looking smug. "I'm telling you, she didn't want to risk being tracked. Care to know what she pulled out of Forton's pocket?"

"Ketamine," he and Jess again replied in unison.

"She turned it over to the deputies this morning," Kurt told him.

"We're trying to determine jurisdiction right now." Jess narrowed his eyes. "You weren't at her place because of the blackmailing case. You were there because of the drugs, weren't you?"

Anders' chin came up. "They're connected."

"Answer the question." Jess pushed the words out through clenched teeth.

"All right." Anders jerked his arms down. "I'd gone to town trying to find obvious places of distribution. I spent a year undercover. This *is* my area of expertise. I saw the man on the bench and was trying to make a determination about whether he was passed out drunk, hurt or dead. Then she came jogging up and went to him. She'd just tucked the packet into her waistband when Davidson showed up. Odd that she didn't give it to you right away, isn't it? She does know you're an NCIS special agent, doesn't she? Logic dictates that she'd be upset at finding a controlled substance and want to turn it over immediately to some form of law enforcement. Even if that law enforcement is you."

"You son of a bitch." Kurt got as close as the desk allowed and leaned into Anders' face. "She found someone she knew beaten within an inch of his life. *Logic* dictates she was upset and trying to find him help. She's a court reporter and knows the letter of the law."

"And how to get around it."

Kurt reared his fist back. Jess caught it before he could follow through. Kurt took a step back.

"She turned it over to the *appropriate* law enforcement personnel at the earliest opportunity," he told them.

"Yet she didn't bother to stay on scene to do so," Anders shot back.

"Because I told her to go home and get out of the cold," Kurt shouted.

Anders had the nerve to roll his eyes. "God only knows how much she really pulled out of his pocket."

Hands fisted, Kurt took another step back before he gave in to the urge to launch himself over Anders' desk.

"Enough." Jess took Kurt's place at the desk. "I don't give a fuck how much experience you have investigating drug cases or how many golden contacts you might have as a result. You are *not* to be involved in this ketamine case *in any capacity*. You have one responsibility *only*. Keep your ass from getting killed so you can testify in court and take down that drug cartel. I threw you a bone by giving you the blackmailing woman case because I knew you were bored. I give you an inch and you take five miles!"

"I have to hit the bars to do that," Anders snapped back. "Do you expect me to turn a blind eye to drug activity while I'm doing it?"

"I *expect* you to report it to us and not get involved." Jess held up his index finger. "*One* job that you couldn't even do."

"I can't very well do that in the daytime." He crossed his arms. "I made preliminary contact with the suspect yesterday. I bought a book at the bookstore."

"Midge isn't a suspect," Kurt said.

"My case. I needed to assess that on my own. Don't worry. I was in disguise yesterday and today."

Kurt laughed. "As someone from the city working on a Saturday. She saw right through that."

Anders smirked. "Yet she didn't recognize me from yesterday." He turned his attention to Jess. "Is this my case or not? Do I not get to rule out persons of interest on my own? I'm more objective than either of you where Staff Sergeant Ellis is concerned. Come *on*." He held out his arms, pleading his case. "You know there's something beneath that dumpy façade of hers. Although, I will admit that if I'd hooked up with her initially, I might be a bit territorial as well."

Jess put his arm in front of Kurt, barring any advance he might make. Kurt was smart enough to remain in place, but it wasn't easy.

Jess shook his head. "Don't you think I would have thoroughly investigated any person my wife wanted to hire? Midge has reasons for putting up barriers. Had you read the investigation, had you noted the individuals who supported her, you'd understand that."

"I pulled up the report. She's got a good reason to get back at men and the military system that essentially screwed her over by retiring the guy instead of making him pay for his crimes. You know she wasn't his first victim — or his last." Anders braced his fingers on the edge of his desk. "Trade places with me and ask yourselves if you wouldn't have done the same thing. I will concede I might have overstepped by trying to gather information on the drug trafficking. Old habits and training."

"Don't let it happen again. And stay away from Staff Sergeant Ellis. That's an order, not a request." Jess pivoted toward the door, motioning Kurt to go before him.

Kurt didn't hesitate and didn't stop either. It was time he read the investigative report and found out exactly what Midge had endured. As much as he wanted to believe in her one hundred percent, Anders had sown seeds of doubt.

"In my office," Jess told him. "It'll save you some time researching it."

He followed Jess, closing the door behind them. Jess called up the information on his computer then turned his chair over to Kurt.

There, in excruciating detail, was all she had endured at Colonel Dean Stanford's hands — not only the attack Zach and Phillip had seen, but also all she'd been putting up with since the day she'd crossed paths with the bastard. There was also a statement from Brian Maynard, her boyfriend at the time, backing her up. What was missing were statements from other victims, and Kurt was certain this hadn't been an isolated incident. The fact that Midge, Zach, Phillip and Brian had received orders elsewhere shortly thereafter supported his theory. He wanted to call it shoddy investigative work. His gut told him those efforts had been highly discouraged. Midge had a lot to be angry over.

Kurt looked up at Jess, sitting in one of the chairs in front of his desk. "Have you talked with Phillip and Zach about any of this?"

"I asked them about Midge when I learned they'd been stationed at Camp Lejeune together. Both said she was a good, dependable worker. As for this" — he pointed to his computer — "they said nothing."

Which was what Midge had told him. The men had her back.

"What's your opinion of Anders' suspicions? Do you think she's capable of doing what he suggests?"

Jess slowly shook his head. "I guess anyone is capable of anything. I've known her to be shy, caring, sweet, honest and is great with animals and kids. She's great at her job and a tremendous asset at the bookstore. Customers like her and trust her book recommendations. Emma says she's very knowledgeable, well read and has no problem pairing a reader with the perfect book. She'd love to have her full-time. But who can really say what's behind the façade a person presents to the world? It took me years to find the person behind your many masks. Do I want to believe what Anders says? No. A better question would be... Do *you* now have suspicions?"

Kurt didn't know how to answer. He didn't want to suspect her. She'd been under his skin for months. Now that he finally had a chance with her, the last thing he wanted to do was screw that up. He cared for her.

The chair creaked as Jess leaned forward, resting his forearms on his knees. "I can see the wheels turning in your head. The fact you defended her so fiercely when you stormed into the building screams of a level of intimacy and caring I've never seen in you before. She means a lot to you. You don't want to ruin whatever is growing between you. But now you're asking yourself if her attention toward you is all smoke and mirrors — a ploy to throw you off."

He pressed his fingers against his temple and nodded, hating that Jess could analyze him. Speaking now was out of the question. He feared revealing too much. *Where is a disguise to hide behind when you needed one?* Raw emotion controlled him, all spawned by his growing feelings for Midge. She was more to him than sex and it pissed him off that he might have been played — that she'd somehow burrowed under his defenses and used him to hide the real person beneath *her* mask.

No. Zach and Phillip trust her.

But that had been three years ago. People change. *He'd* changed.

"You keep your cards close to your chest on this one," Jess told him. "I can check her work schedule at the bookstore against the dates the blackmailer was active. I can also run her financial records."

Kurt nodded. "Check her other duty stations to see if there were similar incidents of extortion and drug activity, too." He felt like a backstabbing bastard.

"I'll let you know as soon as I can. Don't worry. I've got you covered."

"Thanks."

They stood and Jess walked him to the exit. The snow was coming down even harder.

"Drive safe."

"Same to you," Kurt replied.

They shook hands and parted ways. Kurt flipped up his jacket collar and hurried to Midge's SUV. Anders' car was nowhere to be found. He hoped the cocky bastard got stuck in a snow drift.

He's only doing his job.

He cursed his conscience. "He can do it elsewhere."

Kurt knew that if the situations had been reversed, he would have done the same thing. Admitting that didn't help the ache gnawing at his gut. This was Midge they were talking about. But Jess had hit it on the head. After two months of her ignoring him, they were hot and heavy, all because disguises had put them in each other's path and in her bed.

Zach and Phillip believed in her. That had to be enough for him. Though neither knew about these recent developments, Kurt wasn't about to share. One wrong move and he'd either lose a woman he wanted more than anything else or blow his case out of the water.

He kept his closest friends' faith in her uppermost in his thoughts during the slow drive back to town. The roads were obscured, dusk was approaching and the wind didn't help matters. Kurt stopped at his house long enough to pack a bag — a tricky maneuver without power and under the beam of his small flashlight. By the time he was on his way to Midge's, any hint of sun was gone. A drive that would normally take five minutes took twenty.

When he arrived at her condo, he saw a foot of snow had piled against the garage door, making it impossible to open. He parked behind his car on the street, grabbed his duffel and trudged to her front door in the dark. The sound of an engine revving jerked his attention around. He squinted against the snowflakes sticking to his eyelashes. Two headlights blinked on seconds before a truck pulled out of its spot across the street. He followed its progress to the corner then looked away after it had turned out of sight. That was the only activity on the darkened street.

The door opened behind him and he turned. Midge stood in the doorway, backlit by candlelight, her face in shadows. He was struck anew by the lush curves she kept hidden from the world. Jeans and a sweater had never looked better on a woman.

For my eyes only.

Kurt tried to gather his scattered wits and plowed onward as she stood there waiting patiently. His heart was pounding as if he'd run a three-minute mile and not from the exertion of getting through the snow.

"You're going to freeze waiting for me," he said.

Midge laughed lightly. "I've got a cheery fire and you to keep me warm."

He shook off the snow as he stepped into the entryway and shut the door behind him. Midge pulled his coat off.

"Get warmed up. I'll put this over one of the kitchen chairs to dry."

"Your keys are in the pocket."

He left his sodden shoes by the door then headed for the fireplace as she walked to the kitchen. Candlelight flickered inside stained-glass votives on the end tables. An uncorked bottle of malbec with two glasses was on the coffee table. Midge had positioned the chairs closer to the fire. He sank into one and extended his hands toward the flames. She'd left the drapes open on the bay window. Hades sat curled among the red-and-green throw pillows on the padded bench, forgoing his basket. His attention was riveted to the bushes being tossed back and forth by the wind.

"I see Hades has cast me aside for something more entertaining."

Midge laughed. "Enjoy it. Once you warm up, he'll be all over you. We won't be sleeping alone tonight."

"The more the merrier." It was going to be brutal night.

"Wine?"

"Please."

He followed the clink of bottle to glass.

"It's my last bottle. I wish I'd bought more, but there are only so many places I can hide them from Bernadette. As things stand, I could only find the two candles. She's clearly helped herself to the rest at some point."

"Bitch," he muttered.

"Yep."

Midge extended one glass to him, then crawled into the chair behind him.

"That shit needs to stop." He pulled her onto his lap as he scooted back. "We're changing the locks as soon as the snow clears." *Or you could move in with me.* Kurt took a sip of wine to keep those words at bay.

She curled into him. "I called Southern California Edison about the outage. The power is out everywhere, and they don't know when it will be restored. I do have a gas stove, so we won't starve. With this cold, I don't think the contents of the refrigerator will be compromised either."

He cupped her thigh, loving the flex of muscle under his touch. "I'm happy with sandwiches."

"Hungry now?"

He loved that little tilt to her head and the way her long hair framed her jawline. The flickering flames painted streaks of orange, gold and red across her face, stoking a hot surge of desire through him. She was his for now and he was going to hold on to that with both hands.

"Not for food," he replied.

Kurt took the wineglass from her and set it on the floor beside the chair next to his. Midge slipped from his lap, grabbed his hands and pulled him to the thick Oriental rug in front of the fire. He crawled over her body, breath quickening when she hooked one leg over his hip. Another fire greeted him, one he returned in kind.

He reached to caress her cheek. She caught his hand and moved it down to her breast. He dived both hands under her sweater and found a silky shirt beneath. Surprise lifted his eyebrows.

"Did you layer up just for me?"

Midge slipped her fingers up his neck and into his hair. The whisper of her breath kissed his lips. "Why else? Certainly not because of the freezing temps and lack of power."

"Of course not." Kurt loved the humor lighting her eyes. "I'm very excited."

"I can tell." She rubbed her pelvis over his erection and kissed him, slow and deep.

He lost himself in the wonder of her, of how she worked her fingers through his hair and let him have his way with her. Kurt deepened the kiss and clamped her ass, anchoring her to him. Midge draped her other leg around him, rocking her pussy against his cock. The temptation to come overwhelmed him. He broke the kiss and shoved his hands under the silk. Her soft gasp of pleasure sliced through him when he reached her breasts. He pushed her bra up, releasing them. He loved how they filled his palms, how she pushed herself into each squeeze, no matter how subtle or firm.

He stroked his thumbs over her hard nipples. She arched into him, ankles locked around his waist, heels digging into his ass as she grinded over him. Kurt slowly peeled the clothing from her upper body—sweater, silk shirt, camisole, bra. He took the time to admire her then brought his mouth to her breast. She groaned when he pulled on her nipple, setting off tremors deep in his gut. Kurt took his time, loving each breast until she was writhing beneath him.

"Damn, baby, you were made for loving."

"Mmm. So were you. Your turn."

She fisted his shirt and pulled it up. He yanked it off and returned to her breasts. She gasped when he rolled her nipple between his lips and cried out when he sucked it deep. A jolt of electricity shot up his spine and sent a surge to his balls. He grabbed the waistbands of whatever she was wearing and came to his knees to divest her of the clothing.

"I'm about to break my own rule about stripping you slowly. All I can think about is—"

"Coming?"

"Yeah."

It was all he'd thought about for months — coming in her, on her and vice versa. He tugged the clothing down her hips. Though she offered no resistance, she also offered no help.

"You're really going to make me work for it, aren't you?"

Her soft laugh sank into his veins.

"I can't help it. You're so beautiful." Midge ran her fingers from his shoulders down over his flat nipples to the waistband of his jeans.

"And I don't want you to have any regrets that you didn't take your time."

With a gentle push, she had him on his back. Midge leaned down and flicked her tongue over his chest, teasing his nipples to harder points than they already were. She traced her tongue over his ribs one at a time, ending at his navel.

"More?"

The gleam in her eyes would have made a eunuch come.

"What do you think?" he managed to reply.

"Oh, I think a lot of things."

She flashed him a naughty grin and opened his fly button. She dotted hot kisses against his bared flesh. Tooth by tooth she unzipped him. Despite the warmth of her breath, Kurt shivered. He watched, mesmerized, as she tucked her fingers in the waistbands of boxer briefs and jeans and eased them down until his cock was freed. Leaving him bound around his thighs, she wrapped her hand around his erection one finger at a time.

"Fuck," he gasped.

"Soon." She stroked him again. "You feel like hot satin."

He jerked beneath her touch. "Now."

After pushing her gently onto her back on the soft carpet, he stood long enough to remove his clothing and put on a condom. She taunted him by playing with herself — one hand fondling her breast, the other her clit.

"You're killing me."

"Never," she replied in a husky come-fuck-me voice.

He knelt at her feet and nibbled his way up her inner thigh until his lips brushed her curls. The scent of her intoxicated him. He raised her hips with his hands and ran his tongue along her pussy.

She sank back with soft sounds of pleasure, hips twitching beneath his touch. He locked his gaze on her and stroked his tongue over her clit with sure, gentle strokes. Her moans became laced with her pleas for him to fuck her... *now*. Waiting tested his resolve because he did want to fuck now, so hard and deep their bodies made a permanent impression in the rug.

He grunted a response and increased the pressure, licking her clit over and over until she arched upward and cried out, digging her nails into his shoulders as she came. He brought her back to earth with kisses over her soft belly, all the while basking in the contentment on her face.

"Damn, baby, you make me feel like a man."

Midge drew lazy circles around the scar on his shoulder. "My man."

Every primitive instinct screamed for him to take her, to feel her moist heat wrap him in complete oblivion. God, she was beautiful. His body pulsed, demanding to be appeased. Fucking her the way he wanted — and needed — was going to leave them both with rug burns they'd feel for a week.

Kurt drew Midge to her feet as he stood and returned to the chair. Smiling, she straddled his lap, then sank onto his erection. A hot surge of approaching climax tried to take control. Kurt cupped her ass and anchored her to him. They fell into a pounding rhythm that threated to break the chair. Her muscles tightened around him. He managed to shove his hand between them to give her the friction she needed to come again and prayed he could hold on. She tossed her head back on a groan, her long hair tickling his thighs. Images of those silky strands against his balls demolished his control.

"I can't... I'm coming..."

"I'm with you," she gasped.

They hit the high together and Kurt swore their hearts became one as well. He prayed harder than he'd ever prayed in his life that she truly was all he wanted her to be and not guilty of the things Anders suggested. His objectivity was shot. He'd go to hell and back to keep her warm and safe and dry...and loved. *So loved.*

Wrong time, buddy. Too soon.

Kurt wouldn't argue with this conscience. Instead he joined the here and now, loving the feel of her head on his shoulders, his fingers deep in her long hair, and the way their hearts seemed to beat in unison.

Hades' hiss shattered the moment.

They turned their heads in his direction at the same time to see someone trying to peer through the fogged bay window.

Chapter Eight

Midge scrambled for her clothes. Kurt beat her to the door, dressed in only his jeans. A gust of wind and snow blew in, snuffing out the candles. Firelight flickered but held. She ran to the kitchen for his coat. Hades sudden presence at her feet halted her dash. He howled with distress and his puffed-up fur doubled his size.

"I know, big guy."

She knew all too well. Only one person could upset him this much. Their peeper had to be Bernadette. Kurt wasn't going to catch pneumonia over the woman. Sure enough, when she'd reached the front door, she found a footpath straight to Bernie's door and a furious Kurt ready to beat it down.

"I've got this," she called to him. "Get back in here before you freeze to death."

He dropped his fist, shot a final glare at the door and hurried inside. Midge grabbed his coat and draped it around his shoulders when he stepped in.

"Get by the fire and get warm."

"I'm thinking I don't dare disobey."

"I'm delighted to know you have some survivor skills." She pushed him toward the fire. "What the hell were you thinking, running out with nothing on?"

"Whoa. When did you turn into my mom?"

Midge slugged his shoulder. "Stop it. I'm pissed as hell and I'm not going to take another second of this."

"In my defense, I thought it might be that creep who tried to get in your house earlier." He snatched his shirt from the floor and put it on.

"No. A different creep. I *cannot* believe she stood out there watching us have sex. I'm mad at her, not you. I'm only irritated with you."

"That's refreshing."

"If you don't stop the smart-assed remarks, I'm going to slug you again."

Kurt chuckled and wrapped his arm around her shoulders. "Sorry. I rather like the fiery side of Midge Ellis. Help me warm up. You can kick her ass tomorrow. I don't understand why she'd go out in this storm to peek in your window."

She turned into his embrace and tried to rub some warmth back into him. "I bet she saw you arrive and couldn't stand not knowing what I was up to. I learned yesterday she's been reporting my activities back to my mother."

He scrunched his eyebrows. "Seriously?"

"Have you ever known me to lie?"

He laughed. "Never."

She cupped his cheeks and was about to kiss him when Hades' snarl, followed by a bright light stopped her cold.

"That fucking bitch. Of all the nerve."

Beneath the Layers

She stormed toward the commotion, then threw her hands up to protect her eyes from the beam that blazed from the doorway.

"What the hell?" Kurt was by her side in seconds. The light cut his way.

"Well, well, well." Bernadette's venomous tone was laced with sugar. "Our little Michelle seems to be taking advantage of the power outage."

"Get that light out of our eyes," Kurt snapped. "You must be the infamous landlady. Do you have any idea how many rules you've broken?"

Bernadette angled the flashlight downward, highlighting one pristine white sneaker. "I saw a half-naked man running around outside, poking around in my bushes and feared for Michelle's safety. Rather than call the authorities, I decided I'd check up on you and make sure you were all right."

Her sincerity was patently false. She'd meant to intrude on whatever Midge was doing, private or not.

"Clearly that wasn't a good decision." She sniffed.

"By all means, let's call the cops," Kurt said. "I'm sure they could get to the bottom of this incident in record time."

"Yes, let's do that." Midge pushed in front of Kurt. "That way I can explain to them how you've invaded my privacy week after week, even to the extent of spying on me through my front window."

Bernadette turned up her nose and stepped closer. She had to tilt her head back to meet Midge's eyes, but the aggression in her stance made it clear she didn't feel at a disadvantage.

"Are you insinuating I stood outside in the middle of a winter storm to watch you and your boy-toy toss around?" Her squeaky voice ruined her attempt to sound bad-ass. "Don't make me laugh, little girl. I don't need you or anyone else to give me lessons on how to make a man feel good." A smile crawled over her face. "Although you probably could use a few tips yourself, or was that wig the other night a part of your call-girl repertoire? As I recall, it was a different man."

"Nope. Same man." Kurt crossed his arms and rocked on his heels. "I'm shocked that a woman of your *experience* wouldn't recognize role-playing when you see it."

Bernadette narrowed her eyes. "How dare you."

"No," he said slowly. "How dare *you*."

"I should report you," Midge told her.

"Do I look like I've been outside in the bushes in this weather?" She adjusted one blonde curl, held in place by whatever lacquer she used on her hair. "I don't go near them in pleasant weather. That's why I have a landscaping company."

Midge had to concede that point. Bernadette's elaborate coiffure was perfect, not a strand out of place. It was unlikely she could have gone outside, crawled behind the bushes to get to the window and observed the activities inside without completely destroying her hairdo. The time and effort it would have taken to repair that sort of damage was beyond even Bernadette's maneuvers.

Midge's volcanic anger subsided. Her intense dislike remained. "Don't come into my place again without prior notice and express permission from me."

"Don't worry. There is nothing in your rental that interests me." She narrowed her gaze. "Except the quality of people you invite onto my property. I demand to know who he is."

Midge hiked up her chin and stared down her nose at Bernadette. "He's none of your business."

"Oh, but he is, especially if I think there are questionable activities going on. This is *my* property, after all."

She felt Kurt shift behind her seconds before he flipped out his badge.

"Naval Criminal Investigative Service, Special Agent Kurt Davidson."

Despite the dim light, Midge saw Bernie's face pale. She stood there staring at the badge, sputtering for a response before she whipped around and stomped out, making her size five shoes sound like size fourteens.

Kurt tucked his badge into his back pocket then charged to the door and locked it.

For all the good that will do.

"If I thought the hardware store was still open, I'd change the locks for you right now." He turned around, hands on hips. "It's not my place to tell you what to do, but this shit has got to stop. If it were me" — he splayed his fingertips against his bare chest — "I'd be hunting for a new place to live."

Knowing he was right didn't make it easier. "My books."

"I understand. I love books, too, and I've noticed you have an excellent collection of classics and first editions that deserve protecting and displaying." Three strides brought him before her. "But, sweetheart, how long before she realizes the value of them and starts *borrowing* those as well?"

"Then that would be stealing."

He spread his hands, palms up. "And what she's doing now isn't?"

Kurt had a point. She brushed the growing chill from her arms.

"I'm going to put another log on the fire," she told him.

"And I've got a mess in my jeans with this condom."

They were halfway to their respective destinations when the phone rang. Midge ignored it. The only person who called this time of night was her mother. The call could go to voice mail. Four rings later it clicked over with the obligatory greeting.

"It's Zach, Midge. Pick up the damn phone. I know you're home. Claudia's water broke and labor started."

Kurt thundered down the stairs as she snatched up the receiver.

"I'm here," she told him.

Kurt pressed his ear to the phone to hear.

"Thank God. You're closer than Phillip and Rowan. We need your SUV to get to the base hospital. My Jeep is too rough a ride for her."

"We're on our way," she replied.

"We? Oh…*we*," Zach said.

She thought she heard snickers in the background. "Let it go, Zach."

"Yes, ma'am. Hey, you saved me a phone call."

"Whatever." Midge hung up. "At least the impending birth will take the spotlight off us," she told Kurt.

"Not for long." He dashed back up the stairs.

They were out of the door minutes later with him at the wheel. Considering how he was shaking, Midge wasn't sure he should be driving. He was beyond emotionally invested. Zach and Claudia were his best friends and this baby meant the world to him. But driving would give him something to do and help focus his attention better.

His grip on the steering wheel confirmed that as he negotiated a turn onto the main road. What little traffic existed was at a crawl. Californians didn't know how to drive in snow—her included. The heavy snowfall, the wind and iced roads were accidents waiting to happen. She didn't want them to be one of those.

"I think I'm going to fucking cry," he told her. "It feels like someone's squeezing my heart to death. The emotion is...so much."

Midge teared up. *Such devotion.* The guy was tearing down the walls around her heart one at a time. She brushed his shoulder. "It'll be all right."

"Do you know how to deliver a baby?" he asked. "I have first-aid certification but everything's blank."

"I do." *Vaguely.* She wasn't going to tell him that. He needed reassurance, not obstacles. "Does it bother you that they know about us?"

"No." He momentarily took his eyes off the road to frown at her. "Why? Does it bother you? Did you want to keep it a secret? Why?"

"Calm down." She laughed and brushed his shoulder again. "We're good. I'm still a tad miffed that Zach didn't enlighten me about your identity. But you and I are good. I want people to know. You make me feel all glowy inside."

Kurt's tense shoulders relaxed with his smile. "Yeah...glowy. Jess knows, by the way."

"Does he? Ah...your breakfast this morning."

He shrugged. "He knew yesterday when I briefed him on having made initial contact with *her.*" He shot her a side glance. "He didn't enlighten me, either. I'd call them both on their behavior, but Jess is my boss and I want to keep Zach on my good side."

"Because you don't want to be kicked out of the birthing room?"

A grin split his face. "Something like that." His grin faded. "Hey, they didn't call me."

Midge laughed. "You heard what he said about saving him a phone call. I'm sure you were the next on their list. They would want to secure safe transportation first."

"True." His smile lit up. "I love kids."

She cursed the seat belt that kept her from kissing him. "I love kids, too."

He released the wheel long enough to squeeze her hand. "Maybe they'll let us babysit."

"I'm sure they will."

"They trust me to watch their cat, so I'm sure they'd trust me to watch their baby."

"Ah…the infamous Miss Kitty. That explains why Hades was so enamored of you. He must have sensed her on you. She's his love interest, not that he can do anything about it. Miss Kitty ignores him, eats out of his bowl, sleeps in his spot. He watches adoringly, all aquiver."

Kurt laughed. "Wait till I tell him that she and I have slept together."

"I look forward to that conversation."

They were quiet for a few minutes, each locked in their own thoughts. Hers went to their peeper.

"I find it very odd that twice in one day I would have unwanted company at my house. Do you think the peeper is the same man from this morning?"

"It better not be."

She turned as far as the seat belt allowed. "You *know* who was there this morning?"

He drummed his fingers on the wheel. "Another investigator from our office."

"Why?"

"He saw you take the packet of ketamine from Forton's pocket. I set him straight."

"Did you also ask him how in the world he could determine what I pulled from Jeremy's pocket? Clearly, he was some distance away. *I* didn't see him and I would have, because there was little traffic that time of the day. Why was he following me?"

Kurt blew out a breath. "Anders wasn't following you, per se. He was poking around where he shouldn't on a drug case and saw you. He subsequently followed you home, recognized the address from my report yesterday—"

"What report? The one you made to Jess about you thinking I was this extortionist? But Jess knew I wasn't. Anders should have known when he saw my address that I was okay."

"He didn't believe you were okay. Anders had been assigned to the blackmailer case while I took over the drug investigation. He stuck his nose into my drug case, saw you with Forton, saw you go to that address and concluded you were a person of interest."

"Why didn't you tell me this when you came over? You could have at least told me it was another investigator poking around so I didn't have to worry."

His silence was telling.

Midge strained the limits of the belt. "Because you thought I was guilty, too?"

His lack of reply hurt her heart. She jerked back into her seat and stared out of the window. Tears obscured her vision, making her madder. She'd be damned if she let him see her cry.

"Anders dug up the investigation on Stanford. He suggested you might be a ticking bomb and pointed out that you had now been linked to two ongoing investigations. He created...doubt."

She snorted. "How could you even entertain the possibility?"

Another long, drawn-out silence fell. They were nearing Zach and Claudia's house.

"Because, until the other night, you wouldn't give me the time of day and now you're all over me." He snapped his hand up, cutting her off when she sucked in a sharp breath to respond. "And I'm all over you. I know why I want you. What I can't figure out is why you suddenly want me."

Midge rolled her eyes. "How can anyone as good-looking as you are have such low self-esteem?"

"I don't know. You tell me."

He pulled to a stop on the street, jammed the shift into Park and charged toward the house. Zach ushered his wife outside, waving Kurt back. Claudia was bundled up like a kid ready for a day in the snow. Midge didn't know how Zach managed to hold on to her with all the outer garments and still carry her overnighter. Kurt opened the SUV's back door and returned to his place behind the wheel. Midge cranked up the heat. She felt helpless watching them waddle through the snow.

Claudia started stripping off the coat, scarf and gloves as soon as Zach guided her inside. "I am burning up in all this."

Midge could see why. She also wore a bulky Marine Corps sweatshirt—Zach's, considering its size.

"I'll turn the heat down." Midge reached for the controls.

"I'll be fine once I get all this off." Claudia stripped the sweatshirt off and the sweater under it. "I swear the baby's going to want out to avoid heat stroke."

"Very funny." Zach hoisted himself inside, closing the door. "I only wanted you to be warm." He glanced their way. "How's the happy couple?"

"Shut up," Kurt snapped, putting the vehicle in gear.

Claudia's laughter was as beautiful and sparkling as she. Midge envied her poise and class, her blonde hair and blue eyes and the way those eyes filled with love every time she looked at her husband.

"You could have said something yesterday," Midge told him.

"And miss the fun of seeing the two of you bumble along? I see you're getting along as fabulously as always. Not only can I feel the tension, I can see it. I'm not sure I want our child exposed to such negativity," Zach added.

Claudia fanned her long fingers against her throat. "I agree. I say they quit dancing around each other before they realize how much time they've wasted."

That was experience talking. It had taken Zach and Claudia five years before circumstances had finally brought them together.

"I'd like them to kiss and make up," she added.

"You heard the mother of my child," Zach told them.

Midge shot him a glare. "Is that an order, *sir*?"

Zach grinned. "Does it have to be?"

Kurt turned. "You can order her all you want, but you're not the boss of me."

"No, but I am." Claudia's laughter was cut off by her wince as a contraction overcame her.

Zach placed his hand over hers and gently encouraged her to breathe. Once it was clear from the look on Claudia's face that the pain passed, their attention was back on Midge and Kurt.

"We're waiting," Zach said.

Kurt settled into his seat and put the vehicle into drive. "I'll have you there in no time."

"No," Claudia told him. "I want the two of you to kiss and make up *now*."

It appeared they had little choice. They leaned in to comply.

"And not a peck either," she added.

Kurt's eyes narrowed to laser-like intensity.

"I'm scared, Kurt," Claudia softly told him. "I need something to take my head away from the fact that I'm about to push a person from my body, and once that happens, Zach and I are going to have our asses handed to us on a silver platter by an infant."

"This is ridiculous." Midge unhooked her seat belt. "If kissing him is all it takes to get us moving—"

She leaned over the console, grabbed Kurt's face between her hands and gave him a kiss he ought to feel in his toes. She sure did. When she started to pull away, Kurt cupped her head and deepened it. They ended it at the same time, staring into each other's eyes.

Oh, the things you do to my heart, Kurt Davidson.

"Thank you." Claudia's voice trembled with unshed tears.

"Our pleasure," Kurt replied.

Once Midge settled into her seat, they were on their way.

Midge's kiss had scorched his lips. He could feel the burn sizzling in his blood. It settled in his cock and nothing could soothe the burn. Not Claudia's soft moans whenever she had a contraction—which were much too close for his liking, even at *'only five minutes apart'* — not the horrendous drive through a blinding snowstorm in the dark, not trying to determine who had been snooping on them in the bushes, not the rumbling in his stomach echoed by Midge's reminding them both they hadn't eaten since breakfast.

As before, the drive was excruciatingly slow. An hour after they'd left, he was finally pulling up to the hospital's emergency room doors — the closest entrance — and watched Zach help Claudia from the vehicle.

"We'll park and be inside shortly," he told them.

"We'll bring the overnighter," Midge added. "Go."

Zach gave her a sharp nod and swept Claudia into his arms.

"You're going to kill us both on this ice," she said with a light laugh.

"Not a chance, princess." His long strides ate up the short distance to the door.

"I hate that the system forced me to put some distance between them and me," Midge said softly.

Kurt headed for the parking lot in front of the hospital. He wanted to tell her it wasn't the system, it was herself. But that would be cruel…and wrong. The system not only frowned on fraternization between the ranks, it had made it a court-martial offense under the Uniform Code of Military Justice. She was right to put distance between herself and the Taylors. His relationship with Claudia and Zach compromised her and he didn't know what to do about it. Them or her? A choice would have to be made.

"I'm sorry I made you cry," he told her.

Midge tucked her arms across her chest — a classic defensive position. "You didn't make me cry."

"Your eyelashes were damp and spiked. Would you rather I lie to you? If I really believed the crap Anders was spinning, do you think I would have told you? And if you're wondering if I ever would have told you about it before this, the answer is no. Why? Because it'd be like telling you so-and-so thinks you have big feet."

She relaxed, placing her hands in her lap. "I've missed them. Hell, I missed Zach and Phillip the second the case was settled and we returned to our own lives. They feel like big brothers to me."

"You don't need to stay away from Phillip." He'd left the Marine Corps a couple of years ago. His wife had followed his departure soon after Midge had arrived.

"They're a package deal, and you know that."

Claudia was Phillip's sister. The sadness in Midge's voice dived into his heart. He suspected where her thoughts were going—the same place his had. There were few cars in the parking lot. He chose a point as close to the entrance as he could get but left the engine running.

"I refuse to choose between you and them." There had to be a way to have it all.

"I'm not asking you to." She sighed and turned to stare out her window. "I'm so tired of living this way. I see how it is in the office. Officer and senior enlisted are going to the gym, to lunch, hanging out after-hours—men *and* women. No one bats an eye. I always feel as if I'm being watched by Stanford's little spies—all of them waiting for a chance to take me down. Sometimes I feel like making it happen if only to get it all over with, but I don't want to bring Zach down with me."

When Kurt brushed his fingers over her cheek, she turned to him. "First of all, Zach's a big boy and can take care of himself. Second, I won't let anyone tear you down. I don't care what rank they are. I'll fight to my last breath to keep my friends *and* you."

He cupped her neck and dropped a kiss to her parted lips. He longed to deepen it, to drag her into the back seat and take her, to whisper words his heart wanted to say but his brain refused to utter. Logic told him it was too soon to consider the depth of his feelings. Emotion reminded him that it had been two months since he'd first laid eyes on her — the woman of his dreams. Knowing the lengths he'd go to protect her now after so short an association, how would he feel when they were the ones walking into the hospital for the birth of their child? What would she say if she knew how he really felt?

"We need to get their bag inside." She brushed her hand down his arm.

He nodded and cut the engine, laughing when their stomachs rumbled.

"Great minds and empty stomachs."

Midge unhooked her seat belt then exited the vehicle, grabbing for the bag before he could do so. She relinquished it to him when they headed for the building, huddled into each other against the storm. The automatic doors opened as they approached. This close to the entrance there was no snow until they shook off what had gathered on their clothing. Midge pulled her hood back and fluffed her hair.

He leaned close. "Do you know how sexy you look right now?"

Midge giggled and elbowed his ribs. Three feet past the entrance her humor faded. A Navy corpsman blocked their path, eyes narrowed, mouth pinched. Kurt recognized her as one of Midge's companions from the other night—Susan. Midge regarded her with equal displeasure.

"I want my things back," Susan snapped.

"Not a problem." Midge side-stepped her and started walking.

Kurt hurried to catch up. "What things is she talking about?"

"That damn wig and the outrageous outfit she insisted I wear."

So, they are Susan's. Kurt glanced over his shoulder. Susan was already gone.

"You should have seen the boots she wanted me to wear. I refused. I should have refused it all." She stopped and faced him. "But then, if I'd done that, I never would have had you."

She kissed him the way he'd wanted to kiss her minutes before—slow, long, deep. Heat swept down his body, settling in his groin. He damned the coats that kept him from showing her how much he wanted her.

"That you, Davidson? Good God, man, get a room."

Yost's snide drawl jerked them apart. The man was ten feet away and as far as Kurt was concerned, ten feet too close.

"Who's this pretty little filly?" He stepped closer. "You look familiar, baby cakes. We met?"

Kurt could feel Midge's tension. If she made a move to slug the bastard, he would not only let her, he'd swear it was an accident. Although considering how Yost ran a lascivious leer down Midge's body, she might be the one having to back Kurt.

"My lady is none of your business, First Sergeant. Excuse us." He placed his hand on her back as they walked away.

"Don't blame you," Yost called out. "If I had a woman like that rather than my old heifer, I'd be keeping her away from other men, too."

"What a fucking moron," Midge muttered. "See? It never ends."

"Holy shit." Yost's barked laughter rang through the corridors. "Ellis?" More laughter, louder than before. "That's it, Davidson. A good fuck'll help loosen that stick she's got up her ass."

Kurt dropped the suitcase and was on Yost like stink on shit. He grabbed the man by the shirt and shoved him up against the wall. He was so focused on Yost's terror-filled eyes he didn't realize he'd drawn back his fist until Midge pulled his hand down.

"Don't," she said softly. "Please. Come on." She tugged his arm.

He shoved Yost as he released his shirt but moved no farther.

"Please," she whispered. "It will only make things worse."

She had a point, but he didn't like it. Kurt let her ease him away, lacing his fingers through hers when their hands touched. He turned his back on Yost and walked with her to where he'd left the luggage.

"Don't think I won't report this, Davidson," Yost told him.

"Don't give him the satisfaction of a response," she whispered.

Kurt grabbed the bag and kept walking with her. He hated having his back to a man he didn't trust. Rage blinded him to anything else but Midge's hand in his. It dissipated when she dragged him into the women's restroom by the lab. A twist of her hand secured the lock. Midge wrapped him in a tight hug. He released the bag and clung to her, hating himself for not digging in and fighting for her sooner. For someone who claimed to like to peel back the layers slowly, he'd failed when it came to the woman he craved. Not once had he bothered to even try to work his way beyond Midge's barriers. Even now words lodged in his throat, so he did the only thing he knew he could get right. He shoved his hand between her legs and his tongue between her lips.

Midge whimpered and deepened the kiss as she fumbled to unzip his jeans. Following her lead, he did the same and shoved his hand straight to her hot pussy the second he got the zipper open. She broke their kiss on a gasp, arching her neck. He raked his teeth down the column of her throat and pressed her farther back. She gave up her attempt to unzip him and clamped her hands over her shoulders.

"I love when you give yourself to me," he told her.

"As much as you love giving yourself to me?"

She had him dead to rights on that one. Theirs was a mutual exchange of power and pleasure.

"You bet, baby."

"Fuck me," she whispered.

His cock hardened all the more. She didn't plead with him to stop or remind him they might get caught. Not his Midge. She wanted him *now* and damn the consequences.

"Good," he roughly replied. "Because I feel as if I'll die if I don't get inside you right now."

She raised her head. "Damn, you say the sweetest things."

She relinquished her hold on him and pulled away. Before he could comment on how much he missed being inside her heat, Midge was on her knees before him. She opened the zipper, yanked his clothing down and swallowed his cock. She shoved her hand between his legs to cup his balls. Kurt braced against the door, trying his best not to pound into it, but every loop of her tongue around his cock sent his hips rocking with uncontrolled frenzy. He kept one hand against the door and the other clutched in her hair. Climax was close. The fire within him demanded release.

"Stop," he gasped.

Midge released him, fisting his cock instead.

"I can't fuck you if you make me come," he managed to say through pants of breath. "And you did order me to fuck you."

Her grin tightened his balls. "So I did."

She fished a condom from his pocket and started to rip it open.

"If you try to put that on me, I might not make it."

"Oh, the power."

Her husky voice slithered into his veins. He watched through the haze of lust as she stood, wiggled her jeans and panties down to her ankles, then positioned herself at the sink—ass out and all his. Kurt couldn't get the condom on fast enough. He shoved his clothing down as he neared her.

"I hope to hell that sink holds up," he muttered, then slid inside her.

Their breath caught. Neither of them moved. He loved the way her muscles gripped him, as if telling him that he wasn't going anywhere until she was satisfied. He brushed his palms over her ass until she was writhing against him, setting the pace. Then he slipped one hand over her hip and right to her hard clit.

Kurt locked his free arm around her waist to help keep their weight off the sink as much as possible. Eyes closed, he soaked in the feel of her pussy squeezing his cock while her clit grew hotter and harder under his touch. Orgasm rushed over him before he could stop it. He slammed into her under the force of his release, loving that she came with him. They lay draped over the sink, gasping for breath.

"Damn, sweetheart." *Don't say it.* "Just damn."

"I know."

She curled her arm around his head and kissed him.

Chapter Nine

Joy had nestled in Midge's heart hours ago and refused to leave. Watching Claudia give birth to Adam Elias Taylor, feeling love fill the room, holding that tiny bundle of life in her arms made her long for a child of her own.

"I hate leaving them there all alone," Zach mumbled from the back seat.

"They aren't all alone," Kurt gently told him. "Phillip is with them. You've both been up all night. You need the rest. Let your support system support you. Eat and get some sleep. We've got your back."

Midge glanced at Zach's reflection in the visor mirror. He didn't seem appeased, not that she could blame him.

"At least shave, shower and eat something," she told him. "You can always go back afterward and nap in the chair." As Marines, they'd all slept in worse places. "And you'll have your own transportation, complete with car seat, on the off chance they're discharged today."

"True, but they won't be released until sometime tomorrow." He sighed and rubbed his eyes. "I can't believe we had all that snow yesterday and this morning it's nearly gone."

"Desert living," she and Kurt said together.

"Good times," Zach muttered. "Looks like power's been restored as well."

All the traffic lights were operating.

"If you need me to handle your leave request, I can be your runner tomorrow. I don't have to be in court," she told him.

"Not worried about any fallout from helping me out?"

"I have no fucks left to give on that subject. If asked, I'll tell them I'm following orders."

Zach snickered. "There you go. I'll let you know." He leaned his head back. In seconds, he was asleep.

Kurt decreased his speed, giving their friend more time to nap during the drive back to the Taylor house. She'd bet it was the only nap he'd take. He'd feed the cat, shower and shave and be back at the hospital within the hour. Midge hoped he also took the time to eat while he was at home. Food options were limited to the emergency room vending machine on weekends. With the roads clear, though, he could grab a bite elsewhere *if* he could be compelled to leave Claudia and Adam. She doubted it, which was fine. She and Kurt could return with something for him later.

Kurt shot a smile her way. "How does it feel to be an honorary aunt?"

His soft voice seeped into her veins. "Like the best thing ever."

Her smile burst from the inside out. She still couldn't believe that she and Kurt had been allowed to be there for the entire process. Once they'd arrived at labor and delivery, they'd been swept inside by a nurse who referred to them as an aunt and uncle. Emotion had rendered her mute. Phillip hadn't batted an eye when he'd arrived to discover he and Claudia had acquired a brother. Midge learned it was how they'd all planned it since Kurt's coloring matched theirs and his devotion showed a deep connection to Claudia. Now she'd been drawn in as well, with open arms and so much affection. No way was she putting distance between herself and them ever again.

"I can't even begin to describe how it felt to hold the little guy," Kurt said.

"Pure joy?"

His smile widened. "Yeah."

"I love how he snuggled into my arms."

She stifled a yawn. They'd been up all night also. Midge couldn't wait to curl up next to Kurt when they reached her place. At some point she'd dozed off without realizing it. She woke when Kurt pulled to a stop at the Taylor home. Behind her, Zach stretched awake. A glance at the dashboard clock showed an hour had passed.

Zach released his seat belt. "What did you do? Drive to Yucca Valley and back to kill time?"

Kurt twisted around. "Nah. Drove around a bit so you could rest."

"Thanks." Zach leaned forward to give him a hug. Then he did the same to Midge, adding a kiss to her cheek. "We've missed you."

"I suspect you'll be seeing a lot of me now."

He smiled. "Good."

"Want us to take Miss Kitty tonight?" she asked.

"That'd be great. But come get her later. I want to spend some time with her. Kurt has a key, and we have his."

"Later then."

They bid him goodbye and headed to her place.

"I can't wait to crawl into bed," he said.

"That makes two of us, even with the nap."

It didn't take long to get to her house.

"In the garage or out?" Kurt asked, pulling into the driveway.

"In." She fished the remote from the console between the seats.

"I don't see the master in his perch."

"The curtains are closed. Hades is probably pissed as hell about it, too. Heaven forbid he expend the effort to wiggle between the drapes for access."

"I'm sure his basket was in his way."

Giggling, she pressed the remote and the garage door lifted. That was when she saw her kitchen door was open.

"What the... I swear to hell and back, if Bernadette is in my house..." She released her seat belt then shoved open the SUV door and ran toward the kitchen.

Kurt was steps behind her. She jerked to a halt at the kitchen door, horrified at the destruction before her. The cabinets were emptied. Pots, pans, dishes, food lay strewn about everywhere. Drawers were pulled out and dumped. A bag of rice had burst open and grains covered the tile amid shards of glass and silverware. Canisters were upended and their contents spread over the counter.

"Hades would have been petrified. What if he ran out the door?"

Kurt brushed his hand over her shoulder. "Then he would have been in the garage."

"Hades!" She ran toward the living room

"Honey, wait. You don't know what you might be running into."

She froze in the doorway. More disaster, that was what she was running into. Books were scattered everywhere with spines broken and pages ripped. Her couch and chairs spilled their contents from large gashes in the cushions. DVD and CD cases were open and on the floor. Her house phone lay shattered by the fireplace, as if the culprit had hurled it against the wall.

"Why would she do such a thing?"

"Are you certain it was Bernadette?" he asked. "From my perspective, someone was deadly serious about finding something. She doesn't seem like the kind of person to expend this kind of effort. Steal, yes. Physically destroy, no."

Both assessments were true. Bernadette would use that viper-like tongue of hers to destroy. Tears obscured Midge's vision.

"For what? What do they think I have? What if they killed Hades?"

She started for the stairs. Kurt pulled her to a stop.

"What if they're still here?" he asked. "I'll find Hades. You call 9-1-1 then start taking pictures. Try to determine if anything's missing. Try not to touch anything. They may have left fingerprints."

After she nodded, Kurt took the stairs two at a time. The rubble made it impossible to tell if anything was missing. For all her expertise in restoration, there wasn't much to salvage. Somehow she managed to remain calm while reporting the break-in to the dispatcher, but her voice shook with every word. Once she'd been assured help was on the way, she went to the window seat under Hades' perch to retrieve her camera. It was the only place that hadn't been disturbed — probably because it *had* been hidden by the curtains. Getting to it proved a problem. She had to remove everything from the top, yet had nowhere to put it that wouldn't compromise the crime scene.

Hades' pathetic meow drew her attention to the stairs. He clung to Kurt, paws hugging his neck. Even from this distance, she could see him shaking. Kurt trotted down the steps, muttering soothing words while he gently stroked Hades' back. Fur flew with every brush.

"Oh, Hades," she cried.

More wails answered, as if he were telling them all about it. She met them at the bottom, reaching to take him — not an easy task. He didn't want to release his new bestie. Kurt was forced to peel him away and turn him toward her. Once he saw her, Hades leaped into her arms. The force knocked Midge backward. Kurt's quick reflexes kept her from falling.

"It's okay. It's okay. We're here now." She dug her fingers into his fur, as much for her own comfort as his. "Where was he?"

"Under what was left of your bed."

"Is it a mess upstairs, too?"

"It is."

"Nothing insurance won't take care of, right?" Her quivering chin unleashed her tears.

Kurt drew her into a hug. "If it helps, I picked up your sex toys and put them in one of the tote bags."

She leaned into the comfort of his arms. "Bless you." Having law enforcement see that would have mortified her.

"You call it in?" he asked.

"Yes. I was about to take pictures, but the camera's in the window seat and I wasn't sure how I could open it with everything on top and I didn't know where to put the stuff without compromising the scene."

"I got it." He kissed her temple and walked to the window.

"She complains about everything else, why the hell didn't Bernadette report this? They couldn't have been quiet. She had to have heard the noise. Do you think this has anything to do with our peeper? If he was watching the house, he would have seen us leave."

"All excellent questions." He shoved between the curtains, pushed everything on top back and lifted the lid. "Fuck."

Midge rushed to his side and peered over his shoulder. Balanced on top of old photo albums, extra pillows and blankets were gallon-freezer bags filled with packets of ketamine.

"Oh my God. Oh my God. Oh my God." Panicked sobs overcame her. She'd moved back to top of his list as a suspect in his drug case. This evidence was damming. How could she convince him otherwise? "It's not mine, Kurt. I swear to God it's not mine."

Hades dug his claws into her neck. She focused on the pain, not the fact she was losing the best guy she'd ever met and might be going to jail for something she didn't do.

Kurt squeezed her shoulder. "Calm down, honey. We'll get to the bottom of this."

Midge tried to blink away the flow of tears. It didn't work. "You believe me?"

He frowned. "Of course I believe you. If you had a stash like this, you would have put the packet you pulled off Forton in here."

She managed to nod and was vaguely aware of Kurt calling Jess and telling him to get here *now* with DEA and him telling her to say nothing to the deputy sheriffs about it. She watched him start to photograph the scene with his cell phone.

"You don't want to use my camera?"

"I can't get to it."

Because the drugs are on top of it. She needed to sit down. But where? Every place she looked was part of the crime scene.

Hades retracted his claws and burrowed against her neck. Each meow was more pathetic than the last. Midge didn't blame him for being frightened. She was scared to death.

"It's all right, big guy. I'm home now. Everything's going to be fine." She gave him long, soothing strokes down the back and walked upstairs to survey the damage. Petting his soft fur helped calm her, too. Her bedroom was in shambles.

Her mattress had been ripped apart, then shoved aside. The box springs bore gouges resembling hammer-claw marks. Everything from her dresser drawers was tossed about the room. Same thing with her closet. The second bedroom was in a similar state.

She checked the bathroom last. The scent of lilac wafted through the room. The vanity mirror had been smashed. From the broken bottle of bath salts in the sink, she guessed her intruder had thrown it at the mirror. Purple crystals were everywhere — on the sink, the carpeting. At least the intruder had the courtesy to empty the bottles and boxes into the bathtub, not onto the floor. Or maybe that was where he'd thrown them.

It was still going to take forever to clean up. She couldn't do a thing until the various law enforcement agencies, followed by an insurance adjuster, were done.

Midge tiptoed down the staircase. Hades' warbles had finally slowed, but he was still shaking. He'd be clingy for quite some time. She counted her blessings he hadn't been hurt. Kurt stood at the open front door, hands on his hips, ready for battle. She sat on the bottom step—the only inviolate place in the room.

Kurt shut the door and sat beside her, giving Hades a scratch behind the ear. The affection earned him a healthy purr. "That's it. Enjoy yourself now, buddy, and forget about those nasty bad guys."

He moved to the shoulder, then to his paws and the cat finally relaxed. Hades loved to have his feet massaged.

"Should've given them a good whack with one of these, my furry friend. In fact…it looks like you did."

Midge twisted around to see. Kurt studied what appeared to be strands of hair dangling from Hades' claws, then grinned.

"I believe we might have a little DNA evidence here. Keep him still until someone can collect the evidence."

That wasn't a problem. Hades wasn't going anywhere anytime soon. He'd probably wind up sleeping with them for the next two weeks. That was fine with her.

"I'm scared to leave him home alone. Hell, *I'm* was afraid to stay in the house alone."

"You're not going to be alone. You'll be with me. As soon as we can, we'll pack what you need and head to my house. You and Hades will be safe there."

Midge wasn't so sure. "Do you suppose they're watching the house right now? They'll see us leave and might think we took the drugs with us."

He draped his arm around her. "They'll also see the place crawling with police, NCIS and DEA. They'll know the drugs have been confiscated. What I don't understand is why they think or know you've got them — unless Forton hid it and they beat the information out of him."

Midge frowned. "Jeremy was alone for a long time here the other night while Susan and I got dressed to leave. Do you think that's why he called last night, frantic to come over?"

"It makes sense to me," he said, more to himself than to her. "But why tear the place apart if Forton told them where it was? That must mean he didn't...or they beat him unconscious before he could tell them."

"But then how could they have known to come here?" The answer came to her instantly. "They followed me here."

"And waited until we left before coming in."

"Do you suppose that's who was peeping in the window last night?"

"It seems a logical deduction. They sure as hell weren't shy about letting someone know they were here."

"I can't believe Bernadette wouldn't have reported it. She'd think it was me and would be hoping for yet another excuse to throw me out. She comes in here for every other little thing. Why not this? Unless she's the one who did this to scare me into leaving."

"Another plausible theory. We'll figure it out."

They heard cars pull up outside. Kurt picked his way over the debris field and opened the front door. In minutes the place was swarming with more law enforcement personnel than she'd ever wanted to see in her personal space — all jockeying for control. Hades curled into her, quivering at the rush of people. Midge cuddled him, trying to soothe his fears with gentle ear rubs while she watched the power play before her. Full disclosure was next and a decision was made. One sheriff deputy went to talk to Bernadette. Another started a perimeter check.

Midge tried to block the enormity of the mess surrounding her. This went beyond searching for something and well into destruction. It was going to take forever to clean up. She feared her precious collection of first editions was ruined. If it had been intruders hunting for the ketamine, they would have gone right to the source and been subtle about it to avoid detection. There was no way Jeremy could have withstood that beating and not divulged the information.

Kurt, Jess and a third NCIS agent they called Vic engaged in muted conversation with the DEA agent. Every so often they glanced her way. The attention unnerved her. She wanted to scream that she'd done nothing except let people into her life against her better judgment. She leaned against the wall and closed her eyes, willing the nightmare away. Movement near her a few minutes later opened them.

Jess sat beside her. "I understand we have a brave guard-cat here. Mind if I see?" He gently scratched Hades' ears.

He relaxed enough to let Jess pick the hairs from his claws with tweezers and put them into an evidence bag.

"Looks like we've got a little skin here, too. Whoever this cat smacked is going to have some gouges to show for it. Want to tell me your take on this?" Jess tucked the bag in a large tackle box.

"I didn't do this. This isn't me." Midge wanted to scream the words loud and long. Did she need a lawyer? Should she call Phillip? He might be teaching high school now, but he still had his law degree. "Maybe you should ask Jeremy."

"Jeremy Forton died last night from his injuries."

Fuck.

"Your take on this?" he said again.

"Someone hunting for drugs wouldn't have made a mess like this. They wouldn't want to be detected. Whoever did this was sending a message. My landlady wants me gone, but this took stamina and I can't see her expending that kind of effort. What I don't understand is why she didn't call this in. There had to be a hell of a lot of noise. She comes in whenever she damn well pleases, so I'm sure she would have charged in here over this. Hell, she walked in on Kurt and me yesterday."

"Maybe she was out," Jess suggested.

"In that storm? We wouldn't have gone out if not for Claudia. Besides, Kurt had to park on the street last night because of the snow piled in front of the garage door. She couldn't have gotten out."

"We'll see what the deputy can pull out of her. Can you give me a list of who's been in here recently? It will help when we start analyzing fingerprints."

"Me, Kurt, my landlady, Petty Officer Susan Bolotnik and Jeremy. They are the only ones since I've moved here. I clean weekly." *God, the mess.*

He scribbled the names on a small notepad. "Anything else come to mind? Anyone else cause you any grief? Think, Midge. This is the third time in as many days that you've been at the center of an incident."

Fear rippled through her. Midge ordered herself not to panic. That was impossible. There was no coincidence here. Someone was setting her up big time and there could only be one person in the world who hated her enough to do so—Colonel Dean Stanford.

Breathe.

"We've got a body."

Heads whipped toward the deputy poking his head through the front door.

"From the description Special Agent Davidson gave, it looks like the landlady."

Midge's stomach turned. She wanted to run away as fast as she could, to leave all this behind. But there was no place far enough, no time long enough to evade Stanford. He'd said he'd get her when she least expected and had made good on that threat.

Jess patted her knee and walked away. She fought hyperventilation and the terror running through her mind. The next thing she knew, Kurt had his arms wrapped around her and his lips pressed to her forehead.

"Come on." He rubbed her back. "Let's pack you and his highness up and get you to my house. You're not going to be able to take your SUV."

It was part of the scene. She hoped they hadn't destroyed any evidence by parking it in the garage. "I'm afraid to be alone. It's Stanford. He's after me."

"We're considering that as well and will look into it." Kurt tucked his arm around her as they started up the stairs.

"I'm still afraid."

"I don't blame you. I'm not leaving you." He squeezed her shoulders.

She glanced his way. "Don't you have to work?"

He smiled. "I am working. I'm protecting you."

Midge elbowed him. "You know what I mean." She jerked her head toward the activity below them.

"Right now you are my only concern. You come first. There's nothing here I can do that someone else can't. Jess will be by later to brief us. Vic is going to watch us pack your things."

She jerked to a stop. Hades tensed, digging claws into her neck again. "Why? I sure as hell didn't do this. I was with you all night."

"Procedure and precaution. If you uncover something while we gather your things, Vic will be there to record it."

Because he'd be an objective observer.

"All right."

With her words, Kurt called Vic to join them. His ready smile put Midge at ease. He extended his hand once he reached the step below them.

"Special Agent Vic Brownell. It's a pleasure to meet you."

He looked like he meant the words. She accepted his handshake, trying to smile and failing.

"I wasn't aware Kurt was seeing anyone. My wife will be beside herself with excitement. Don't worry. I'll do my best to keep her enthusiasm contained until you're ready to meet. Helen has a tendency to get ahead of herself sometimes. She's been trying to fix Kurt up since she met him." He shrugged. "My little matchmaker."

The light in his eyes said love.

"We're...new. Space would be appreciated."

"Come on." Kurt put his arm around her shoulders and they continued up the staircase. "We'll get you packed then we'll head to Zach's to get Miss Kitty. She should be able to take Hades' mind off all this."

She snorted. "And who's going to do that for us?"

"Us?" He winked. "You get your clothes. I'll get what you need from the bathroom."

"I don't think there's much left."

"Then we'll get more."

She closed her eyes and leaned into the kiss he pressed to her temple. "Everything is such a mess, Kurt. I feel sick inside at the thought this person has touched my things, my clothes." All her toys were going in the trash.

"I would feel the same way. I've got a washer and dryer at my house."

"Bless you...again."

Midge kissed his cheek and walked to her bedroom. Vic kept a respectful distance behind her as he followed.

She spotted the red wig lying in a puddle of crimson on the floor the moment she crossed the threshold. The color of the wig reminded her of the blood on Jeremy's face. A wave of nausea washed over her.

"You okay?" Vic touched her back. "You look a little pale."

Midge nodded. "I just want to get this done."

I just want my life back.

Chapter Ten

Midge studied her reflection in the bathroom mirror. She looked as if she'd pulled an all-nighter. Shadows underscored her eyes. Claw marks ringed her neck from Hades' grip. He'd refused to release her until Kurt had walked out of Zach's house with Miss Kitty in her carrier. Only then had Hades allowed Midge to put him in his. He'd spent the short ride from the Taylor house to Kurt's telling Miss Kitty everything. For once, his love interest hadn't ignored him. The two had curled into Hades' basket once things were set up at Kurt's. Miss Kitty had wasted little time grooming him.

She'd been expecting a bachelor home, but Kurt had nested very well. Blues and creams were his color choices — soothing, safe...a sanctuary. They'd put her things in the second bedroom. He'd promised to make room in his closet and drawers for her clothing right before he'd gathered her delicate items for washing. He'd nested in her heart as well. Midge didn't try to dissect the love blooming there. It would either last or it wouldn't. She'd take it as her right and treasure every second for now.

Live in the moment, not the past.

Even if the past was hurtling her way... Dwelling on it wasn't going to make things better.

"Those scratches look nasty," Kurt said from the doorway.

"I've got ointment in my things."

Kurt had managed to salvage her toiletries and they now occupied space throughout his bathroom. He'd even remembered to grab the box of tampons she'd had under the sink. The man had 'keeper' written all over him. It was a wonder he hadn't been snatched up long ago.

"Let's get a shower. We're both getting a little ripe."

"And the cat hair covering us doesn't help."

"Probably should have waited to wash clothes. You can go first."

"I'd rather we shower together," she told him. "I don't mean to sound like a baby, but I don't want to be alone while you shower. And don't go all logical on me and say I can sit on the toilet and wait for you — or that you'll have me memorize the code for your gun safe if I need a weapon."

"I wouldn't dream of being the voice of reason right now." Smiling, he stepped up behind her and slipped his arms around her waist. Their gazes met in the mirror. "But I am giving you the code for the gun safe on the floor of my closet. I want you protected at all times. Also, for the record, I'm not thrilled about leaving you alone, either. I was going to follow Hades' example and wait on the other side of the door while you showered."

Midge managed a laugh, draped her arms over his and leaned against him. Kurt kissed her cheek, then patted her hip.

"You get the water warmed up. I'll get a towel and washcloth for you."

He moved back and pulled his shirt over his head. She followed suit, stripping herself of clothes as he did. While she reached to twist on the shower, he gathered an extra set of towels from the closet by the door. They stepped under the spray together, wrapped in each other's arms. Warmth seeped into her bones, chasing away residual chill. It was a shame it couldn't wash off the bad. Too soon, he released her. They reached for her washcloth at the same time.

"Let me do the honors." He slipped it from her fingers. "Relax, sweetheart. Let me give this to you. I promise I'll wash all your worries away."

Midge didn't think that would be possible, but she gave herself over to him. He rubbed the soapy washcloth in slow circles over her, leaving no spot untouched. She closed her eyes and leaned against the stall, content to let him stroke the tension from her body. He even washed her hair, making her feel treasured and decadently spoiled.

She peeled her eyes open to watch Kurt wash. His cock stood at attention, something he seemed to ignore since he merely scrubbed and rinsed. The way it bobbed in front of him felt like a call for attention and though he might ignore it, she couldn't. She wanted him, wanted to feel the heat of his cock in her hand and against her body.

"Is that for me or is it your going-into-battle erection?" she asked.

His eyebrows arched. Midge liked that she'd surprised him. Hell, she'd surprised herself with the question. It wasn't like her, and since he hadn't answered, Midge worried she might have crossed a line.

He slipped his arm around her, pulling her against him. His erection was hot against her belly. Her body begged to have it.

Kurt kneaded his fingers deep into her butt cheeks, stoking the fire that built between her legs.

"It's one I've never experienced before. The best description I can give is that I'm hard because I have the hot woman of my dreams and I will die to keep her safe and protected from harm. I've had relationships before, but I never put that person before my own goals and job...until now. *You* are my priority. I'd say screw the job, but I need it to protect you."

He'd rendered her speechless. How could she respond to an admission like that? Telling him that her feelings for him were growing with every minute they spent together would be premature.

She moved to kiss him and he met her halfway. The touch of their tongues gliding together stole her breath. Midge prayed that over-the-hill-too-fast feeling never faded, that years from now his kiss would still make her breathless.

"I want you, Kurt. I need you. Right here. Right now."

He rubbed his erection over her stomach. "Let me go get—"

"I'm on the pill. No need. Or just come on me."

"Damn, baby." He growled low in his throat. "Do it, sweetheart." He pushed her hand to his cock. "Make me come."

Midge wrapped one hand around his dick and cradled his balls in the other. Kurt's groan gave her more of the power she'd missed in her life. She pushed him against the wall.

"Too bad there isn't a towel bar in here." She traced her tongue over his nipple, loving how he whimpered. "I could bind your wrists and give you a real treat."

"First thing tomorrow," he gasped.

She tightened her grip on his cock. "Don't disappoint me."

"Never."

"Good." She licked her way down his torso, pausing near his cockhead. "I bet you'd like me to suck you off."

He stared down at her. His arms were now over his head. Midge loved how he played at being captive.

"I'm yours," he told her. "Do as you wish."

"I see." She released her hold and cradled his dick between her breasts. "Then come on my tits. You know you want to."

She squeezed his balls, pressed her finger into the puckered flesh behind them and writhed against him. Kurt came fast, painting her skin with his semen. Midge wiggled her way up his body, dragging her mouth over his flesh until she reached his lips. He cupped her head and thrust his tongue around hers, quickly switching their positions.

There was nothing leisurely about his excursion down her body. He went right to the source, spreading her thighs with his shoulders. He clamped his mouth over her clit, then shoved his thumb into her pussy and two fingers up her ass. Climax swept over her with his first suck and left her spent.

* * * *

Kurt closed his laptop when he heard the vehicles pull up to the house. It was either Jess or the pizza delivery guy. Considering how many car doors he heard close, he was betting on Jess and that he'd brought company.

He hated like hell to wake Midge, but she'd want the information his team was bringing. Plus, there was no way she'd be able to continue to sleep on the couch with them here. She'd fallen asleep shortly after they'd come into the living room. He'd draped one of his mom's afghans over her then sat in his recliner with his laptop to research Dean Stanford. Hades and Miss Kitty had wasted little time curling up next to her.

Kurt liked the comfort of having her near him. The break-in and Bernadette's murder had rattled him. Clearly the busybody had interrupted the would-be burglar and been killed as a result, although Kurt was sure Bernadette had her fair share of enemies. Any of them might have finally had enough. But during a snowstorm and during the same time someone was ransacking the adjoining house? Highly unlikely.

"Hey, babe. Gotta wake up." He tweaked her big toe, loving her cat-like stretch and that sexy wake-up smile. "Jess is here with company."

The cats jumped down as she sat up and stretched a little more. "I'll go make a pot of coffee. Whoa, it's dark out. What time is it?"

"Six." He gave her a quick kiss. "I ordered a couple of pizzas about thirty minutes ago. They should be here soon."

"Good. I'm ravenous."

They exchanged another kiss—longer this time and interrupted by the knock on the door. Kurt cupped her face and kissed her once more before they parted — she to the kitchen and he to answer the door.

Jess, Vic and DEA Special Agent Everest stood huddled against a breeze growing colder by the second. Kurt waved them in then waited outside when he saw the pizza delivery car stop on the street. By the time he completed that transaction, Kurt was chilled to the bone and grateful he'd trusted his instinct and gotten two large pizzas. Midge had steaming mugs, paper plates and napkins on the coffee table and the afghan draped over the back of Kurt's recliner. He was going to need the warmup. As if she'd read his mind, Midge walked to the thermostat and turned up the heat.

"Dig in, guys." Kurt put the boxes on the table, helping himself to a slice of the barbeque chicken pizza.

"Thank you for this last indulgence before Emma comes home tomorrow." Jess glanced up from under his eyebrows as he reached for a slice. "I trust my secret is safe with the two of you?"

Midge crossed her heart. "I sure won't tell." She grabbed a slice and curled into the chair across from him. "What did you find?"

Vic pulled in a breath before he began. "Evidence has to be analyzed, so we're hoping for a hit on the fingerprints. Coroner puts time of McFee's death between six-thirty and nine-thirty last night. Her throat had been cut. The knife — one of her own, it appears — was left beside her. Whoever did it had strength enough to knock her to the floor, hold her in place and yank her head up by her hair to expose her neck. We suspect it was a man. Large bloodied handprints were on the inside of her back door, another on the side of one of the storage containers outside. Both were broken into and searched."

Midge pressed her fingers against her forehead and closed her eyes. "All my Christmas decorations —"

"Strewn across the yard," Jess replied.

A tear slipped from beneath her lids. Kurt hated the distance between them, short as it was. He wanted her beside him where he could comfort her from this hell.

Jess went on. "Based on what you and Kurt told us, we're surmising McFee heard the noise and came over to investigate. She caught the person in the act and ran home. Her door adjacent to the garage had been opened with such force the doorknob broke the wallboard. The killer grabbed a knife from the butcher block on the kitchen counter, tackled her and cut her throat."

"There would be blood on him. Blood that would have transferred over to my place," Midge told them. "Did you find any?"

Vic and Jess shook their heads.

"He might have wiped his hands on his clothing," Kurt suggested.

"It'd be a reflex action for him because he certainly didn't care about anyone knowing he was there. Or he could have taken off after the murder," Vic added.

Midge sniffed. "His actions were overkill, if you ask me. I can't help feeling someone was sending me a message, trying to demoralize me and break me down."

Jess looked at Kurt. "Did you find anything along those lines?"

"Not yet," Kurt replied. "It's as if the man disappeared from the face of the earth."

"Or is very good at hiding," Midge muttered.

"Who are we talking about?" Everest asked.

It was the first time he'd spoken during any of the discussions Kurt had been privy to. The fact he was here now suggested he had information. Before Kurt divulged anything about Midge's past, he wanted that information.

Scowling, he snapped, "Why are you here?"

Everest sighed and tossed his empty plate to the table. "Jeremy Forton was one of our men. We'd been working with the Provost Marshal's Office to embed him in one of the units. As things progressed, the commanding general highly suggested we needed to bring NCIS into the fold to cover all our bases."

"But, *apparently*, we didn't warrant full disclosure," Jess snapped.

The fallout from that would last a long time. Kurt knew Jess wanted to tell them all to go to hell and that NCIS was stepping aside. His professionalism wouldn't let him do so. Kurt wasn't feeling so magnanimous.

"Then why the *fuck* was he hiding drugs in my girlfriend's home?"

Everest raised his palms. "Calm down."

"Calm down?" He shot to his feet. "A woman is *dead*. Midge's place is in ruins. Do you have any idea of what you've put her through?" He stabbed his finger at Everest. "I swear to God, if any of those first edition vintage books of hers are ruined, your people are paying for every single one *and* all of her furniture." He pointed to his neck. "These scratches around our necks aren't from crazy sex. Her poor cat was terrified and wouldn't let go until we picked up *his* girlfriend. I need a fucking beer."

He headed for the kitchen before he gave in to the urge to punch Everest's too-perfect face.

"Make that two," Midge called to his back.

"Three," Vic and Jess shouted.

Kurt grabbed the six-pack from the fridge and plopped it between the pizza boxes. He opened a bottle for Midge, another for himself, then returned to his chair.

"I'm still waiting for an answer." He took a long swallow, gaze locked on Everest. The man didn't so much as blink.

"We can only surmise that Forton had just made the buy and needed a place to hide it," Everest replied. "Although how he managed to get that many bags into her place without it being seen has us wondering who knew what and when."

"I didn't know shit." Midge perched on the edge of the chair, eyes shooting fire. "He was by himself for a good hour while Susan and I got dressed to go out. They came over by cab. Maybe she knows something. I sure as hell don't. He was never without that olive drab duffel bag. Now we know why. That also explains that scratch I saw on his hand that night. He must have tried to get into the window seat while Hades was on top of it. Honestly, it's hard for me believe that buffoon was a DEA agent. And another thing" — she punched her index finger into the cushion — "if he was one of your people, why the hell didn't he call you on Friday night if he was in trouble? Why call me? Where were *you* when he needed help?"

"My guess is that he called you in order to retrieve the ketamine and take the next step, whatever that was. Our goal was to find the top man."

Everest was calm personified. *Does nothing rattle him?*

"Well...clearly Jeremy was made. Good job, Special Agent Everest." Acid-laced sarcasm dripped from her voice.

Pride swelled Kurt's chest, but anger took the forefront. "You've put her at risk, Everest. I'm not happy."

"Really? I had no idea. You hide it so well." Everest rolled his eyes and grabbed a beer.

"All right, now that all cards are on the table" — Jess pinched the bridge of his nose before he continued — "we searched Forton's room yesterday afternoon. Someone had been there before us and torn it apart, as they did yours."

Kurt frowned. "So, he didn't give up where he'd hidden the drugs during the beating. Then why would someone go to Midge's?"

"We don't know," Everest replied. "Maybe they followed him to Miss El—"

"That's Staff Sergeant, not Miss," Midge snapped.

Everest's lips twitched as if he was trying to hide a smile. "If they followed him to *Staff Sergeant* Ellis's house on Thursday, they might have gone there after a search of his quarters revealed nothing."

"We did find a couple of surprises in his room," Vic said. "A computer-generated blackmail letter was among some bills. It was similar to the one Parsons and the other victims received. We're running it for fingerprints right now, but since we haven't found any on the other letters, we don't expect to find any there, either."

"What did it say?" Kurt asked.

Jess rubbed the back of his neck. "Same words. 'You know what I have. Pay up or I send it to your command.'"

Kurt frowned. "Why would Forton's command care if he was having sex with someone? He wasn't married, so it wasn't a case of adultery. Doesn't make any sense...unless this person knew about the drugs and was holding it over his head."

Midge shrugged one shoulder. "Not that he would care, since it was all part of his undercover work. What was the other surprise?"

Jess leaned forward, forearms on knees, eyeballing the pizza. "He was renting a house in town and, judging from its looks, I'm guessing it was part of his undercover work. We searched it as well. It's very sparse and looks more like a porn set, which might explain the blackmail letter."

Everest rubbed his neck. "We authorized the rental. He'd found a lead and was trying to milk it."

"The question now is... Was he killed by the blackmailer or by the ketamine ring?" Vic asked.

"Or are they the same person?" Everest sighed then glanced at Midge. "What do you know about Susan Bolotnik?"

She shrugged. "Not much. I met her when I arrived in Twentynine Palms. She was very persistent in forming a relationship with me. Jeremy was always with her. It was a package deal. They'd been a couple once. I'd gotten to the point where I found them pushy and tedious and broke off the friendship after the debacle of Thursday night."

"What debacle?" Vic asked.

"Both were insistent I go out with them. Susan wouldn't rest until I put on the disguise she'd brought with her."

"The red wig was hers?" Jess asked.

"Yes."

Susan felt the heat of her deceptions and was using a decoy to clear herself. Kurt had started to put the pieces together earlier, but Adam's birth and the destruction in Midge's home had sidetracked him.

The other men were nodding. Kurt suspected a plan had been made long before they'd arrived. Dread churned his stomach. He knew what they were going to say and had his response ready before any of them could utter a word.

"No. It's too dangerous. Midge isn't trained for these situations."

"She's our only link and she'll be able to draw Susan out." Jess' tone tolled defeat for Kurt. He'd made up his mind and nothing would change that.

"Or you could bring Susan in for *questioning*." Visions of all the many ways this could go wrong filled his head. He would *not* risk Midge's life.

Now Everest assumed Jess' posture. "Jeremy hooked up with Susan for a reason. She has to be crucial to his investigation or he wouldn't have kept up the façade. These are careful people. We don't want them spooked."

"What do you want me to do?" Midge asked.

Kurt sliced his palm through the air. "Did you *not* hear what I said? I will *not* have the woman I love put in danger."

He watched her eyes widen and it still took precious seconds for him to realize he'd outed himself. His fear for her was nothing compared to the fear he'd screwed up and lost her.

She recovered her composure and leaned his way. "And how do you feel about visiting me in prison? Someone is setting me up for these crimes. I'm not going to sit back and let it happen without a damn good fight." She eased back with a slow, measured breath, then looked at Jess. "What do you want me to do?"

"We want you to go back to the bar tomorrow night in the disguise she gave you," he replied. "Invite her to go with you."

"I'm going with her." Kurt stood, facing the four of them down.

Midge glanced up at him. "You can't. She's seen you in disguise and out of disguise. The only way I can convince her to meet me is to tell her that she was right and it didn't work out between us."

"We'll send Anders in to guard her," Vic said. "We'll set up surveillance across the street in the van. You can be in there with us."

His glare had no effect on any of them. Their attention was on Midge.

"Tell her everything," Everest told her. "Make her believe she's your best friend in the world. You'll be wearing a wire, so we'll pick up everything."

Kurt parked his fists on his hips. "She needs to be rehearsed."

"All planned." Vic flashed him a shit-grinning grin. "We'll clear her absence with the Staff Judge Advocate tomorrow and practice here."

"Fine." It wasn't as if he had a choice. He plopped into his recliner and grabbed his beer.

Vic smirked. "You could always dress up as Kiki and watch over her."

"Fuck you. I'm not running down a perp in high heels." He brought the bottle to his lips.

"Not even for me?" Midge asked.

Mischief danced in her eyes, rousing the beast in his jeans. He took a drink and used the bottle to cover his predicament.

"I've put on weight in the last year. The clothes no longer fit."

Vic laughed. "Don't fall for it, Midge. He's a talented tailor and can make the adjustments in record time. Hell, he helps out with costumes for the local theaters. He just doesn't want to shave his legs and pits."

"I know exactly how he feels," she replied.

Her response surprised him. Kurt had been expecting her to say that she'd help him shave.

"I have a closet full of disguises," he told them. "I'll find something else, because she is *not* going into that bar without me backing her up. And if I have to resign in order to have my way, I'll do it."

"Everyone calm down." Everest fanned the air. "He's not wrong. Someone needs to be in there with her and since it seems the blackmailer and drug trafficker cases are converging, I'd rather it not be Anders. If something happens to him before the case goes to trial, we're screwed and another drug lord is back on the streets."

No one argued, but Kurt could tell by the toothpick Jess shoved into his mouth that he wasn't pleased. He was thinking Kurt was too emotionally involved. He wasn't wrong. All Kurt's emotions were on the table. But he was going in with her, either as a current member of NCIS or a former one.

"She might be suspicious if I call her from my cell. I've never given her the number, only the house phone."

"Which was shattered into dozens of pieces." Everest leaned back. "Use the break-in to your advantage. Tell her that you and Kurt got into it and you ended things, that you came home to ruin and are sure he did it. Tell her you think he killed the landlady. Using your cell should back you up."

"It's going to have to wait until tomorrow," Kurt told them. "If she calls tonight, she runs the risk of Susan wanting her to come over and stay with her. That's not happening."

"Kurt's right. It might be easier if I talk to her in person. I told her I would be returning her things to her on Monday. It'll make more sense that way and I can ask to keep the wig. *If* the SJA approves my being involved."

Jess chuckled. "At this point it will be all in a day's work for him. Been there, done that."

"Yes, I've heard the stories." Midge finished her beer then stood. "Anything else? It's been a roller-coaster ride of emotions the last twenty-four hours. I need some time to process everything. And we're beyond exhausted."

"Would you at least sow the seed and call her?" Jess pleading was a sign of how desperate they were to close this case.

Midge sighed, retrieved her phone from her purse then sat on the arm of Kurt's recliner as she dialed. He slipped his arm around her hips, silently offering his support, even though he didn't want this.

"Put it on speaker," Everest told her.

"Nope. Not going to risk one of you making noise."

Midge didn't spare him a glance. He was proud of the way she'd dug in her heels, even while he hated what she'd agreed to do. He'd wanted to see the woman beneath the mask she wore for the world. *No sense faulting her for being strong and independent.*

"She's not picking up," Midge told them.

"Leave a message," Everest replied.

Her long, beleaguered sigh signaled displeasure. Nevertheless, she did as he'd asked.

"It's Midge. Call me. You were right and I was wrong. It didn't take long for everything to go to shit. He" — she feigned a sob — "he's a monster. I really need a friend. I'm so sorry for acting the way I did. Let's call it the hornies and leave it at that. I'm sure you've been there. Call me."

She rattled off her number, ended the call and placed the phone on the side table. "Good?"

"It's a start." Everest pulled his business card from his shirt pocket. "Here's my number."

Midge ignored his outstretched hand and started clearing the table. "Kurt will call his people if something noteworthy happens."

"It's a *joint* investigation, Staff Sergeant Ellis." He stabbed the card back into his shirt.

"Only when it's convenient for you." She stared a hole through him. "I'm Team NCIS all the way. If you'd read them in from the start, you might have closed your case months ago."

Yeah, baby. That's the way to put someone in their place. Kurt's pride doubled. He loved the smirks on his coworkers' faces. "Midge needs her vehicle. Is the scene clear?"

"Not yet. Locals are working on the homicide, trying to piece together what happened." Jess ducked low, catching Midge's gaze. "You know the family can help the two of you set things in order and be more than happy to do so — or help you pack up if you want that. Don't hurt our feelings by refusing."

She smiled. "I won't. Help is greatly appreciated. But don't mention the rest of it to Phillip or Zach. All they need to know is that a determined robber broke in. I don't want them worried or, heaven forbid, involved."

"Nor do I," Jess replied.

Yet putting Midge in harm's way is all right? Kurt let it go. There was no way he was going to win this argument, though he held out hope that Colonel Scott would refuse to let yet another Marine from his office become involved in an NCIS investigation.

"If you don't mind, it's been a day." She stacked the boxes and grabbed three empty bottles in one hand.

They headed for the door with Kurt behind them, firming up plans for the morning. He'd bet Colonel Scott would know about all of this well before then. A trill from Midge's cell phone jerked everyone to a stop and their heads around. The little device shuddered on the end table. Midge had paled.

And they expect her to pull off being undercover?

"Answer it," they told her in unison.

She set her load down and picked up the phone. "It's my dad."

Kurt watched her chin quiver before she turned her back on them.

"Hi, Daddy."

"What the hell's going on?" Her father's voice rang loud and clear. "Your mother's gone insane with worry. She called Dee, for crying out loud."

"Out," Kurt told the men and hurried to her side.

They wasted no time leaving, giving Midge privacy. He guided her to his chair, kissed her forehead then cleared the remains of their meal while she told her father about the break-in. She assured him that she was safe and would call with updates later. There was no mention of anything else—not the cases, not Bernadette…and not him. He was almost to the kitchen when he heard her say…

"No, Daddy, please don't come up here. I'm fine... I swear." She blew out a hard breath. "Daddy, stop. Listen. I've met someone... Two months ago..."

He glanced back to find her rolling her eyes and starting to pace.

"Yes, I'm with him now... And last night, too... All night, Daddy... Yes, his place... Hades loves him... Kurt Davidson... NCIS Special Agent. I'm sure you'll meet him soon... I'll call her right now... I *promise*. I'll talk to you later. Love to Dee and the kids."

She ended the call, scowled at the phone and punched in another number. Judging from the anger in her eyes, Kurt suspected this conversation wouldn't be pleasant. He gave her privacy and walked on to the kitchen. It wasn't far enough to mask her mother's screeched, "How dare you ignore my calls."

Midge followed with a rebuttal that silenced the woman, even hinting that Bernadette might still be alive if her mother hadn't asked her to snoop. He heard the phone *thunk* to one of the tables. Midge didn't join him. He guessed she was taking a moment to calm down. But when the minutes ticked by and she still hadn't come into the kitchen, he decided to go to her. He found her sitting on the foot of his bed, head buried in her hands.

Kurt leaned against the doorjamb. He wanted to say he'd never been this unsure of himself but that would have been a lie. He'd been off-kilter since the day he'd met Midge, more so when she'd rejected his sorry attempts at getting her attention. Now he'd laid his heart bare. Reminding himself that she was only three days into their relationship while he was two months involved didn't help, nor did his pathetic excuse that he'd been worried sick about this plan and the words had spilled out before he could stop them. Kurt refused to take them back. He'd meant every word. But he also didn't think it was wise to bring further attention to them.

"Family dynamics," he offered in sympathy.

"I've been the prize in an emotional tug-of-the-war since I was three. I wish to hell my dad had gotten physical custody of me from the beginning. He was trying to keep peace between them." She raked her fingers through her hair as she raised her head. "I can't even call his wife 'Mom'. If my mother caught wind of it, Armageddon would pale in comparison. I call her Dee to avoid slip-ups. I love her and my half brother and sister."

"I know she's your mother, but sometimes you have to save yourself and cut negative people from your life for your own peace of mind."

"She'd only take it out on Dad and Dee, like she did tonight. I can't put them through that."

"Then it's time to lay down the law with her and stand by your convictions." Kurt pushed away from the door and squatted down before her. "If it helps, think about your future children." *Our children.* "You're the one who needs to take a stand. Otherwise, she'll find someone else to attack like she has your father and Dee. Everyone else is at fault but her. That's her view of the world and I can't see her changing, not if she convinced Bernadette to spy on you. You have to change your interactions with her in a firm, noncombative manner."

"Wise *and* handsome. Do you know what that does to a woman's heart?"

She cupped his face and kissed him. If someone had told him a week ago that a simple brush of her lips would set his soul on fire, Kurt would have laughed them off. Now he lived for her touch, for that glimmer in her eyes when she looked at him, for the joy of being near her that an hour away from her felt like an eternity. He loved her, pure and simple, and he longed to tell her the right way this time.

"Midge, I—"

She pressed her index finger over his lips, silencing him. "I love you, too. It doesn't make sense that I'd feel this way so soon, but there it is."

Relief demolished his tense muscles.

She laughed. "In essence, I've been sleeping with you for two months."

"Man, the images you just put in my head."

More laughter. "I'm all yours."

She cupped his face and kissed him lightly. "Exhaustion is etched in your face. I'll get the lights, check on the cats and make sure the house is secure. Crawl into bed and let me be the hero right now."

He wouldn't argue. "Thank you."

Kurt undressed and crawled under the covers as she walked off. Sleep slithered over him. He was conscious of only two things—the minute Midge spooned her naked body against him and the cats joining them seconds later.

Chapter Eleven

Midge put the finishing touch on her mascara, then double-checked her appearance, liking what she saw — the real her, the person her family and close friends knew. Her coworkers were in for a surprise. Gone was her mousy façade. There might be a few who would attribute the change to Kurt. She didn't give a damn what they thought or said behind her back. He loved her. She loved him. Her feelings were real and not the result of some killer sex and the rush of returning to the real world.

Kurt ducked his head into the bathroom. "How the hell can you make cammies look so fucking hot? First wearing the contacts and now this. I think I liked it better the other way. I don't want everyone to know how hot you really are."

Midge tried not to laugh and failed. "Don't worry, big guy. I'm all yours."

He grunted. "Could you at least lose the French braid and go back to the bun?"

She patted her hair. "After all your hard work putting it in?"

He rolled his eyes. "Why do I have the feeling that's going to come back to haunt me?"

Her cell phone vibrated on the sink vanity, setting her heart racing. *It could be Susan finally returning the phone messages I left last night and again this morning.* They glanced at the caller ID—her mother.

"Can I answer it?" He pleaded like a kid wanting a new toy.

"Knock yourself out. Put it on speaker."

He tapped the button. "Midge's phone. Kurt speaking."

"Who the hell are you?" Her mother's haughty tone demanded answers.

"As I just said... I'm Kurt. Who the hell are you?"

Midge smothered laughter under her hand.

"I'm Michelle's mother. Don't get smart with me, young man. I've heard about the shenanigans going on with my daughter. Bernadette McFee was very informative."

"I bet the thieving old biddy was. Did she also tell you she violated several California State laws regarding her tenant?"

"Let me speak to Michelle right now."

Midge shook her head. His smile broadened.

"She can't come to the phone right now. It's not *convenient*...for either of us."

Her mother sucked in an outraged gasp. "How dare you engage in intercourse while you speak to me!"

"Intercourse?" His light-blue eyes sparkled with mischief. "Oh...you mean sex. No, we're done with that for now. You just missed it, though. Made us run a little late. But I could go for a nooner. Why don't you call back at lunch?"

That left her mother sputtering. Before she could recover, Kurt jumped in again.

"Is there a message I can give to Midge when she gets done washing sweat and other various bodily fluids from her body?"

Midge bit back a shriek of laughter.

"Tell her to call me." Then she was gone.

Midge released her pent-up laughter. "Well, what do you know, Kurt Orin Davidson? You *do* have your uses."

He winked. "And I kill spiders, too."

"What more could a woman ask for?" She batted her eyes.

"Whatever it is, I'd find a way to deliver." He kissed her quick. "Come on. Breakfast is ready, as per your specifications."

Peanut butter on toast—something they had in common for workdays. "Be right there."

He kissed her again then left. Midge stuffed her makeup into its little bag and followed. When she walked into the kitchen, he picked up a piece of toast and handed it to her. His expression turned solemn as he poured coffee into travel mugs for them. He handed Midge one, then reached up and wiped his index finger over the corner of her mouth.

"Peanut butter." He licked it off.

Midge's heart tumbled. How could such an innocent gesture feel so intimate?

She stretched on tiptoe, he bent closer and their lips met somewhere in-between. He tasted of peanut butter and coffee. Or was that her? It didn't matter. They were one.

"We need to get going or we'll both be late for work," he said.

"I didn't realize there were could be so many pluses to cohabitation. You braided my hair, made breakfast and now you're chauffeuring me. It's a rare treat to actually be able to eat and enjoy my coffee rather than gulp it down or do without. Tell me, hot stuff, what do I have to do to get you to iron my cammies?"

"Don't push it, baby." He squeezed her ass as he walked by. "Come on. We have to be in the SJA's office by seven-thirty."

"You know Jess called him last night." She snagged her duffel bag of workout gear and followed.

"I know." Hand on the doorknob, he shrugged. "That ought to save some time this morning. He would have made up his mind, but he's still going to make us work for it."

That much was true. Colonel Scott would want to hear all arguments pro and con, despite his decision. He'd weigh all sides carefully before rendering a verdict. He'd make a hell of a judge one day.

They gave the cats goodbye ear rubs before heading to Kurt's car parked in the garage. Midge would have felt better if she had her vehicle, but local law enforcement had yet to release the scene, though they'd promised to do so sometime today. Jess had snagged the wig from the day before and secreted it out of her house. The plan was to drive her as far as the strip mall outside the base where an NCIS vehicle — another white sedan — awaited her use. On the off-chance Susan was at Midge's office, Midge would tell her it was a rental. She would also explain the meeting with SJA and NCIS personnel was to lodge a formal complaint against Kurt.

They ran a small risk that Susan might see them driving toward base. The only other choice would have been for her to call a cab. But it would have been out of character for Susan to be here since she was mad and not returning her calls. Plus, if she suspected a net was closing around her, Susan would be cautious. She might even have the license plate numbers from the vehicles Kurt had driven—his own and the agency's vehicle he'd used their first night together. The white sedan might be camouflaged in a sea of other white cars, but the license plates would give them away every time. Whoever they were after wasn't stupid or they would have been caught long before now.

"You were researching Stanford?" she asked as Kurt backed into the street.

"Damn straight I was. The level of destruction in your place was off the charts. It was either personal or someone so desperate and stupid they weren't thinking straight. I can't connect the latter to a criminal who's evaded authorities this long. And since the only other stupid person I would suspect is dead..." He flipped up his palms in a semblance of a shrug.

She clutched the travel mug between her hands and stared ahead. She'd despised Bernadette but hated that this had happened to her.

Kurt rubbed her thigh. "Try not to be scared, honey."

She glanced at him. "Because you're scared enough for both of us?"

"Nailed it. I don't fuck around with anyone's life, and when it's someone I—"

He clamped his mouth shut on the rest of the sentence. Midge scuffed her hand over his thigh. All too soon they were pulling into the strip mall. Her assigned vehicle waited. The key was in a magnetic box in the wheel well.

She opened the door when he came to a stop. "I'm kissing you goodbye in my head."

"And I'm kissing you back. See you in a few."

To the outside world and whoever might be watching, they were nothing more than friends. Fifteen minutes later, Midge was seated in Colonel Scott's office on the rose-colored love seat with Kurt by her side and Jess and Vic occupying matching chairs across from them. Everest wasn't present, since her working with NCIS wasn't his business, and that was fine with her. It was going to take her a long time to forgive DEA for stepping all over NCIS.

She didn't have too much interaction with the Staff Judge Advocate, but she sure did like him. He had a compassion for his people, combined with a toughness no one could doubt. He laced his fingers before him while Jess and Vic laid out the plan to which Kurt still vehemently objected. Midge remained silent. When the last word died, Colonel Scott pursed his lips and nodded.

"Agent Davidson, I understand that a relationship has developed between you and Staff Sergeant Ellis?"

"It has, sir." Kurt's tone defied him to say something against it. "But that doesn't change the fact that we're sending in an untrained—"

Colonel Scott raised his palm. "I get it. You've made your feelings very clear." He focused on Midge. "You know the risks. I'm sure NCIS briefed you thoroughly. Is there anything I can say to make you change your mind?"

She kept her chin level. "Sir, my home was violated and my household goods destroyed. I feel strongly that someone is trying to frame me. It surely can't be a coincidence that I've been made the center of all this. Only a direct order from you would stop me from going under."

He leaned back in his big chair and drummed his fingers on the armrests. "All this planning and you've yet to make contact with your target. Aren't you concerned about playing your hand too early?"

"I've left messages for her, sir." Midge folded her hands in her lap. "It's unlike her to leave them unanswered. She and I had a bit of a falling out recently and she might still be mad about that. I've apologized and told her she was right. She might not be answering, but she wouldn't miss the chance to rub this in my face."

"In this falling out, was she right?" he asked.

"No, sir. She was dead wrong."

"Did you try her at work?"

"Not yet," she replied. "She would have arrived at the same time we were due in your office."

"Call her."

Midge looked to Jess for confirmation and received a slight nod. She pulled her flip phone from her trouser pocket and dialed Susan's office. Someone else picked up.

"I was trying to reach Petty Officer Bolotnik," she said.

"Called in sick this morning," the woman replied. "Sounded bad. I hope it's not that damn flu. People are toppling right and left. I sure don't want—"

"Thank you. I'll try her at home." A glance at Jess gave her the okay, so she tried Susan's cell for the third time. "Me again. Heard you were sick. Call me if you need anything. I'm still going out tonight. I hope you don't mind that I'm using the wig. As you'd probably say, 'time to get back on the horse.' There are certainly a lot of stallions to choose from."

"Really?" Kurt said once she'd put the phone away.

Midge shrugged. "Just trying to play the game the way she would."

"I'm sure you're the only stud in Staff Sergeant Ellis's corral right now, Agent Davidson," Colonel Scott said.

She tried not to giggle but the red flush crawling over Kurt's face was too much. They all had a light laugh at his expense.

"Glad I could break the tension for all of you," he muttered.

Colonel Scott rested his forearms on his desk, looking resigned. "Why should I be one to stand in the way of justice and a strong-willed woman? Just try to keep her safe and in one piece, gentlemen. I don't want anything to happen to one of my best Marines."

Dismissed, Midge filed out with the men and ran right into Zach. He clutched leave papers in one hand and a bag of Godiva dark chocolate in the other. His smile faded to a frown.

"What's going on?" he asked.

Telling him would involve him. Midge refused to let that happen. She pointed to the chocolates.

"Are you going to pass those out or hoard them for yourself?"

Zach grinned and opened the bag. "For the newly designated Aunt Midge? You may have two."

"Good. I'm taking three." She shoved her hand in the bag and took four.

"Major Taylor, come in and tell me all." Colonel Scott waved him in.

"On my way, sir," he called out. "I'm going with full disclosure, Midge."

"Do it." She added a sharp nod.

"And I expect full disclosure from one of you at some point." He passed a slow gaze over each of them. "I suspect something's going on that I'm probably not going to like, and it's well beyond the fact that someone broke into her home."

She held her breath waiting for Kurt to spill everything. He was sure to have Zach on his side. United, they'd be a formidable force, especially when Zach tattled to Claudia and the extended friend-family.

Kurt clapped Zach's shoulder. "Go be a dad. It's just another day in the life here."

Zach's narrowed gaze called him a liar, but he walked away and stepped into Colonel Scott's office.

"Don't the rest of us get candy?" Vic asked.

"I'm pretty sure she took four. Share." Zach winked and closed the door.

Three palms shot out in front of her. Midge reluctantly put a chocolate in each hand.

"Go, Team NCIS," Vic said, and the men exchanged high-fives.

* * * *

Kurt stood in front of his bathroom mirror and made the final adjustments to his gray-streaked beard. A similarly colored shaggy wig and nondescript clothing completed the over-the-hill look. He'd fit in well with the stool-hugging old-timers who always lined the far side of most of the bars in the area—even ones with loud, obnoxious music. They'd watch young people from the shadows, perhaps a little envious of what they were missing, nursing their drinks in silence while they longed for days gone by. It would be the perfect vantage point to keep an eye on Midge.

His final appeal had failed, as Kurt had suspected it would. Kurt had no choice but to agree. Midge would do what she wanted to do. Nothing and no one would stand in her way. He'd learned that fast from working with Claudia.

If he and Midge were going to have a future together — and they damned sure were, as far as he was concerned — he had to accept that quality in her. He already respected it, even admired her for it. Now all they had to do was get her safely through this evening's sting.

They'd gone their separate ways once they'd left Colonel Scott's office to perpetuate the myth that they were combatants for anyone who might be watching. Kurt hated it, hated that Vic would be the one to tape the wire to her torso, hated that she had to go elsewhere to keep up the appearance that they were finished. In this case, elsewhere had meant Vic and Helen's place, since her home had yet to be cleared of the crime scene. With their help and that of Anders, they'd have her dressed for her role. Hearing that Anders had been drawn in pissed him off. Anders wasn't supposed to be involved in any way. Everest had made that very clear. And if having him help prep her meant that Anders was the one securing the wire to her and not Vic…

Kurt pulled in a deep breath. Getting angry would make him sloppy. He had to be at the top of his game tonight. Satisfied with his disguise, Kurt put the earbud in place. He'd be able to hear the men surveilling, but not Midge. His own wire under his shirt would allow him to communicate with them as well. Anyone looking at him would think it was a hearing aid.

Beeps from his phone announced it was time to go. His team would already be in place across the street from the bar in the shadow of a long-abandoned restaurant. Midge would be leaving Vic's place five minutes afterward. The gap would give him time to get into position.

He grabbed his keys, said goodbye to the cats and left. To the best of his knowledge, Midge had never heard from Susan. The whole charade could be for nothing. He didn't want to think about what they'd do then.

It didn't take him long to reach the bar. He parked three blocks down then assumed his role as an elderly man and shuffled the rest of the way, hunched forward. Dougie greeted him with a nod and a smile, then opened the door for him. Loud music hit him in the face. He made his way to the bar stools and found one facing the door. In less time than it took to think about it, he had a bottle of beer and a bowl of pretzels in front of him...and was counting the minutes.

Kurt's heartbeat triple-timed when Midge walked in. Skintight jeans and black stilettoes accentuated her shapely legs. The red wig clashed with her long-sleeved red top. Men turned to gape at her when she cleared the entrance. She paused there, scanning the room before she stepped into the sea of people and aimed for a vacant table. Kurt wondered if she was scared. He sure was.

Midge trembled inside. What had sounded great in planning now terrified her. She prayed she could play her part well and that her voice didn't quiver and give away her fear. Spotting Kurt at the bar in the disguise he'd mentioned helped quell her nerves. Her red top would make it easy for him to keep track of her.

She passed her gaze over the Marines at the bar. They laughed and made sport of the old men seated on the other side. So far, no Susan. It'd be like her to play coy and show up. That was fine. *Whatever it takes to get this done.*

The noise had slammed into her the second she'd walked in. She couldn't understand how someone could put up with coming here night after night. Warmth had curled around her next—a welcome comfort from the cold outside. For the sake of her get-up, she'd forgone a jacket. She was racking up stupid points tonight.

"Okay, guys, here I go," she said softly, then stepped into the fray of men and women, weaving through the crowd until she reached a table near the bar. A waitress zoomed up before Midge's bottom could touch the seat.

"What'll you have?"

"Diet cola. I'm driving."

"At least that's the plan, huh? Who knows? Maybe you'll get lucky, especially dressed like that."

The woman flashed a smile and was back in seconds with a tall glass. Two cherries were plopped on top. Midge picked up one by the stem and yanked it off with her teeth. The other soon followed. Still no Susan, nor had she shown by the time Midge finished her second drink. She wished Jess would pull the plug on all this so she could go home.

She sighed and motioned the waitress over. "Another, please, and could you save my table while I run to the ladies' room?" To ensure her assistance, Midge slipped the woman a five and walked away when she nodded.

Signs pointed the way to the restroom and an exit she'd been advised was one-way — people could leave but couldn't come in. A rock wedging the door open took care of that issue. She'd tell the waitress once she was done.

As she wrapped her hand around the handle for the ladies' room, Midge heard footsteps behind her. She glanced over her shoulder in time to see someone duck into the men's room, then she stepped into the ladies' to take care of her needs. A quick peek under the stalls revealed she was alone. She hated the thought that the team would hear her pee but was sure they'd heard much worse. Still, she gave herself the illusion of privacy, hoping one of them would be waiting outside the door to tell her this was a wash.

Maybe even Kurt.

Tamping down her smile, Midge finished her business, cleaned up then slung her purse over her shoulder and walked out. The men's bathroom door swung open, blocking her way.

"Going somewhere, girlie?"

She stared at the big Marine blocking her. He was solid, built like a boxer, with overly muscled arms that strained the seams of his shirt. His hands were huge, his shoulders doubly so. His flat dark eyes were fixed on her face with unnerving intensity. Fear twisted her gut.

"Let me pass or I'll scream."

He shook his head slowly. "You expect to be heard over this noise?" He gestured toward the din that pounded down the hallway from the dance floor. He smiled, revealing a row of white, even teeth. "You and I have some unfinished business, baby."

Fuck, he thinks I'm Susan.

"I'm not who you think I am." God, the man was huge. All the self-defense training in the world wouldn't help her bring him down. The best she could hope for was to stall him until her backup realized she was in trouble. "You're making a mistake. This is going to land you in very serious trouble." She tried to dive back into the women's restroom, praying he wouldn't follow.

He snagged her biceps in a grip of steel. "You're coming with me."

Midge smacked the small purse against his head.

He laughed, an oddly high-pitched sound for a man of his size. "Yeah, I know how you like it rough, Red. I'm more than ready to play."

He backhanded her with the speed of a viper. Midge's head snapped back from the force of the blow. Her cheek burned. Shock stole her breath. Tears blinded her. Her head swam. She pulled in a gasp, praying someone in the club would hear her scream. He merely laughed again, stuffed a gag between her lips and yanked her arms behind her back. He put his face close to hers, breath hot upon her cheek.

"Now we'll see who's in serious trouble, Red."

* * * *

Kurt nursed his bottle of beer. Every so often he'd bring the opening to his lips and feign a drink. The liquid hadn't dropped below the top of the label. That was the good thing about a dark bottle—unless someone looked carefully, they'd never notice if it was full or empty. So far, no one had paid him much mind. Even the bartender ignored him, probably not expecting a scruffy old guy to spend much money on beer, much less tips.

He glanced toward the restrooms, wondering how much longer Midge was going to be. Not that it mattered since their prey had failed to show. He was ready to call it quits.

"We've got a problem." Vic's voice crackled into Kurt's earpiece. "She's shouting at a man. He called her Red. We think he's got her. Go!"

Kurt jumped from the stool and shoved through the crush of bodies. It might as well have been an impenetrable wall of thorns. He saw a flash of red in the restroom hallway and watched in horror as Parsons ducked out of the exit with Midge tossed over his shoulder. A zip tie bound her wrists.

Kurt broke into a cold sweat as he shouldered the packed crowd aside in a wild attempt to reach her. He shouted into his own transmitter. "Parsons is taking her out the back. I can't get through. I can't get to her."

He thought he heard Vic scrambling. It was hard to tell with all the noise.

The music changed. The tide of people shifted. Kurt shoved through a gap and sprinted for the back exit, snatching her purse from the floor in the process. He burst into the cold, dark night, chest heaving, and spun around.

Parsons' dark sedan careened across the dirt parking lot toward freedom. Kurt raced after it. He caught movement from the corner of his eye as Vic approached from the van. Weapon drawn, his friend took a stance in front of the onrushing vehicle.

"NCIS! Stop! Now!" Vic shouted.

Dirt and gravel spat from behind the car. Kurt watched, horror-stricken, as Parsons plowed headlong into Vic. His friend bounced off the hood like a crash-test dummy, landing in a crumpled heap ten feet away.

"Man down! Nine-one-one!" Kurt prayed Jess or Everest were aware and moving. As he raced to his friend, he saw Parsons' red taillights disappear into the night. There was no way he'd be able to run to his car three blocks away and give chase.

Everest skidded to a stop beside him. Kurt jerked his head around, pointing in the direction of the departing vehicle.

"That way. Now. He's got Midge. Dark sedan."

Everest ran off. Kurt prayed he had a vehicle close by. In his heart he knew Everest would never pick up their trail in time. Despair and fear twisted his gut at the thought of Midge in Parsons' demented clutches.

Jess dashed across the street from the surveillance van. "Police and paramedics are on the way."

When Vic groaned, Kurt grasped his hand. "Hang on, buddy. It's going to be okay."

"Helen…" Vic muttered.

"We'll call her," Jess reassured him.

Vic's eyes flickered to Kurt. "Her wire's still running. You might get some clues."

"They're out of range by now. My guess is that she's knocked out cold. Everest followed. They went east. If I leave now, I might be able to catch up. We could have the police run the plates under Parsons' name. Put out an all-points bulletin for his car." Kurt realized then that he was rambling aloud and wasting precious time.

Jess stared up at him across Vic's body. Worry deepened the lines in his face, but he was also clear-headed about the reality of the situation, something Kurt couldn't be right now. This was *his* woman. Hard as it was, Kurt forced himself to take a giant emotional step back and evaluate things objectively with more common sense.

Someone needed to call Helen and tell her about Vic before she found out from the local radio news. Someone needed to monitor the van's equipment in case they were closer than Kurt suspected. If there was a chance Midge could give them a clue as to her whereabouts, they needed to take it.

He swallowed hard. "I'll be in the van."

"Good. I'll meet you there as soon as the paramedics get Vic on his way to the hospital. I need you to call Helen. Have her meet them at the emergency room."

"Will do." Kurt ran across the street. Flashing red-and-blue lights signaled the arrival of the deputy sheriffs. Paramedics closed the gap behind them. He slipped his cell phone from the deep front pocket of his baggy jeans.

Helen took the news without hysterics, but her voice was strained and high. It had to be a nightmare for her, considering she'd lost a dear friend in a similar accident the year before. Kurt prayed Vic would be all right. After repeating Jess' instructions to Helen, he disconnected.

He stopped two feet from the van's back door. The pointlessness of his actions overwhelmed him. He should be following, giving chase, trying to find Midge, not sitting in this damned van feeling as if his hands were tied behind his back. The thought resurrected the image of Midge being hauled from the bar. Her hands *were* tied behind her back. He didn't want to think about what Parsons had planned for her. The man was obviously insane. Anything could happen.

To hell with it. Kurt did a one-eighty and ran down the street. He couldn't sit still and wait. It might be like searching for the proverbial needle in the haystack, but he had to do something to find her. He tore off the disguise piece by piece as he ran the three blocks to his car. By the time he reached it, only the baggy jeans remained. He tossed everything else to the back seat and started up the engine.

As he combed the streets looking for any sign of Parsons' vehicle, Kurt tried to think like a madman. If he were Parsons, where would he take Midge? Parsons wanted the blackmailer to leave him alone. He would want all the blackmail pictures and videos Susan had taken, and Kurt didn't doubt he'd use force to get them. This was a man who acted on impulse, not on common sense. Kurt was counting on that fact to help find them.

"Hang on, honey. Just hang on."

* * * *

By slow degrees, Midge pulled away from unconsciousness. The taste of blood in her mouth turned her stomach. The gag didn't help. She was in a car. Judging from that crisp, one-of-a-kind smell, it was new. The man had tossed her in the back seat like a bag of dirty laundry and she lay crumpled, facedown on the floor. At least she could be thankful it was a new car. She didn't have to deal with the filth from an old one.

Still, being on the floor, stuck in this discarded rag-doll position, was no treat. With her hands tied behind her back, moving was impossible. The carpet scuffed her burning cheek. It was hard to breathe and her head throbbed from the blow he'd delivered a second time when she'd spat his gag back at him. It probably hadn't been one of her smarter moves, but did he actually expect she would allow him to kidnap her without a fight?

She opened her eyes, blinking several times to settle her contacts in place. How long had she been out? Were they still in Twentynine Palms or one of the other nearby towns? Surely she hadn't been unconscious long. She wiped her face against the carpet and got the gag free. That helped her nausea. The car was riding smoothly, so she knew they were on a hard-surface road. She lifted her head and was able to see out of the window. Street signs passed at regular intervals — *still in town somewhere*. Few vehicles passed them — *not on the main thoroughfare*.

Who was this man? One of Susan's victims out for revenge, one of Jeremy's associates wanting the ketamine or some a crazed fool? It didn't look good for her, no matter who she was. If she could talk to him, reason with him... Midge didn't want to think beyond that and refused to speculate on what he had planned for her.

She maneuvered to her knees. The pull of the wire taped to her torso reminded Midge that she wasn't alone. The range on the device wasn't far, but if NCIS was monitoring her, she might be able to give them a clue as to her location.

Midge dismissed the idea. Talk might antagonize him. The man had knocked her out once. He obviously meant her harm. The longer she played dead, the better her chance for survival. She had to survive, had to give Kurt a way to find her, somehow, some w

Her determination was nearly squelched when her captor hit a deep pothole. She fell face-first and another jolt bounced her hard against the floor. Midge gritted her teeth to keep from crying out. He swerved around a corner, knocking her head into the door. Another sharp turn and he jerked the vehicle to a stop.

He cut the engine and opened his door on silent hinges. Then the rear door swung open. Icy air swirled about her. Midge prayed she could suppress a shiver. He grabbed her shoulders. She had to stay limp, keep her eyes closed, make him work to get her out of the car, delay whatever fate he had in store for her.

When he couldn't lift her shoulders up and through the door, he grabbed her bound wrists and pulled. A hot spear of pain stabbed Midge between her shoulder blades. She prayed he couldn't see her grimace. He yanked again. Sheer will kept her silent, but she wasn't sure how much more she could take.

Muttering a curse, he wrapped his hand in the wig and pulled, cursing when he realized the futility of that action. He yanked the wig cap off her head, fisted Midge's hair and tugged. Strands ripped from her scalp. Tears slipped from beneath her lids. She sent up another prayer of thanks when he finally gave up. Next, he grabbed a handful of her shirt. Seams ripped as he hoisted her higher and higher then dropped her onto the seat facedown.

The car sagged as he crawled in beside her. Cold metal touched her hands. There was a tug and she was free. He'd cut the plastic from her wrists, probably in an attempt to better carry her.

Now what? Did she try to make a run for it? *Not yet.* She'd wait until he actually got her out of the car.

He yanked her arms forward and wrapped his thick hands around her wrists. With one long pull, he heaved her out onto the driveway. Concrete ripped a hole in her jeans and scraped her knees.

The man squatted down beside her, rolled her to her back, straddled her and grabbed her wrists once more.

Now!

Midge head-butted him and plowed her knee into his balls. His howl of pain ripped the night and he toppled to his side on the concrete. She was free. Midge kicked off her high heels and sprinted down the street. A few darkened, fenced houses surrounded them, but she had no idea whether or not the gates were unlocked or if anyone was home. She decided she couldn't risk being trapped inside a fenced yard, so kept running and began shouting.

"Help! Somebody help me!"

Nothing. Not so much as one light clicked on.

Aim for the cross street. Aim for where the lights are.

Midge knew the futility of such a goal. The desert played tricks with distance. The safety she thought she could see could be miles away, not blocks. Asphalt cut into her bare feet. Still she beat a path toward what she hoped was help.

Run. Run.

Her steps echoed off silent houses. Fear struck when she realized it was no echo. The man was coming up fast behind her. She tried one last, desperate attempt.

"Help! Fire!"

A flying tackle smashed her to the ground. Air whooshed from her lungs. He yanked her head up by the hair, weighed her body down with his groin indecently pressed to her backside. A porch light clicked on, glinting off the blade of a pocket knife in her captor's hand. He pressed the tip against the pulse at her throat.

"One word and I'll cut you here and leave you to die. It doesn't much matter to me how I get you out of my life. I just want those pictures and videos."

So, this *was* about Susan's blackmailing, not the ketamine. That gave her something to work with, but not much. She felt his erection growing against her and prayed it wouldn't come to that.

The porch light went out, and with it, Midge's last hope of quick rescue. As much as she longed to cry out, the knife against her throat was too great a risk.

He waited a few minutes longer. With a slash, he cut off one of her sleeves and bound her wrists together.

"Now we're going to play things my way." He hauled her to her feet.

"I'm telling you that you've got the wrong person."

"I saw that dude pick you up at the bar the other night. I followed. I've been following you ever since. I've got the right woman all right. Red hair... Brown hair... It doesn't matter. I know it's you. I'm sick and tired of them dragging their heels with you. This shit's gonna end tonight."

With the knife blade poking her ribs, he forced her back to the house. His grip on her elbow grew a little tighter, more intense with each step. She realized that as angry as he was now, it was a wonder she was still alive.

As they walked up the driveway, Midge saw yellow crime tape draped over the front door. She tried to take note of the house numbers, the yard, the house itself and those around it. Black film covered all the windows. No one could see in or out of the place.

"You didn't think I'd remember, did you, Red? But I did. I sat outside your little home last night and thought real hard about where you took me the night you fucked my brains out."

He shoved an evil leer in her face. "I was pretty drunk that night, but it finally came to me. It took a little street-by-street searching, I'll admit, but I'd be damned if I'd let someone like you get the better of me. And now, we're back. Aren't you glad to be back?"

He tore the tape away with a swipe of his knife then reached above the sill and pulled down a key. He unlocked the door and shoved her inside. Midge stumbled and fell onto the dusty carpet. A flick of his wrist flooded the room with dim light from a bare bulb hanging from the center of the ceiling. Other than a large couch and a beat-up dinette set in the kitchen, there was no furniture.

"On your feet." He grabbed her arm and yanked her up. "Into the bedroom with you."

"No...please... You have the wrong person."

He grabbed her by the hair and pulled her in that direction, flipping switches as he went. "Where are they, bitch?"

Midge struggled to keep her wits about her, to not show fear. It was impossible. Her abductor wouldn't listen to reason.

He kicked open a door at the far end of the hall. Mirrors covered the walls and ceiling. A four-poster king-size bed with a black and gold velvet bedspread dominated the room. The whole thing looked like a cheap porn set gone bad. He shoved her against the mattress.

She stumbled. He didn't give her time to recover. Smashing her down, he cut off the other sleeve, tore it in two, bound one leg, flipped her to her back and bound the other.

Midge stared at the huge mirror hovering over her. Her own reflection stared back, cheeks bruised and red, eyes huge dark smudges. She'd give anything to not be able to see what he was about to do to her. She'd recorded testimony of such events too many times. She knew what was coming. Tears threatened. Closing her eyes, she gathered her courage and thought of Kurt.

There was a violent tug against her shirt followed by the sound of ripping material. Cool air brushed her exposed skin.

"What the hell is this!" He grabbed the edge of the tape holding the wire in place. "Trying to get more ammo against me?" With one yank, he tore the wire away and her skin with it.

Midge cried out.

"Shut up. That's the least you'll get if you don't give me what I want." He nestled the blade between her breasts, slicing her bra in two. And, finally, he cut away her jeans.

"There. Now you're gonna give me what I want."

Can't the monster see I'm not the same woman? We're nothing alike. Why doesn't he see?

He covered her body with his. Midge bit back bile and squeezed her eyes tighter.

"Scared?" He laughed. "Good." His hot breath grazed her neck. His teeth were next. "Where are the pictures, the videos?"

"I don't know." She sobbed.

He shifted to her right breast. "Where?"

"I swear I—"

He bit hard. Midge screamed. He bit the other breast harder. Her stomach. Each mouthful mocked her lack of power, her inability to escape.

"Please, don't. I don't know. Please."

Lower he slipped, viciously biting her thighs, her calves, then he settled between her legs. His breath curled against her pussy.

"Tell me or I swear I'll bite it off. Then I'll start cutting that pretty little face of yours."

"No, I'll take you to where they are," she cried.

Damn Susan. Damn her to hell.

* * * *

Kurt had driven down this same street half a dozen times. No sign of the vehicle, Midge or Parsons. He'd passed Everest earlier and they'd split the town. Jess' appearance soon after divided the area in smaller chunks. Every so often, they'd crossed paths to exchange information. Nothing.

He spied the surveillance van approaching ahead. Jess flashed his lights, telling Kurt to stop. He obliged, pulled up alongside and buzzed his window down.

"Anything?"

"Possibly," Jess replied. "Everest called. He went by that house Forton rented and found Midge's heels in the driveway. Told us to meet him there. He's already searched the house. There was no sign of her, just her clothes."

Kurt did a fast three-point turn and sped in the direction Jess gave him. What the hell reason would Parsons have to take her to Forton's? Was he involved in the ketamine, too? His head spun.

Within minutes, he braked to a stop in front of Forton's rental. Jess was close behind. Local law enforcement had beaten them to the scene. One barred their march to the house. A flash of a badge and a wave from Everest gained them entry.

"What did you find?" he demanded to know. "Is there any sign of her?"

Everest motioned him passed the crime scene tape into the barren kitchen, then waited for Jess to catch up.

"I found her high heels discarded in the driveway. The tape on the door was ripped away. After calling it in to the locals, I went in. They were already gone. I found drops of blood leading from the bedroom to the living room door."

His locked his gaze on Kurt. "Her clothes were torn off her and left behind. The bedspread is gone. He might have wrapped her in it."

Kurt grabbed Everest by the front of the shirt. "Are you saying she's dead? Is that what you're saying?"

Jess peeled his hands away. "Calm down, son. If she were dead, there'd be a whole lot more blood than a few drops."

Kurt shrugged away Jess' hand. "Not if he strangled her or cracked her skull with his sledge-hammer sized fists." He took a deep breath. "All right. What made you decide to come here?"

Everest smoothed his shirt. "Forton rented this house at Bolotnik's request. Since he felt she was a possible link to the ketamine, coming here was a logical conclusion."

"This isn't about the ketamine." Kurt clenched his jaw.

Everest lifted an eyebrow. "Isn't it?"

"Fuck, I don't know anymore." He raked his fingers through his hair.

"All right, let's dissect this logically," Everest said. "What does Parsons want?"

Kurt released a frustrated sigh. "The video and pictures Bolotnik's been using to blackmail him."

"He's obviously not the brightest star in the sky. Patience isn't one of his virtues, if he has any. So, he jumps to conclusions and take matters into his own hands." Everest stared into space and rubbed the dark stubble on his jaw. "Does Midge know where Susan lives, and would she give her up to Parsons?"

"Yes." Kurt ran for the door. Midge wasn't stupid. She was a survivor. Now all they had to do was get to her in time.

* * * *

Wrapped in the bedspread, Midge drove the man's car to Susan's house. Her captor never once took the knife from her throat. An unfilled pothole, a hard turn and she'd be dead. His huge hand jolted when Midge drove over a dip in the road and a hot line of blood trickled down her neck and over her breast. The nightmare drive seemed to stretch out forever, but she saw her turnoff and pulled to a stop in front of Susan's darkened house.

He shoved her against the car door and ordered her to do as she was told—as if she had a choice. Shaking, she crawled from the vehicle, clutching the heavy bedspread around her. When she lifted her hand to the doorbell, he smacked it down.

"I'll take care of this." He smashed his booted foot against the wood. It splintered beneath the force.

"In."

Grabbing her once more in that paralyzing grip, he yanked her across the threshold. Light poured from the bedroom down the hall. He hustled her in that direction. They met Susan halfway, fumbling to tie the belt on her pink robe. She gasped and tried to run to her room. The man grabbed a fistful of her hair and hauled her back, stripping her of the robe. Susan was naked beneath it, a fact she didn't bother to hide. Surely now he would notice Susan was the woman he'd sought.

"What the hell is this about?" Her voice was arrogant, rude, queen-like.

"I want those pictures and videos."

A sneer curled her lip. "I don't know what you're talking about. Midge, what have you dragged me into? You two had better get the hell out of my house or I'm calling the cops."

A growl exploded from him. He smashed his fist across Susan's face once, twice. Her head snapped with each blow. Blood spurted from her nose. The confident look from a moment before was replaced by pure fear. Midge shook off her shock and dashed for the door. The man grabbed her hair before she could get two feet.

"In the bedroom…both of you. I'm going to get what I want, one way or the other."

They had to do something. They were two against one. They could surprise him, outwit him. But Midge couldn't pull free of his inhumanly strong grip, and Susan was too dazed to understand the severity of their situation.

He bound them to Susan's bed, tying Midge's leg to Susan's, spread-eagle. He paced at the end of the bed, staring, laughing, aroused and rubbing his cock through his jeans.

"Working together, I'll bet. Taking turns with the troops. Eeny, meenie, minie, moe." He pointed to each one, settling on Susan. Crawling between her legs, he unzipped his jeans. "This is how you like it, isn't it, pumpkin? I could do this all night…to both of you."

The bed bounced for what seemed an eternity. Midge squeezed her eyes shut against the horror and wished she could do the same to her ears.

Susan cried out for help, for mercy. It only made him wilder.

His grunts, his laughter, his cry of victory when he finished… It was a nightmare forever etched in her memory. And her turn was coming.

She dared a peek at Susan after he was done. She stared into space, wide-eyed, vacant, a zombie. If not for her shallow breathing and trickling tears, Midge would swear she was dead.

Cigarette smoke drifted her way. Midge focused her gaze to its source, to *him*. That evil leer split his features. He strolled toward her, cigarette poised, a thin silver stream drifting up from its burning end.

"Now…where shall I start? I know…on that pretty little face of yours." He took a deep drag of the cigarette and leaned over her with its red glow trapped between his fingers.

Midge stared in horror as the ember grew closer and closer. She could feel the heat.

"Get the hell away from her!" Kurt hurled himself across the room and smashed full-force into the man.

Midge saw another flash of movement, more men. Jess…Everest. Why the hell didn't one of them untie her? Instead, they swarmed around her captor, taking him down and cuffing him. It was Everest who started to cut them loose. He helped Susan up first. All she did was crumple to the floor. Then he reached for Midge.

Kurt shoved him back. "Don't touch her. She's mine."

His expression was painful to see as he loosened the cut ropes then reached for the edges of the bedspread. His gaze passed over her, pausing at the bloody bites that marked her body. He paled then flushed crimson. His eyes blazed like blue diamonds.

"Son of a bitch. Fucking son of a bitch!"

Kurt whirled around on the man, pounding blow after blow into him, chest, face, gut. Midge clutched the cover around her and scrambled to the far side of the room. Jess and Everest shouted at him to stop. Nothing pierced Kurt's rage.

He hauled the big man up by the shirt, lifting him off his feet. Midge had never seen such strength. He hurled the man against the bed then continued his assault, kneeling on the man's chest, pounding him with blow after blow. The force of the struggle, their combined weight, broke the bed. With a groan and a shriek of tortured wood, the entire thing collapsed.

Jess and Everest grabbed Kurt from either side, trying to haul him off the man.

"Stop it! You're killing him!" Jess roared.

Midge sobbed. Kurt loved her. Nothing would make him stop until she was avenged. Nothing except…

"Kurt, please," she somehow managed to say. "Please. I need you."

He froze, dropped his bloodied fists and staggered from the bed. Two strides brought him to her side. He wrapped shaking arms around her.

"I love you, Midge. God knows, I love you." He cradled her to him, rocking her gently while brushing kisses over her cheeks.

"I love you, too," she whispered.

A low whistle of surprise pulled their heads around.

"Look what we found," Jess said.

DVDs spilled from the broken box springs. Susan, now wrapped in her robe, stood with a deputy sheriff, staring into space.

Jess cupped Kurt's shoulder. "You all right?"

Kurt nodded.

"Why don't you take her to the hospital? You know what has to be done. We'll finish up here. Paramedics can take care of Bolotnik."

Kurt scooped Midge into his arms. When she tucked her head against his shoulder, he carried her out to his car.

"What has to be done, Kurt?" she asked.

He swallowed hard. "They have to photograph you. Take evidence. Do a rape kit."

She shook her head. "He didn't rape me. Only Susan." She let out a small sob and clutched him tighter.

"The rest has to be done, sweetheart. Evidence."

"You, Kurt. Only you. No one else. *Please*."

"Only me, Midge. No one else. I swear it."

Chapter Twelve

"Are you ready, honey?"

Kurt didn't know if *he* was ready. How could he ask Midge that? They'd been given one of the two private rooms in the ER to photograph her injuries. The bedspread was evidence. He'd had no choice but to call Zach and ask him to bring her some clothes. Kurt was told he'd arrived and was wearing a groove in the floor of the waiting room.

"I'm ready."

Her voice was just above a whisper. Despite her consent, it still took her a while to open her hospital gown. When she did, a new wave of rage washed over Kurt. He did his best to put a lid on it, for her sake. She didn't need anger right now. She needed understanding and support. He steadied his shaking hands as best he could, then lifted the NCIS camera Jess had shoved into his hands before they'd left the scene.

"We'll start from the top." He gave her what he thought was a reassuring smile.

She nodded and tilted her head to one side. "He held a knife to my throat. I hit a bump in the road and it cut me." She shifted slightly on the paper-covered examining table to give him a better view.

Kurt saw a trickle of dried blood and zoomed in on the area.

Press the button. Done.

Take pictures of the finger bruises around her upper arm. Press the button. Done.

That was the easy part. The livid bite marks covering her breasts and stomach weren't.

"Can I at least hide my nipples before you take a picture?"

Her chin quivered and tears pooled in her wide eyes. Her pupils were dilated, the gray irises no more than a thin rim around them. Kurt longed to tell her she didn't have to be brave, that she could fall apart, but his Midge was a strong, proud woman. She wanted to maintain her dignity and he wouldn't take that from her.

"Of course, sweetheart."

Swallowing hard, she pressed her fingers over the peaks of her breasts. Kurt snapped the pictures as quickly as possible. Parsons had broken skin. She'd have to be on antibiotics. Human bites were the worst and the risk of infection great.

Kurt felt ill. Now *he* wanted to cry. Instead, he made a big show of concentrating on adjusting nonexistent camera settings so Midge wouldn't see his distress. When he was sure he was in control once more, he moved to the bites on her stomach, then to the various bruises and scrapes marring her torso, arms, legs and face.

"Anything else?"

Midge nodded, took a deep breath and slowly parted her legs. Kurt froze. He wanted to throw up. He tore his gaze from the bites dotting her inner thighs. A single tear rolled down her cheek. He caught it on the tip of his finger and held her in his arms.

"It's okay, honey. It's all over. I've got you. You're safe."

She nodded and gently pulled away. "Please finish so they can treat me and we can go home."

"And take a nice long soak in the tub?"

Midge forced a smile that didn't quite make her eyes. "Sounds heavenly." A leaden response.

She tucked the hospital gown over her intimate area and let him photograph. As he did so, one question kept nagging Kurt. He hated asking it but had no choice.

"I'll make sure the nurse does a rape kit."

"I told you he didn't rape me. Why would I lie about something like that when it would affect us? Kurt" — she wrapped her fingers over his arm — "I'd never lie to you about anything. I'd never withhold *anything* from you."

He brought her fingers to his lips and kissed them. "I'm sorry. I'm just—"

"My hero? My knight in shining armor? You *did* save the warrior queen, you know." Another tear spilled down her cheek.

He wiped it away with his thumb. "Always. Forever."

Midge gripped his wrist. "He raped Susan. I saw scratch marks down her neck, too. She seems to be in shock, not communicating. I thought someone should speak for her. She may have been blackmailing men, but she didn't deserve any of this."

Neither did you.

He kissed her forehead. "I'll let the doctor and nurse in now and get your stuff from Zach."

She touched his arm before he could leave. "I presume I'll also have to make a statement of some kind?"

Kurt lifted her fingers to his lips and kissed them. "Your statement can wait until tomorrow." He couldn't handle hearing a detailed account of what had happened tonight. Reliving Midge's horror and his own guilt at having let her put herself in danger was too much.

After giving her another gentle kiss on the cheek, Kurt slipped from the small room. Medical personnel swarmed the ER. Jess paced near the check-in counter. Military police hovered around the curtained examining areas, obviously guarding Parsons and Susan. Vic had been taken down to Desert Regional in Palm Springs.

Jess motioned him to the adjacent waiting area. Zach charged into their space. Jess ignored his presence and leveled a no-nonsense stare at Kurt.

"You realize you could be facing disciplinary action for what you did tonight. You could've killed him."

"I know," Kurt replied. "I got carried away. I don't care. Midge is *my* woman. No one lays a hand on my woman." A burst of adrenaline shot through his body. He'd attack Parsons all over again, given the chance.

Jess merely shook his head. "Is she all right?"

"Barely. And the others?"

"He's banged up pretty bad, but it doesn't look like you broke any bones. Your fists have got to be hurting after all that." Jess pointed to Kurt's hands.

Kurt stared at them. His knuckles were scuffed, turning a dark reddish-purple. They hurt. He hadn't noticed until now. His sole focus had been Midge.

"Susan?" he asked.

"Still in major shock. Hasn't said a word. Just stares ahead."

"Is it an act? She *is* in a lot of trouble right now."

"If it's an act, she can't hold it forever. Everest is at the crime scene helping us log in all the evidence. Now that these two are in the MPs' capable hands, we need to get back there ourselves. I'm going to have Anders question Parsons."

"I have to stay with Midge."

"You have to do your job, Kurt. If you two are going to be together, Midge must understand that sometimes — often — your job comes first. She needs to grasp the dangers involved. If she can't accept it, the relationship will never work."

How could Midge understand when he was having such a hard time of it?

Zach cupped Kurt's shoulder. "I don't know what the fuck's going on, but I've got her. I'll take her to our house. Claudia is beside herself with worry."

"The cats—"

"They're already at my place," he said. "I took them over when I picked up Midge's clothes. Go do your job."

It seemed he had little choice. Kurt knew they were right and hated it. "I need to tell Midge I'm leaving."

"Don't be long," Jess said and walked out.

Kurt returned to the examination room to give Midge the news. He felt like a hypocrite. He'd told her that she came before the job. Now he was deserting her for that job.

"Okay. I'll see you when you're done," she softly replied when he'd finished.

Her voice was calm. No tears. No hysterics. No pleading. No accusations of desertion. Kurt's heart swelled with love. He was almost through the door when she called him back.

He returned to her side and brushed one errant wave of hair away from her pale face, trying not to cringe at the bruises there. "Yes, honey?"

Midge curled her fingers in his shirt, pulled him to her and kissed him gently. "Be safe. And remember, I love you."

And I'm supposed to go back to work now? "I love you, too. I'll come over to Zach and Claudia's as soon as I'm done."

"That's the least of my concerns."

Kurt didn't ask what her biggest concern was. He knew it was getting this all behind them. She might not have been raped, but the physical assault would leave emotional scars for a long time to come—for both of them. After they exchanged another kiss, he left.

Zach gave him a bear hug before he got two steps into the waiting room. "Don't worry. We'll take good care of her."

Kurt managed a nod and left, dogged by his guilty conscience.

* * * *

Midge tugged her hospital gown closed once the nurse finished dabbing antiseptic on the last of her wounds. The bag with her clothing waited by her feet. Other than the tetanus shot and prescriptions, she could have tended her own injuries. But she was evidence and evidence had to be catalogued. Doing so made her feel like a piece of meat, no matter how gentle Kurt had tried to be. All things considered, she would hate to have endured what Susan had.

"How's Petty Officer Bolotnik?" she asked.

The nurse tossed the cotton swab into the trash. "Still in shock. She hasn't said a word, just stares into space. They're talking about transferring her down to Balboa to the psychiatric ward. We're keeping her overnight and making a decision in the morning."

That's one way to get out of being court-martialed.

Midge couldn't believe she'd thought that, but she wouldn't take it back. Susan *had* tried to frame her. She didn't trust her. They had her on the blackmailing, but what about the ketamine? Jeremy had clearly thought she was a connection. Why else continue the association?

"May I see her?"

For the first time since she'd started treating Midge, the nurse looked her in the eye. "I suppose it wouldn't hurt. We have her in a private room. You can get dressed. I'll have a corpsman bring your prescriptions then we'll send you home."

Midge waited to dress until the woman left. Leggings and a sweatshirt had never felt sweeter and she blessed Zach for his help, even while she dreaded that it was confession time with him and Claudia.

She'd struggled when Kurt had told her he had to go to work. One part of her wanted the opportunity to fall apart in privacy. The other part wanted to cling to him and never let him go. It was the torment in his eyes that let her release him without a murmur of dissent. He couldn't worry about her. He had to know it was all right. He wouldn't go unless he knew she truly didn't mind.

Who wouldn't love a guy like that?

After slipping her feet into socks and sneakers, Midge grabbed her bag and shuffled from the room. Her feet were cut from her mad race down the road. It hurt to walk. Hell, her whole body hurt. None of this would have happened if it hadn't been for Susan.

She made her way to where Susan was, ready to give her a piece of her mind. The sight of her sitting there, eyes wide and unblinking, hair tangled and stringy, changed her mind. Midge left the door open and walked to her side.

"Susan?" She flinched when Midge touched her shoulder. "It's okay. You're safe." She smoothed back a lock of Susan's hair. "Why would you do such a thing? Surely you knew you'd get caught someday. You had to know you'd run into a man who'd want to get even. Then, to try to frame me? Why?"

Any answer remained locked in Susan's presumably troubled mind. Midge didn't believe it for a second. Standing here wasn't going to get her anywhere either. She was hurting, exhausted and still had to face the Taylor inquisition.

Fighting tears, she left the room and signed for her prescriptions. Zach did a crisp about-face when she entered the ER lobby. He was next to her in two strides, slipping his arm around her shoulders.

"Ready to go?"

"More than ready."

She leaned into the kiss he pressed to her forehead, longing to wash the feel and scent of Parsons from her body. But the nurse had told her that the antiseptic needed to stay on for a good twelve hours or the risk of infection would be high. The thought of an infection from the germs in Parsons' mouth made her skin crawl. She'd follow orders.

* * * *

Everest spared them a glance when Kurt and Jess returned to Susan's house. He was surrounded by piles of DVDs and binders filled with documentation.

"Glad you two made it back. There must be at least a hundred tapes here. Look at all her notes and ledgers. It's going to take forever to sort them all out."

Kurt started his search from the opposite end of the box springs. Each DVD was dated with the Social Security number of what he presumed was her victim listed on it in neat black print.

Everest glanced up from a pile of papers. "I don't know how she managed to get this level of detail about her sexual partners." He gestured to the documents in his hand. Each one was a meticulous spreadsheet describing various men and included information from their private military files.

"Not hard," Kurt answered. "Susan worked at the Naval Hospital and had access to everyone's medical records."

Jess nodded and picked up the storyline. "Bolotnik would target servicemembers at the Lost Oasis, enticing them into having sex. Whether she used alcohol or drugs to cloud their good sense, we'll never know. She may have even used the ketamine in her schemes. Of course, horny too often trumps common sense." He shook her head. "She'd have sex with them, record the encounter then get detailed information on them through their military hospital records—

marriage status, command, whatever she needed to put the squeeze on them and their wallets. Have you found any tie to ketamine yet?"

Everest shook his head. "Not yet. I've searched the house and can't find anything." He looked up at Kurt. "How's Midge?"

"Badly shaken but holding up."

"She's a strong woman," Everest said. "Brave."

"Yeah. She is."

They settled down to work. The volume of evidence was staggering. There was no telling what they'd find when her computer was searched. Four hours later, back at NCIS with fast-food bags scattered over Kurt's desk, they were finally able to evaluate everything. There were hours upon hours of video to go through, yet none of them had the energy to get started. It sounded like a great job for Anders.

As if sensing Kurt's thoughts, Anders poked his head in the office. "I just finished interrogating Parsons. With a lawyer present, Parsons admitted to everything — the liaison with Susan Bolotnik, the break-in and killing Bernadette McFee. He'd followed Davidson and Ellis to her place that first night when they were both wearing those disguises. He believed she was his blackmailer and subsequently saw your true identities when peeping through the front window. He broke in when the two of you left that night, hoping to find the evidence against him. McFee caught him. He chased her down, killed her then got the hell out of there. She interrupted him before he could get to the second floor."

That meant someone else had been searching for something up there. Kurt bit into his breakfast sandwich to keep from voicing his opinion. As much as he disliked his coworker, Anders' perspective was objective, something Kurt had lost the second he and Midge hooked up.

"Evidence backs him up," Anders continued. "We got hits on the fingerprints. Parsons' were all over the first floor, as were others we expected. His were also a match to the bloody print at her landlady's, but his prints weren't upstairs. Those prints belong to those we expected — Ellis, Davidson, Forton, McFee and Bolotnik. However, Petty Officer Bolotnik's prints were also on the storage boxes outside."

Jess finished off the remains of a cup of hot coffee then leaned back and rubbed his reddened eyes. "The women were acquainted. Midge indicated they were on that floor a couple of nights before. We'll have to ask her about the storage box."

"Let's pretend Bolotnik didn't have access to the storage and broke into those," Kurt said around a mouthful of food. "Forton thought she was a tie to the drugs. What if Susan knew he'd hid the ketamine? She saw me and Midge at the hospital and would have easily learned we would be there a while. That would have given her ample time to search the house. This woman is methodical and an opportunist. She knew Forton had been taken down. She might have suspected he'd hidden the drugs — "

"Or been told by whomever beat the information out of him." Everest popped a hash brown nugget into his mouth.

Jess stood and stretched his back. "She was trying to blackmail Forton for something. It makes sense it would have been the ketamine. He had to be buying from someone, maybe even her. Now that he's dead, she's going to want the drugs to sell."

"Or to retrieve them for someone else. She's not the top dog or this case would have closed months ago." Kurt thought a moment. "Her prints are upstairs. It sounds like we have two people in Midge's house, searching for two different things. And we know why. What we don't know is the when."

Nods went around the room.

"I'm getting too old for these all-nighters." Jess stifled a yawn.

Kurt crumpled his empty Styrofoam cup in one hand and tossed it to the trash can. "Bolotnik could have easily searched Forton's BEQ room for the ketamine then moved on to Midge's house when she saw us at the hospital."

"Now we have to figure out a way to trip her up. If she's faking, that is." Jess clapped his hands on his thighs and stood. "Let's see what Parsons has to say for himself. Anders, you start going through those DVDs and see what you can find."

"Bolotnik doesn't know me," Everest said. "I can go in and question her."

Kurt snorted. "She's not going to talk to you."

"She doesn't have to talk. She only has to listen. I'm going to need your girlfriend's help, though."

Anger bubbled up inside Kurt. He wanted to smash his battered fist on the desk and tell Everest to go to hell. In the end, it was Midge's decision and he wouldn't take that choice from her.

"What do you need her to do?"

* * * *

Midge surfaced from a hard sleep. Every muscle in her body protested. Exhaustion coupled with the drugs had made her oblivious to the world. She occupied a twin bed in what would one day be Adam's room. At present, he slept in his parents' bedroom, so they could better care for the newborn. There was no telling how long she'd slept or what time it was. She tried to stretch the stiffness from her body and found her movements blocked by two solid, warm objects. It made her smile that Hades and Miss Kitty were curled against her. Though she longed to snuggle deeper under the covers, nature demanded otherwise.

She opened her eyes and fumbled for her glasses on the small table beside the bed. That was when she saw Kurt sleeping in the blue rocking chair. A glance at the clock showed it was eight in the morning. All was silent.

Midge managed to extricate herself from the bed without disturbing her companions and hurried to the bathroom. At least her feet didn't hurt as badly. The scent of coffee drifted her way, making her dry mouth water. After taking care of her needs, she wandered toward the kitchen and saw Claudia sitting in Zach's recliner, nursing her baby. Longing, pure and deep, settled in Midge's heart.

"Good morning." Claudia smiled up at her. "Coffee's fresh. I'm sure you could use a cup."

"Thank you." Midge helped herself, then returned to the living room and tucked into the corner of the couch to enjoy her first cup.

"I see Kurt finally got here," Claudia said.

"He's sleeping in the rocker." But then, Claudia would have seen that. "Do you know what time he got here?"

"We were asleep and he was quiet. How are you feeling this morning?"

"Stinky. Sore. Frustrated that with all my training I still couldn't bring down that beast of a man. Angry that I was betrayed and used and that she's still playing games trying to get out of it." Midge knew Susan well. Despite the trauma, she would normally have come up fighting.

"I'm glad to hear you say that," Kurt mumbled from behind.

Before she could turn around, he was beside her on the couch, reaching for her coffee. Midge let him have a drink then took one of her own.

"We've got a plan and need your help," he told her.

"I'm in."

He chuckled. "You haven't even heard what it is."

"Don't care. I want her taken down. I want her held accountable for *all* of her crimes. It must not be too dangerous or you would have already put your foot down and refused my services."

A glimmer of mischief lit his eyes. "Baby, I'd never refuse your services."

Claudia cleared her throat. "Audience, people. If you're going to get frisky, take it to another room and keep the noise down."

Midge laughed lightly. "What's the plan?"

Kurt helped himself to her coffee again. "You'll go to the hospital with a bouquet of flowers for Susan. You'll be given a bug to hide so her actions can be monitored. Anders will be near the facility listening. Try to engage her in conversation, even if she's unresponsive. At some point, Everest will arrive to question her in his capacity as DEA. He'll feed her information, ask you some questions. You play along. It'll require some improvisation. Once he's gone, you're going to tell her where you would have hidden the ketamine. Then we'll see what she does with that information once you leave. Jess and I will be waiting at your house to see who takes the bait."

"And to the world, you and I are still finished?" she asked.

"Yes. We brought your SUV over here. My car's parked two blocks down. I brought you more clothes. I saw Zach was pretty thorough in gathering your toiletries."

"I'm going to wear my glasses. I want her to think I am sufficiently humbled." She took her mug back and drained it.

"Should I anticipate seeing the hair bun again?"

"I'm not that humbled." She nudged his thigh with her foot. "Mind if I use your shower?" she asked Claudia.

"Not at all. And this little guy is done." With her words, Adam relinquished his hold on his food source, mouth agape, drooling milk and sound asleep.

"I've got him." Zach swooped in to retrieve his son.

"Thanks. I'm starving. I'll get us some breakfast." Claudia reached for the footrest.

"I'll do it." Kurt jumped up and headed for the kitchen.

"Adam and I will keep you company." Zach followed him.

The love in the air and in their actions nestled deep into Midge's heart. "Nothing like being spoiled by the people you love."

Claudia smiled and snuggled into the recliner. "Get used to it. Accept it as your due. Now go shower. You stink."

"What time did you get in?" Zach settled into one of the kitchen chairs. Adam was nestled deep in his arms. At present, the baby was the perfect combination of his parents, though his eyes promised to be Claudia's deep blue.

"About two hours ago." Longing welled up in Kurt. He covered the emotion by gathering what he needed to make breakfast. The rattle of pans brought the cats into the kitchen.

"Thanks for taking Hades last night." He dumped frozen hash browns into a pan. "This should be all wrapped up soon." *I hope.* "One of us will pick him up afterward."

"No rush," Zach replied. "He's doing a great job of keeping Miss Kitty's attention off the new addition. She's not too sure of Adam yet."

"Did Midge tell you everything?" he asked.

"That's a little hard to answer since I don't really know what the heck is going on."

Kurt almost laughed. A day ago Zach would have thrown out 'fuck' instead of 'heck'. Having a baby changed everything. He made a note to watch his language, too.

"Given your closeness to each other and past history, I'm going to presume she did."

He gave the potatoes a stir and started cracking eggs into a bowl. He would have preferred to make omelets, but when Claudia said she was starving, meltdown generally wasn't far behind.

"It made me sick inside to see what he'd done to her." His shoulders slumped with his confession. "I love her so much. I want her more than my next breath. And now I'm scared to death to touch her."

"I know how you feel."

Kurt turned and leaned against the counter. "What do I do?"

"Just continue to love her. Tell her how you feel. Take your time with each other." Zach's gaze fell to Kurt's battered knuckles. "What happened there?"

Midge didn't tell me everything. Maybe she didn't remember, being in the state she'd been in at the time.

"I pulled him off her and beat the hell out of him. Jess and that DEA agent had to pull me off. I'll probably lose my job over it, but I don't give a sh…a da… Not cursing is very hard, by the way."

Zach chuckled. "I know."

"The least I can hope for is suspension and reprimand. He purposefully plowed his car into Vic. Then to see what he'd done to Midge… What he was trying to do to her…" He scrubbed his hand down his face. It didn't erase the memories. Each time he thought about it, Kurt got sick inside. "What if Midge thinks that's who I really am?"

"Trust me. That's the furthest thing from her mind."

"And what's the closest thing on her mind?"

Zach smiled. "You're going to have to ask her. I'm going to put Adam in his bassinet. Claudia's not the only one who's starving."

Kurt returned his attention to cooking…or tried to. Midge filled his mind, his heart, his soul. Then he felt her slip her arms around his waist and press her cheek to his back.

"And he can cook, too. Goodness, you *are* a keeper."

He didn't know what to say. Well, he *did* know what to say but was afraid to do so. *Marriage proposals should be intimate and romantic and given after a longer association than we've had…right?* But Kurt found himself turning in her arms, taking her hands in his, starting to go down on one —

"I've got a present for you." Zach charged into the kitchen, phone extended to Midge.

Her eyebrows scrunched closer as she took it. Kurt read the text over her shoulder.

Stanford wife divorced soon after his retirement. Took half of his retirement, too. Others stepped forward after Ellis's complaint. What little rep he had tanked. He committed suicide two years later.

Midge lifted tear-filled eyes to Zach. "Where did you get this?"

He shrugged one shoulder. "I told you I was going to give Colonel Scott full disclosure. I've seen him mad before but never as mad as when he heard the backstory. Said he was going to find out what he could about the ass."

She returned the phone and gave him a tight hug. "You're the best."

Zach hugged her back and winked at Kurt. "Back at you."

Midge pulled away and squared her shoulders. "Now to get these other bastards."

Kurt hoped their children were as fierce. If they had children... *If* he could find that perfect moment to lay his heart before her.

Chapter Thirteen

Midge took yet another deep breath to calm her nerves. She was determined to sell this act and equally determined to see Susan was held accountable for her actions. Going in shaky and nervous couldn't happen. At least Everest had found a way to put the bug on the vase and she didn't have the pressure of trying to hide it. The device was part of a fleur-de-lis glued to the cobalt-blue vase. She plastered on a smile when she stepped off the elevator. Head high, shoulders back, she walked to the nurse's station.

"I'm trying to find Petty Officer Bolotnik's room."

The nurse's smile brightened her dark features. "Last one on the left."

"How is she doing?"

"Much better than when she was brought in."

"Good." Façades—if that was what she'd been doing—were hard to maintain. Midge knew that firsthand.

Susan was watching TV when Midge walked in. No smile greeted her, but Susan did turn off the TV.

"How are you feeling?"

"How the fuck do you think I'm feeling?" Susan snapped.

"Don't get an attitude with me. I was there, too, and I wouldn't have been if it weren't for you. As far as I'm concerned, you brought this on yourself."

She frowned. "Why aren't you at work?"

"I've been given the week to recover." Midge strode to the small bedside table to place the flowers. "These are for you. I honestly don't even know why I came. You've got some explaining to do. Why the hell were you trying to frame me?"

Susan closed her eyes on a sigh. "It wasn't like that."

Midge crossed her arms. "Then what the hell was it?"

She turned her head and opened her eyes. "It was fun and addictive. All those idiots cheating on their wives. They deserved what they got."

"Like you deserved this?" Midge waved her hand at her. "I certainly didn't do anything to deserve what that creep did."

"Well, if is matters, I'm sorry for that. I just thought"—she shrugged—"I thought it would be something we could do together. We could be partners. You got laid. Quit complaining."

Unbelievable.

"What I got was me being used, my heart stomped on, my house broken into, hours of interrogation from NCIS and my landlady killed."

Susan's eyes widened. "Bernadette's dead?"

"Yes."

"Well, that's not on me." She turned away and stared ahead.

"Parsons did it. She surprised him when he was searching my house for your blackmail videos and pictures. I'd appreciate it if you were upfront with NCIS about what you did when they come to talk to you. It's the least you owe me for what you put me through."

Susan jerked her head around. "It's not like I have a fucking choice, since the evidence was under my bed." Anger lit her eyes.

A throat cleared by the door—Everest, right on time. Midge turned. He flashed his badge and walked in.

"Petty Officer Bolotnik, I'm Special Agent Everest with the DEA. I'd like to ask you a few questions about Private First Class Jeremy Forton."

"Go on," she replied.

Midge stepped away from the bed and sat in the only chair in the room. She crossed her legs and pulled a nail file from her purse, feigning disinterest in the conversation.

Everest pulled out a notepad. "What was your relationship?"

"Friends only, though we did have sex from time to time."

"Were you aware that he was dealing drugs, specifically ketamine?"

Susan sniffed. "It wouldn't surprise me. He was constantly in trouble or looking for it."

"Our sources suggest he'd acquired a large amount of ketamine. Do you know anything about that?"

She frowned. "Why would I?"

"Just asking questions, ma'am."

"He asked me the same ones." Midge kept filing her nails. "It's been a long night."

"Yeah, it's been a cake walk for me," Susan replied snidely.

Everest tucked his notepad away and stared at her. "Here's the thing, ladies. We know he purchased a lot of ketamine for distribution but died before he could do anything with it. You two seemed to be the ones who spent the most off-duty time with him. Was there any time in the days prior to his death that he might have had the opportunity to hide that in either of your residences?"

"Really?" Susan laughed. "NCIS is tearing my place apart right now. Don't you think they would have found it? The bastard who did this to me apparently tore through *her* place, too. Do you really think he left no stone unturned? I'm quite sure if he'd found that much ketamine, he would have sold it himself and left me alone."

He plucked his business card from his pocket and placed one on the nightstand. "If you think of anything, let me know." He handed one to Midge as well. "I might come by later with more questions."

"Knock yourself out," Susan replied.

He gave them a nod and walked out. Midge listened to his footsteps fade, then sighed.

"What a nightmare." She tucked her file in her purse and stood. "My home and most of my possessions have been destroyed. Hell, if I found that much ketamine, I'd be tempted to sell it myself."

"Jeremy was alone for a long time the other night," Susan said. "Do you think he really did hide it?"

Midge squinted her eyes, pretending to consider the possibility. "The best place would have been the window seat."

"What window seat?" Susan asked. "I didn't know there was one."

"Hades is generally on it, watching the world outside."'

"I hate that fucker." She ran her fingers over the scratch on her neck.

Now we know whose DNA is in Hades' claws.

Midge tilted her head to one side. "Hmm. I don't recall anything on top of the seat being disturbed. The curtains were drawn, so that's probably why Parsons didn't mess with it. Of course, he wouldn't have known to look there. I found it by accident myself after I moved in." She frowned at Susan. "Do you think I should tell the DEA?"

"I wouldn't. I'd get a lawyer first. You don't want them putting the blame on you, do you?"

"You're right." She glanced at her watch. "I wouldn't know who to contact."

Susan snickered. "You work for legal. I'm sure one of them can steer you to a civilian attorney. I appreciate the flowers, but I'm exhausted and need to rest. So, if you don't mind…"

"Not at all. I'll stop by later."

"I'd rather you didn't."

A feeling Midge echoed. "Fine by me."

She walked away but was tempted to hover outside the door to see if their plan had worked. She'd find out soon enough. There would be no do-overs with Susan. They'd made it clear to each other their relationship was over. Midge couldn't wait to testify against her in court—Parsons, too.

The closer she got to the exit, the more she picked up the pace. As she reached one set of automatic doors, Midge tried to look beyond to the parking lot to see if

Everest and Anders were still there. She needed to know if Susan had taken the bait. She was so focused that she nearly ran into two Marines walking in. They all drew up short to avoid a collision. Her heart jolted to find McConnell and Clark in front of her. They muttered apologies and walked around her.

Midge willed her heart to stop pounding and thanked her lucky stars they hadn't recognized her from the Lost Oasis. She had been without glasses then and wearing the red wig. She continued on and spied Anders waving her to come to his vehicle — the same silver sedan he'd driven during his inept attempt to spy on her. Beyond him, Everest was driving away. It looked like their little sting operation had succeeded.

Anders leaned over and opened the passenger door when she neared. She recognized frantic when she saw it and prayed Kurt was all right. Pasting on a smile for anyone watching, she slipped into the seat.

"Who were those men?" he asked.

"Their names are McConnell and Clark. They came on to me at the bar the other night. Kurt intervened. Why?"

His gaze wandered to the building. "I saw them on those videos we confiscated last night."

Midge scrunched up her face. "They were having sex with Susan?" What use would she have had with them? She didn't think either were married.

"No. With each other. Sometimes another older man was with them. Do you know anything else about them?"

That explained why Susan might be blackmailing them. "Nothing. But if they're here, do you think Susan is in danger?"

"I don't know. Let's find out."

He put his earplugs back in. To anyone watching, he was listening to music.

Midge cracked her knuckles while they waited, earning Anders' side-long scowl. "I presume Special Agent Everest is headed to the other scene."

He nodded and lifted his palm for silence. With each second, the furrow between his eyebrows deepened.

"She's not in the room. Shit, they're going to kill her."

He called for backup from the Provost Marshal and dashed off, badge in hand. The automatic doors parted before him. Two doors down, Susan walked out, dressed in dark blue sweats.

Midge debated her actions while Susan scanned the parking lot. Susan's eyes narrowed when she looked in the direction of Midge's SUV, but her attention shifted quickly and she hurried off. Staying low, Midge watched Susan go to her flashy red sports car. A few minutes later, she drove off.

"Oh no, you don't. You're not getting away."

She started to open the door when she saw that Anders had left the keys in the ignition. Midge took advantage of it.

Easier to ask forgiveness than it is to get permission.

* * * *

Kurt hid in Midge's bathroom. It was the closest he could get without being seen. There was no place to hide on the first floor. Adrenaline buzzed along his nerves. Susan hadn't taken long to call her cohort, and in doing so, revealed the full extent of her involvement by saying, *'And don't send those fucking idiots. You get it or you know what will happen.'*

Kurt couldn't wait to review the videos of her sexcapades. He had a feeling it would be a who's-who list of individuals who had a lot to lose. It'd been thirty minutes since she'd made her call. He was getting antsy and knew Jess — watching the back entrance from his car — would be as well. Everest had arrived fifteen minutes before and taken his position in the front. Backup was on standby a block over. Comm links for all were operational.

"Got a hit," Jess said in Kurt's ear. "Male, black jeans, olive-drab sweatshirt, ski cap and gloves. Bulge at lower back. He's carrying. Can't ID him yet. Heading to the back door. He's picking the lock. Come on, you fucker. Turn around. He's in."

Kurt barely heard the door open. It was more like the pressure in the house changed. He drew his weapon and crept to the edge of the staircase for a peek. The man Jess had described stood before the window seat. A military duffel bag lay on the floor beside him. Without pause, he opened the curtains, tossed the pillows aside and reached for the lid.

"Hello? Anyone here?" The woman's high-pitched voice was reminiscent of Bernadette. Cat claws on a chalkboard were less irritating.

"Got a problem," he whispered into his headset. "Woman walked in."

Jess muttered a string of curses. "Coming to the back."

"Got the front," Everest added.

Kurt crouched against the wall, trying to keep watch below. The man spun around. *Yost.* Kurt told the others and watched in horror as Yost reached for the weapon at his back but didn't draw it.

"I saw you come in the back and dashed right over." The Bernadette clone thrust out her hand. "I'm Gloriana McFee. My mother was Bernadette."

Yost ignored her greeting and she awkwardly dropped her hand. "I'm the owner now. I wanted to talk to your girlfriend about keeping the lease."

No way in hell.

"I also wanted to apologize for my mother's actions. She could be annoying on her best days. I won't be like that. I won't even be here. I'll be renting out the other side as soon as it's cleaned."

She started to fidget under Yost's unblinking stare. "Goodness, this *is* quite a mess. Don't worry about your security deposit. I know it will be cleaned and all. It's not like you have bloodstains to worry about like I do."

Man, she's as cold-hearted as her mother.

"But it doesn't look like you have much left," she said. "I'd be glad to give you Mother's furniture. It's hideous and I sure don't want it."

Will she ever shut up and leave?

"Bolotnik's here," Everest told them. "Ellis followed her. Where the fuck is Anders?"

Breathing his last as far as Kurt was concerned. His job had been to keep Midge safe.

"She's headed to the front door," Everest added.

Kurt assumed he meant Susan. Midge knew they were inside and had things covered. At the sound of the door unlocking, Yost grabbed Gloriana in a chokehold and put the weapon against her temple. He relaxed his hold when Susan walked in, dressed in blue sweats. She tucked a lockpick kit into her pocket.

"What the fuck, Susan?" Yost snapped.

"I told you I'd be here. What the hell is taking so long? Who the fuck is she?"

"The landlady's daughter, I guess," he snapped back.

"Grab the stuff and let's go. They'll know I'm missing by now."

"What do you want me to do about her?" He shoved Gloriana away from him. The woman crumpled to the floor in tears.

"What do you think? She can ID us. Kill the bitch."

"I'm not killing anyone. What's she gonna tell? They already know you're involved in shit up to your eyeballs. Once they see those videos, I'm done, too. You've left loose ends."

"Yes, I have." She yanked a pistol from under the back of her sweatshirt and shot him.

Gloriana's scream pierced Kurt's ears. Shock widened Yost's eyes. He clutched his chest and fell.

Kurt moved in. "NCIS... Put the weapon down."

Susan jerked the gun in his direction. He froze on the bottom step.

"You heard the man," Jess said. "Put the weapon down."

Her gaze darted between them. Indecision flitted across her face, but the gun she leveled his way didn't waver. Her lips thinned to a tight line when Everest came in the front behind her.

"You're surrounded. Drop the gun," he told her.

"There's plenty to go around, gentlemen. I don't have a problem sharing."

"Tell that to the man you shot," Kurt said.

Susan glared at him. "I've had just about enough of you. You've ruined everything. Too clever for your own good."

"You shoot me and you'll go down next," he told her. "Both of them are dead shots. You won't make it. Is any of this worth dying for?"

"You tell me."

Kurt saw her finger flex. Shots rang out—his, hers, Jess' and Everest's. She had the nerve to look surprised before she fell. Clouds from outside darkened the room.

Odd. I thought the sun was out.

He couldn't catch a good breath. Pain swamped him. It felt like he'd been hit with a sledgehammer. Kurt slumped against the stairwell then sagged to the steps. He was vaguely aware of Jess rushing up, of Everest attending Susan.

She shot me.

"Midge. I need Midge," he gasped.

Someone must have heard him over comm because she burst through the door in short order. He wanted to reach for her but couldn't. She grabbed his hand and squeezed. Tears poured down her cheeks. Jess squatted down beside them, smiling.

"He's going to be okay. Vest caught the bullet. I can tell you from experience that it hurts like hell. He's going to be sporting a bruise and might have a busted rib or two."

He squeezed Midge's shoulder and walked off.

"Don't you ever scare me like that again, Kurt Orin Davidson. I'm not done with you yet. Do you understand?" Her voice shook with every word.

He smiled and fumbled to cup her cheek. "Yes, ma'am, I do."

She pulled in a deep breath then released it. "Oh goodie. I get to be on top for a while."

He started to laugh. Pain stopped him short. "Just be gentle with me."

She leaned in. "Now where's the fun in that?" she whispered then pressed her lips over his.

* * * *

Activity buzzed around Kurt and baby Adam. They were ensconced in the remains of one of Midge's chairs while she and their friends packed up her possessions. Three cracked ribs had put him on two weeks of no duty then four-to-six weeks of light duty. Kurt wanted to complain but all he felt was relief. Convalescence would give him time to seriously think about his chosen profession. Right now, while the others toiled, he had the best task ever — caring for Adam, who ate, slept and gave him crooked grins from time to time. Kurt was in love. But then, it didn't take much for him to love kids.

"You doing okay?" Jess offered him one of the two bottles of water in his hand.

"Yes and no." Kurt accepted the water, tucking it beside him next to Adam's bottle of mother's nectar.

Jess sat on the couch arm. "Talk to me."

"I'm beginning to feel like a bullet magnet." Admitting that took a weight off his shoulders. "I can't help wondering if I'm playing Russian roulette with my life. I think it might be time for me to quit before I get killed."

"I know how you feel." Jess leaned in. "Emma and I talked about it. I'm putting in my retirement papers."

It was comforting to know that someone else felt as he did. "You've been working some long hours lately, Jess. I don't think there's been a day this week that you didn't look exhausted."

Jess chuckled. "That was more play than work." His cheeks flushed. "I've been going down to San Diego every night to be with Emma, then leaving at o-dark-thirty in the morning to back here for work."

Kurt fought laughter and failed. "Damn, you're killing my ribs."

"Sorry." Jess smiled. "Anyway, I've been asked to choose my replacement. I'd like you to apply for the position."

Excitement momentarily canceled out the pain drugs couldn't touch. Reality slipped in on its heels.

"That right should go to Vic. He's been doing this longer."

Jess shook his head. "He's in bad shape and looking at eighteen months of healing and rehab. He's most likely going to be medically retired."

"Parsons should be locked up for that alone." Kurt's cracked ribs paled in comparison to Vic's injuries.

"Think about it. Talk to Midge."

"Talk to Midge about what?" She jerked to a stop halfway out of the front door with a box.

Jess chuckled and brushed his finger over Adam's cheek. "I love babies." The grandfatherly gleam in his eyes backed him up.

"Me, too," Kurt replied.

"Tell Midge what?" she asked again.

Midge stood over them now, hands on her hips and ready to do battle. He'd seen that stance too much the last couple of days when she thought he might not be following doctor's orders. Damn if she didn't make him hard as hell every time…like now. Too bad he couldn't do anything about it.

"Back to work for me." Jess lightly touched Kurt's shoulder and walked away.

Midge took his place. "What's going on?"

"Jess is putting in retirement papers and wants me to apply for his job. He's been tasked with finding his replacement. Vic's injuries will force him to medically retire."

"That's too bad." She frowned. "But why do you need to talk to me? It's your life."

Now or never, Davidson. "And yours, too…as my wife."

Her eyes widened, mouth dropped open. He focused on that surprised expression and not the bruise still emblazoned on her cheek.

"Sweetheart, I wanted you from the second I laid eyes on you. I want to go to sleep every night with you in my arms and wake up in the morning the same way. I want to have babies with you…so many babies. I want us to laugh and love and cry and cling to each other for the rest of our lives. I want the very last breath I ever take to be in your arms."

Tears trickled down her cheeks…and his. Kurt drew in a shaky breath.

"You hold my heart in your hands. I love you, Midge. There aren't enough words in the world to say how much. I want to be with you forever and beyond. I want to marry you. Right here. Right now."

"As tempting as that sounds…"

Oh fuck.

She knelt before him and put her hand on his knees. "There's no way in heck we're going to get out of a big wedding."

"Oh my God…you're saying yes?" Joy filled his soul.

Midge smiled. "I'm saying yes. And I want lots of babies, too—sooner rather than later."

Zach reached between them. "Give me Adam and kiss each other, for crying out loud. You've got us all in tears."

Indeed, their friends stood scattered around the room, blinking tears from their eyes.

"Freaking voyeurs," he said with a laugh, then kissed his bride-to-be with as much enthusiasm as she did him.

Epilogue

Kurt smiled from the inside out. Today he'd married the woman of his dreams and the room was packed with well-wishers, much to the delight of her father and stepmother. Midge's mother had refused to attend *'with that woman there'* and that was fine with them. Midge had cut the cord between her mother and herself, for her own peace of mind as well as his. That decision also allowed her to do what she'd always wanted — call Dee 'Mom'. The woman deserved the honor. She doted over Midge and her siblings, got along very well with Kurt's family and had taken a lot of the wedding planning off his and Midge's shoulders. The family had wanted the big wedding. He and Midge had only wanted to be married. Plus, they'd had other things to occupy their time, and she needed to conserve as much energy as possible. Keeping *that* secret had been impossible since it had required multiple alterations to Midge's wedding dress. Everyone at their reception knew they were expecting a child and he had a feeling that most of the wedding gifts—which he and Midge had asked their guests not to bring—reflected that.

So many things had happened over the last four months. While Susan had recovered from her gunshot wounds, NCIS and DEA had continued to gather evidence against her. She'd had quite the racket going with blackmail, drug trafficking and murder charges. Susan's trial would begin shortly after they returned from their honeymoon. The list of conspirators was long and all had been compelled to assist her under the threat of blackmail. Parsons was already serving his sentence in Leavenworth. Yost was recovering as well and still hoping for immunity, which wasn't going to happen. He was complicit in the beating death of Jeremy Forton. McConnell and Clark were going down for that. Susan had coerced all three into helping her, threatening to expose their little threesome.

Jess had retired at the first of the year. Now Kurt had the honor of being in charge of the unit. The bump in pay would help immensely since Midge would be leaving the Marine Corps at the end of her enlistment, come fall. She'd already been offered a full-time job at the bookstore as manager. Vera was leaving the area with Colonel Scott around that same time. He'd been beyond surprised to learn the two had been a couple, soon to be husband and wife.

Midge slipped her hand over his and leaned in. "It's time. Let's do this. I'm so excited I can't eat."

He'd noticed she'd picked at her chicken and had put it down to morning sickness that cropped up at every hour of the day *except* morning.

"All right then."

They exchange a kiss, clasped hands and stood. All attention shifted their way.

"We have an announcement to make. We would like to introduce" — he and Midge placed their hands over her belly — "Amanda and Abigail."

It took a few seconds for the words to filter in, then squeals and laughter replaced the silence.

Zach and Claudia wrapped hugs around them as the moms rushed the table.

"Showoffs," Zach whispered.

"We're scared to death," Midge told them.

Claudia's bright smile washed over them. "We've got your backs."

Then the horde descended.

Want to see more from this author? Here's a taster for you to enjoy!

To Die For
Caitlyn Willows

Excerpt

Fear clawed at Zoe's gut, fighting its way to the surface. Prickles of the monster she'd buried zinged beneath her skin, searching for a way out.

People. She had to be around people. If she went home, another monster might be waiting. Zoe wouldn't risk it — not until she had control firmly in her hands, not until she could face whatever hell awaited her with dignity and strength. Having her .38 in ready reach wouldn't be bad either.

Gun trumped knife every time. Too bad she'd gotten out of the habit of carrying the weapon. Zoe would rectify that once she got home. Being without threat had made her careless. If she wasn't diligent…

Dead. She'd be dead.

No. That was why she had the black belt — to protect herself.

Could she keep her wits about her and remember how to use those skills? Besides, all the martial arts moves in the world couldn't win over a gun. She needed that weapon in her possession.

Zoe gasped for breath, fighting hyperventilation.

Burt's Diner. That was where she could go. Open all night. Always someone there. A favorite place for cops. She'd grab a bite and order her thoughts — make a game plan.

Zoe scanned the jumble of signs, looking for that familiar red one. *Have I passed it?* She'd been so upset that she barely remembered leaving the station. *Where the hell am I?* Certainly not pointed toward home. She nearly wept with relief when she spied her beacon a block ahead. A Holiday Inn Express was across the street from it. That was an option she hadn't considered. She'd check in for a night — maybe two — get a room on the top floor and hole up until this was over.

She snorted at her foolishness. This was *never* going to be over — not until one of them was dead. Zoe didn't plan on that being her.

She eased into the parking lot and found a spot next to the restaurant. Maybe luck was on her side tonight. Pulling in slow breaths to calm her shattered nerves, she cut the engine. Xavier didn't know where she lived. Chances were slim he'd recognize her on the street — as long as she kept her mouth shut. The encounter had been an isolated incident. Why would Xavier care? He was rattling her to show he was a big man, nothing more. Old fears ran deep, though. Too deep.

He knows where you work now.

True. Zoe wondered if her subconscious had steered her to take an alternate route home.

Silly. The shooting was across town. There's no way he could —

She cut off the thought. There was always a way for a determined person, and he'd sounded damned determined. Thank goodness, her parents were vacationing in Maui and her sister visiting friends in New York. They were safe from him. Xavier couldn't have picked a better time to make his move. For another panicked moment, Zoe wondered if he'd planned this. Just as quickly, she dismissed the idea. Xavier never planned anything. He was volatile, driven by rage and a very short temper.

Damn it all. She'd thought this was in the past. Now she'd inadvertently crossed paths with him. His threat wasn't an idle one. Xavier would hunt her down. It was only a matter of time.

Not if the cops get him first.

Zoe was counting on that. Talk about determination. Xavier had killed a police officer tonight, seriously wounding another. *He* was a marked man. She prayed they got to him before he got to her.

A thorough look around the parking lot confirmed her safety. Still, she didn't let her gaze or attention wander as she looped her purse strap over her shoulder, clutched the hobo bag against her side and stepped from her F-150 truck. Her rubber-soled ankle boots thunked on the sidewalk. Zoe wasted little time getting inside. Once the doors closed behind her, she let the hostess's smile scatter the dark shadows lingering in her mind…at least for the moment. The woman's nametag identified her as Jennifer.

"One?" she asked.

"Yes, just one," Zoe said.

Jennifer plucked a menu from the box attached to the pedestal behind her. "Table or booth?"

Under normal circumstances, her answer would be 'table,' but Zoe didn't want to be that exposed tonight. "Booth. Away from the window." Her back against the wall with a clear view of the entrance.

"Right this way." Jennifer led her down the aisle, nodding to other diners as she took Zoe into the bowels of the restaurant.

Zoe saw the men and women too late. Twelve police officers and detectives occupied a large section of tables in the back room where Jennifer intended to seat her. Zoe plucked at the woman's long white sleeve in a vain effort to subtly catch her attention. Again, too late. One by one, the men and women stopped what they were doing, all gazes latching on to Zoe. Chairs slid over the carpet as they stood and applauded her.

She wanted to crawl into a hole and never come out. The only thing that kept her feet rooted in place was the pride on Frank Ludwig's face. Zoe's heartbeat triple-timed.

"Come join us." Officer Joanie Robertson yanked over a chair from a nearby table, while Frank's partner, Theo Garcia, waved Zoe toward them.

Only that morning, Robertson had gone out of her way to avoid her. Zoe was their hero tonight. Tomorrow, things would go back to how they had been. Zoe didn't want to muddy the waters by socializing.

She'd heard what some of her coworkers said behind her back. A few even said it to her face. Some of them meant well, but others didn't. Zoe'd learned to live with scathing remarks, dirty looks and *kindhearted* suggestions. After all, she had only herself to blame for the way she looked. She wasn't a small girl. But Frank — hot Frank who shared her bed in Zoe's nightly fantasies — accepted her with no questions, no attempts to change her. Their friendship was unconditional.

"No, thank you." She combined her refusal with a polite smile she didn't truly feel. "It's been a long shift. I need to decompress."

Jennifer motioned to a booth just inside the room. "How's this?"

"Perfect." She could sit with her back to them and still have a clear view of the front door. She slid onto the narrow seat and accepted the menu from Jennifer.

"Anything to drink?"

A bottle of your cheapest wine – and put a straw in it. "Iced tea, no lemon."

"Coming right up."

Zoe stared at the menu. Conversation behind her fell to whispers. Words swam before her eyes. *Damn.* She was going to start bawling right here. A shadow blocked the light. The second she glanced up, Frank slid in beside her.

"Scoot over." He butted his hip against hers.

"What are you doing?" Zoe refused to budge.

"I'm sitting with you. What does it look like?"

She flicked her fingers toward the opposite seat. "Then sit there."

"You know I can't sit with my back to the door."

"It looked to me like that's what you were doing over there." She motioned to the party behind them.

Frank shrugged. "I lost the toss. Only fair way to determine seating when you have a table of cops." He nudged again. "Scoot."

It occurred to Zoe that she could move to the other seat, but that meant depriving herself of the brief joy of having Frank next to her. The man made her feel all kinds of crazy happy inside – safe and sheltered, small and feminine. Worry and fear didn't dare bother her with Frank by her side. His sheer personality warned them away. She wanted to lean into his solid body and cry her heart out.

"How nice you ran into your husband." Jennifer put down a tall glass of iced tea.

Reality slapped Zoe's daydreams to bits. "Oh, he's not my husband."

Frank plopped his hand over hers and squeezed. "Not yet."

Jennifer's smile drained the power grid. "When's the wedding?"

"We're not engaged, either." Zoe slipped her hand from under his and grabbed her straw.

"Not yet." Frank dropped his hand to her thigh, shocking Zoe senseless. Her clit cheered at how near he was to it. Juices flowed in anticipation of more. "I'm still trying to get her to notice me."

Jennifer's gaze ping-ponged between them. Her smile dimmed while she probably pondered a response — or planned how she could get Frank for herself. Although he was a bit old for her. Hell, he was a bit old for Zoe, too, but that didn't stop her from lusting after him. She'd calculated around a ten-year age gap. Her fantasies of him pressing her to the nearest wall and fucking her senseless didn't care. A thread of jealousy twined its way to the surface. If Jennifer started flirting—

Home of Erotic Romance

Sign up for our newsletter and find out about all our romance book releases, eBook sales and promotions, sneak peeks and FREE romance books!

About the Author

Blessed (or cursed) with a vivid imagination, award-winning author Caitlyn Willows eventually learned to turn that talent inward. Readers will find deep emotions and sizzling sensuality seamlessly woven into her action-filled stories. Believing life is to be lived and felt, not merely watched, Caitlyn delivers real-to-life characters in unforgettable tales of love, adventure, and always steamy passion. No one is more surprised than she at the direction life has taken her. She is also a mosaic artist and an avid crafter with a passion for cross-stitch. Caitlyn lives in the beautiful desert of Southern California with her husband (a genealogist). She is always on the lookout for the next interesting tidbit that will help fill her writing well.

Caitlyn loves to hear from readers. You can find her contact information, website details and author profile page at https://www.totallybound.com